Love's Second Bloom

by

L. M. Gonzalez

Love's Second Bloom

Cover Art by *Kristian Norris*

The Wild Rose Press, Inc.
PO Box 708
Adams Basin, NY 14410-0708
Visit us at www.thewildrosepress.com

Publishing History
First *Last Rose of Summer* Edition, 2017
Print ISBN 978-1-5092-1634-5
Digital ISBN 978-1-5092-1635-2

Published in the United States of America

The kids left the room, all of them furious or crying. Gloria glanced at Matt, feeling as if she'd been physically battered. Her whole body ached, especially her chest. She wanted to slump on the sofa and sob her eyes out as Patsy had. The kids' angry voices echoed around the room, though now silence reigned.

Matt put his arm around her. "That didn't go so well."

"You think?" She blinked to prevent tears, but she wasn't successful.

"Aw, Gloria." He pulled her into a tight embrace. "We'll find a way. We have to. I love you."

"I love you, too," she murmured against his broad chest. The whiff of his cologne and his nearness evoked sweet memories. After what had just transpired, maybe memories were all she'd ever have. "In this case, I'm not sure love's going to be enough."

"It will be," he said, his mouth near her ear. "These kids, our kids, were brought into this world with love and have been loved all their lives. They'll understand."

"I hope so."

He kissed her. In his kiss was the love he had for her, his want, and his need. Her heart swelled with love, but it also ached with pain for her sons, because the decision to remarry had driven a wedge between her and them, between Matt and his daughters. And at the moment, she saw no way this could be resolved.

Praise for L. M. Gonzalez

"Love can happen at any age and this story [*TOO LATE FOR ROMANCE?*] proves it!…This is a beautiful story that is enjoyable for the wonderful things that happen. It is humorous as well for the simple fact of getting the kids to get along."

~Krista Reviewer for Coffee Time Romance

~*~

"Matt and Gloria meet [in *TOO LATE FOR ROMANCE?*]…The attraction is instant…I enjoyed the realism in the story, it wasn't all a bed of roses (if you'll excuse the pun) and it pointed out real problems that occur in this day and age when it comes to relationships and romance. Is it ever too late for romance?"

~Mimi, Night Owl Romance Reviews

Dedications

To the San Antonio Romance Authors
for their support and wisdom,
~*~
To The Next Chapter writers, and to Mary Lou Solis,
who never stopped asking
when they could read more about Matt and Gloria,
~*~
To the best dad, Alberto M. Morales,
~*~
To my sisters,
Amelia Garcia, Nora Morales and Dora Calderon—
thanks for not disowning me
during the past seven years,
~*~
And always, always
To my son, Albert Daniel,
who never wavers in his belief
in his crazy writing mom,
~*~
Thank you from the bottom of my heart.

Chapter One

Will you marry me?

Gloria Amaya stared down at Matt Cerda's dark, chocolate-brown eyes. He knelt in front of her holding a diamond engagement ring that sparkled in the dim light of the lamps in his living room.

"I've never been engaged before." Oh, she'd been married before, but never engaged.

"That's not what I'm asking, Gloria." He lifted one knee and then the other from the floor before settling on both again. "I hate to rush you with your answer, but my knees are killing me."

She burst out laughing. "Then how can I say no?"

"Is that a yes?"

"Yes!" She held out her hand so he could put the ring on her finger.

He stood, pulled her into his arms, and kissed her. Because they'd been dating for several months, his kisses were familiar now. Familiarity did not mean boring, however. Anything but. This man who'd come into her life when her roses were dying had not only coaxed her flowers to bloom in the South Texas heat, but he'd also helped her see she wasn't as content as she'd believed.

"Yes, yes, yes," she murmured against his lips.

"You've made me the happiest man on earth."

"I think the line comes from a song." She stayed

within the circle of his arms.

His low laugh rumbled in his chest against hers. "So when will it be?" He pulled her down to sit beside him on the brown leather sofa.

"Let's get married tomorrow." Gloria cuddled against him. His spicy cologne and manly scent mixed and excited her.

"Don't you want a big wedding?"

"I never had one." She looked away from him and stared at a button on his blue shirt.

He raised her face. "I know. You eloped."

"Guess I shouldn't do that again, huh? Look how doing it that way turned out."

"I had the big wedding with Angela and look how that turned out."

She sighed. "I do want a big wedding. Well, maybe not big. But I want my family to be there—my sons, your daughters, everybody. I don't want to start my married life with any regrets this time."

Again, she looked away from him and couldn't help but remember her ex, Eddie Amaya. She'd thought she'd loved him, so she'd agreed to elope. The wedding had taken place at the courthouse with two witnesses she barely knew. Then when the marriage hadn't worked out, she'd been crushed. But now with Matt, things were different. She'd gone into this relationship with both eyes wide open. She'd also learned any relationship took a lot of time and love to make it flourish, like Matt's plants.

From far away, she heard his voice.

"Gloria…"

She put her arms around him and nestled her head on his shoulder. "I love you so much. I'm glad Tanya sent you to me when my roses were dying."

"I love you, too," he whispered against her ear.

"I'll have to buy a dress." She lifted her head from his shoulder. "And you have to have a tux. Do you want a tux? Well, maybe a nice suit. Oh, and flowers, the cake…" Warming up to the subject, she reached for her purse to get a notepad and pen. "I'd better write this down."

Matt laughed. "You're beginning to like this big-wedding thing."

"Well, just a wedding thing. It doesn't have to be big." She flipped open the notepad. "What colors should I have my bridesmaids wear? Lynda had turquoise. I have to call her and ask her to help me."

"Do you think your sister will say no?" he teased.

"Of course not." She turned her gaze from the notepad to Matt and found him grinning. "Oh you! I'm just so excited."

His answer was to pull her close and kiss her again. "I am, too. But first, we have to tell the kids."

The growing anticipation regarding her upcoming wedding diminished. The kids were the first huge challenge because their happiness was so important. She'd been single so long Dex had recently told her he couldn't imagine her with a man. He'd been in elementary school when she and Eddie had separated. Gordy would be more of a problem than Dex, if that were possible. He and Matt's daughter Julia had a stormy relationship. Julia wouldn't like the idea of her dad remarrying either. Amber and Patsy accepted her more readily, though how they'd react to their dad marrying was debatable.

"We'll tell them together next weekend. The girls

will be with me," he said, once again bringing Gloria back from her troubling thoughts.

"Do you think that's the best way to do it?" She flipped the pages of the notepad without even realizing she did it until Matt placed his hand on hers.

"If we tell one set of kids one day and the other set the next day, they might get together and gang up on us. They do talk to one another now, you know?" he reminded her.

"At times, I think they're becoming used to each other—and to us."

"Maybe it won't be so bad. Maybe we're worrying for nothing."

"I hope so." She set aside the notepad.

Telling the kids was the first hurdle, and she'd never been very good at sports.

****

Matt's gaze landed on the flowers and shrubs in his front yard. Gloria loved the red roses from the moment she saw them. He would feel eternally grateful to Tanya for sending him to Gloria's the day she called Wayne, Tanya's husband, to ask for help with her roses. He had known Wayne for a long time. The man had actually been his mentor as he'd started his own landscaping business.

Matt had fallen in love with Gloria almost instantly, and once he was able to explain his aversion to sickness, especially heart problems, they'd been able to develop their relationship. He carried a phobia for sickness ever since, as a teen, he'd found his mom dead in her garden after they'd argued. Now that Gloria knew about it, he could talk to her, and she'd try to understand. His ex-wife, Angela, never had.

When he'd found out Gloria had high blood pressure and was on medication, he'd left her. Now he cringed whenever he remembered how close he'd come to losing someone he loved. This time it would have been his fault.

After he entered his house, he walked to the refrigerator to make sure he'd stocked it with everything his daughters liked. In the middle of the dining table, pride of place was taken by the ceramic bowl Julia had made for him when she was in elementary school. The thought made him smile. His oldest daughter was seventeen and constantly reminded him she was almost an adult.

A glance at the clock confirmed they'd be home soon. And that's what he'd tried to do—make his house a home to his girls, too, even though they lived with their mother.

He walked down the hall to their rooms. Julia had her own room, and the younger ones, Patsy and Amber, shared another. He'd let them decorate the rooms however they'd wanted. Julia's was pink. Every time he went in there, he thought he'd fallen into a bottle of Pepto Bismol. Lately, she'd been adding black touches, a lampshade, a pillowcase. At first, it hadn't bothered him because he liked black. But now she'd also become a bit withdrawn.

Patsy and Amber were frequently at odds about how to decorate their room. Patsy was older by three years and wanted more-feminine things. Amber was still into toys, although lately she, too, had exhibited signs of growing maturity and leaned toward liking the same things Julia and Patsy did. Eventually, Amber and Patsy would both need separate rooms. He planned to move his office to the utility room, section off a part of it anyway. The washer and dryer had to fit in there somehow. His office could be Amber's room.

But life had a way of changing plans. He'd met Gloria, and he wanted to marry her. Julia still had one more year of high school before she went to college, if she even went. Patsy and Amber would be with him a while longer. Maybe even Julia. And Gloria's sons still lived with her.

Could they all coexist in one house? Which house? Neither house was big enough for all of them. But those were logistics that could be ironed out later.

"Daddy, we're home."

Matt heard Amber's voice before she ran into the room. The other two followed more slowly. "Have a good day?" he asked as he hugged all three of his girls.

"I'm glad it's the weekend," Julia muttered. "Though I wanted to be with my friends tonight. But we had to come..." She looked at Matt, a stricken expression on her face.

Even though a part of his heart hurt to hear how she really felt, he understood and he told her.

"Sorry, Dad." She fumbled with her purse and didn't meet his eyes.

"I'm glad I'm here," Patsy said. "Mom is acting funny."

Angela was frequently weird, in his opinion, so he would believe whatever freakish attitude she'd taken on now.

"Mom told you not to tell Dad anything," Julia scolded.

"Tell me what?" He looked first at Julia, then at Patsy. When no one answered, he said, "You know you have to tell me, right?"

Julia glared at Patsy, who walked to the sofa, dragging her tote bag, and turned away.

"Mom's been crying and crying, then gets angry," Amber piped up. "When we ask what's wrong, she tells us to leave her alone."

"How long has this been going on?" He turned to Julia for an answer.

"Since the last time we came here."

Two weeks. What was wrong now? Angela hadn't called him, so he hoped it was a good sign. Usually, she needed money. If so, sooner or later he would hear from her. But what if it was something else? He decided not to quiz his girls anymore. He'd call her himself. For now, he had something else to tell his daughters.

"Girls, let's take your things to your rooms, and then we'll come back here. I have something to tell you." He picked up a pink suitcase.

"Gloria and her sons are coming over tomorrow," he said when they were all back in the living room and the girls seated.

"Not again," Julia said.

Patsy smiled. "It'll be nice to see Gloria."

Amber jumped up from the sofa. "I like Gordy. He let me play his football video game last time."

"What do you know about football?" Julia asked.

"I know what a safety is," Amber said. "And he dressed this player in my favorite colors, orange and green." She sat down, clasped her hands, and sighed. "He's like a big brother to me."

"Shut up. He's a jerk." Julia elbowed her sister. "All boys are."

"Julia hit me, Daddy," Amber yelled.

7

"Settle down, girls," Matt said, hoping they could avoid problems. "It's happening tomorrow. How come you seem against this? We've been getting together at least once a month pretty regularly. What's up?"

No one spoke. Again, a twinge in his gut warned him a problem was coming.

"We don't have to be one big happy family, do we?" Julia said. "It's just you and Gloria, right? Keep us separated."

"I'm afraid I can't, girls."

"Why are we getting together tomorrow? Is it someone's birthday?" Patsy finally spoke.

"No…" He hesitated, unsure what to say. He and Gloria wanted to tell the kids together. "We just wanted to be together this weekend."

"What for?" Julia asked.

"Ah…well…"

"Oh no. Please say you didn't." She groaned.

"What?" Both Patsy and Amber shouted.

"Let's wait until tomorrow." He'd lost the battle. He didn't feel a twinge in his chest anymore. Now his heart hammered inside him.

"You're marrying her, aren't you?" Julia demanded. "That's why Mom has been so upset lately. Oh, Dad, how can you?"

"Your mom doesn't know anything."

"So I'm right. You did propose." She glared at him.

He had to be honest. There was no way he could avoid answering her direct question. "Yes."

"Oh…" Patsy looked away.

"Gordy is my brother now." Amber bounced up and down on the sofa.

"Great," Julia muttered, but he knew she meant the exact opposite as she stormed off to her room.

He thought about going to her but decided to leave her alone for a few minutes. "Let's order some pizza and watch a movie." Maybe he could still enjoy the evening with his daughters.

"I'm okay with this, Dad," Patsy said. "I love Mom, but I understand you can't be happy with her... Sometimes, neither can I. I want you to be happy."

He walked to his daughter and hugged her. "You're a girl of few words, but when you speak, you say the nicest things. What do you mean sometimes you can't be happy with your mom?"

Patsy buried her face in his chest. Then she lifted her head and edged away. "Aw, don't listen to me, Daddy. I'm okay."

"You sure?"

"Yeah," she mumbled and let go of him.

"Patsy?"

"Mom told Patsy she was a disappointment to her," Amber said in spite of Patsy trying to hush her by covering her mouth. "Well, she's told me, too. She's always saying Julia is just like her and why couldn't we be as well."

"I think it's time I talked with your mother," he said.

"Oh, Dad, please don't say anything," Patsy begged. "Amber should have kept her big mouth shut."

"I won't say specifics, but I know how she can be, Patsy. I've known your mom for a long time. And I've seen how she favors Julia. She won't be surprised when I question her." He walked to the kitchen and picked up the phone. "So do we order pizza and watch a movie?"

9

"What about Julia?" Amber asked.

"She'll come out when she gets hungry," he said, wondering if she really would. Something was up with Julia as well, more than just the proposal. She was preoccupied with her friends. Who were they?

The divorce bothered her more than the other two, at least lately. Now he'd proposed to Gloria, and he was afraid this could affect her in ways he couldn't even imagine. He hoped Gloria fared better than he had.

What would happen tomorrow?

****

Gloria was on cloud nine. She'd never have believed it if someone had told her she'd marry again. Eddie had killed the desire in her. She'd become content with her life, her sons, and her job. Now all that had changed. Matt wanted to marry her. What was even more surprising was she'd actually accepted and couldn't wait to be his wife. Her past bad relationship with Eddie didn't concern her as much as her sons and their reactions to her engagement.

Lately, they seemed okay about Matt, that she'd go out with him—somewhere else. Whenever she and Matt decided to plan family get-togethers, however, both sets of kids balked. Somehow, they managed to get through it, though, with only minor struggles and mishaps. How would they react upon hearing of his proposal?

When her sons arrived, she gave them each a kiss and a hug. She took a deep breath before speaking. "Matt and I are planning a get-together this weekend."

"Aw, Mom, not again." Gordy dropped down on the recliner and fiddled with the remote.

"What's this with a get-together every few weeks? Can't you keep us separate?" Dex asked.

"You know better," Gloria said, her heart in her throat, butterflies in her stomach. Why did she dread this so much? "We just..." She sat on the sofa and clasped her hands in her lap. She'd turned the ring around so they couldn't see it. She'd thought about taking it off, but she didn't want to. Matt had placed it on her finger. "We want to tell you something."

"Oh no," Gordy said.

Dex, who'd been standing by the love seat, came around and sat down. "Please don't say it."

She should have known her sons would be able to see right through her. They knew each other so well it'd always been hard to keep secrets from each other, even good ones like surprise birthday parties.

"Would it be so bad?" She picked up the notepad she'd left on the coffee table.

"Yes," Dex yelled. "If you couldn't stay with Dad, what makes you think you can make it last with this dweeb?"

She knew he remembered his pain when she and Eddie had divorced. Back then, he'd accused her of not loving his dad enough. Through his adolescent and teen years, the accusations resurfaced. However, for a long time now, he hadn't said anything. Somewhere deep in his soul, Dex still wished for his parents to get back together. If she married Matt, the dream would be gone.

For a few minutes, she didn't know what to say. "I care for Matt. Besides, he's helped both of you a lot since we met." She bit her lip. She'd said the wrong thing.

"So now we pay him back with you?" Gordy muttered.

"Oh, boys, please be happy for me. He makes me

happy. I haven't felt this way in a long time."

"Spare us the details." Dex sneered. "I'm not living with him in this house."

Gordy stood. "Those girls will probably always be around, too."

"We haven't even talked about where we'll live." She wrinkled her brow. So many things to think of. But she needed to regain control of the conversation. "This is just the first step. We're not getting married next weekend."

"Why marry him at all?" Dex asked. "Like I said, you tried it once and failed. Leave it alone."

In spite of herself, her eyes filled with tears. "Dex, I'm so sorry things didn't work out between your dad and me."

"Forget it. You'll do what you want anyway." He stomped from the room.

"Gordy?" She turned to her younger son. "Please try to understand."

"It's going to change things," he said. "I like things the way they are." He threw the remote on the recliner and left the room.

Had Matt's daughters figured out their plans, too? She wasn't supposed to have said anything yet. Would he encounter the same problem?

****

On Saturday evening Gloria drove to Matt's house—after arguing with her sons, who at first refused to go. She hoped her eyes weren't still red from crying. Her mind flashed back to the scene only a few minutes ago.

"I'm not going." Dex had planted himself on the love seat.

"If he doesn't go, I'm not either," Gordy said.

"Boys, we talked about this. We want everyone present so we can talk about everything—how it'll affect everyone, how we can work things out."

Dex was only half listening. His head was turned away, and his stony expression said it all. Gordy looked at her but didn't say a word.

"All these years I've loved you, cared for you, and provided for you, and I wouldn't trade them for anything in the world. You'll always come first in my life, no matter what, no matter who. I'm just asking for your love and support in this."

"Dad said you would never love anyone but him. Matt is just your…well…whatever…"

She wanted to remain calm, but her body stiffened. "When did you talk to your dad?"

"Last night," Dex admitted.

"I told him not to call when he was upset," Gordy said. "You know how Dad is."

"What business is it of your dad's anyway? He's had so many floozies in his life even during…" She stopped, remembering her vow never to speak ill of Eddie, no matter the provocation.

Dex sprang up. "I don't want any part of your life with this character. I'm going to get my own place. It's past time I did anyway. I'm almost finished with college, and I have a full-time job."

"I'll move in with you, bro," Gordy said.

"No," Gloria yelled. "You will not move out like this. Gordy, you haven't even finished high school."

"But I will this year. Hopefully."

"I can't stay in this house," Dex said

"Plus, we'd have to deal with those sappy girls,"

Gordy added.

"Boys, please." She looked at her watch. "We're going to be late."

"No, you are." Dex stalked from the room.

"Gordy…" Gloria said.

"I'll go talk to him," Gordy said and left the room in a calmer manner than his brother had.

Her eyes filled with tears. She dragged herself to her room and sat on the end of her bed. The dresser was right in front of her. On top, among the bottles of lotions, perfumes, and hair spray, she spotted the latest family picture she and her sons had taken a few months ago. In the picture, Gloria sat on a chair with her boys positioned behind her. That's how it'd always been. She'd stood in front of her sons to protect them from all harm as best as she could.

For so many years, they'd been a family with no man in the picture, except for Eddie whenever he felt like it. And John, her brother-in-law, had always been there for her sons. But no man in her life. And she'd been content. Until now. With Matt.

The picture blurred as hot tears spilled out of her eyes. She loved her sons more than anything, and their happiness and well-being were vital to her. They were older now, and they could live on their own if they insisted, but she didn't want them to leave in anger. She wanted her sons to participate in her new life with Matt. She wanted them all to be a family.

Dex told her she looked at life through rose-colored glasses in spite of the slaps and hard knocks it had given her. But who was she kidding? It was just too late. Maybe it would have been easier if she'd found a man when her sons were little. They would have grown up with him around. And they wouldn't have been able to leave.

A knock sounded on her door. "Mom?" Gordy's voice penetrated. "We'll go with you."

"Really?" She opened the door.

Gordy hugged her. "Your eyes are red. I'm sorry, Mom."

Over Gordy's shoulder, she saw Dex standing in the small hallway, but he didn't say a word.

"Let me just wash my face, and we'll go." She patted Gordy on the back and released him.

"Don't make this long and drawn out," Dex finally said.

As she turned to go into the bathroom, she heard the front door slam.

Gordy gave her a small smile. "He'll be okay, Mom. I talked to him."

"Does the proposal bother you, Gordy?"

"Apparently not as much as Dex. He just lived with Dad longer."

"And he's always wished we could get back together. I guess this means the death knell."

Gordy shrugged.

She had repaired the damage to her face, and now here they were in front of Matt's house. She braced herself for whatever might happen. After her sons' reactions, who knew how Matt's daughters would react?

Chapter Two

Gloria reached the door first. Her sons followed more slowly, obviously dreading entering the house. Matt must have been on the lookout for her because he opened the door before she could ring the doorbell.

"Hi." Although he smiled, he looked anything but happy. "You've been crying."

"Allergies," Gloria lied.

"Gloria?" He looked past her to her sons.

Dex and Gordy looked as if they were nearing the guillotine. "We had a problem getting here," she said.

"We should have known better than to think we could hide the reason for this get-together. They're smart kids. Mine know already, too."

"So…"

"We still need to talk." Matt hugged her and stepped aside so her sons could enter. "Come on, guys. I've got drinks and snacks."

"As if that's all we need to like him, like dogs. Man, he's a dork," Dex muttered.

Thankfully, Matt gave no indication he had heard.

"God, I wish this was over," Julia said.

Gloria heard the comment as she walked into the living room behind Matt, and her stomach sank.

"Do you want to eat first?" Matt looked at her and her sons.

"Let's just talk." Dex made the *quotes* gesture with

his hands. "So we can get outta here."

"Sounds good to me, too," Julia said.

"At least you agree about something," Matt said.

Julia glared at him, even though she went to stand by his side. Dex and Gordy huddled near Gloria. Amber pulled Gordy down to sit beside her on the brown leather sofa, but he remained standing. Patsy sat on the arm of the sofa.

Matt held out his hand to Gloria, and she left her sons' side. Actually, she realized she'd been standing slightly in front of them as in the family picture on her dresser. Now she'd gone to stand by Matt's side, and she no longer protected them. Her heart wrenched at the thought, but then she looked up at his face. She wanted him in her life. Why couldn't they resolve this?

Matt cleared his throat. "I've proposed to Gloria, and she's accepted."

No one spoke, barely moved.

"We'd like your support," Gloria added.

"You don't have it," Dex said.

"Who are you to speak for all of us?" Julia demanded. "Though in this case, I agree with you."

"I'm not speaking for you. I'm saying how I feel."

"It's your mother's fault," Julia cried.

Dex sneered. "That's certainly mature, tossing blame."

"What can you expect from her?" Gordy said.

"Boys, please," Gloria said. But as she stood next to Matt, she debated turning around and telling him to forget it. What had she expected?

"Amber, get up. Don't align yourself with the enemy," Julia said.

"Julia, no one's an enemy here," Matt said.

"I like Gordy…and Dex, too," Amber shouted.

"You're a baby, and you're too young to know what's what," Julia said.

"If anyone's at fault here, it's Tanya." Gordy let go of Amber's hand and joined Dex.

Gloria stared at Gordy. She'd thought he was on her side.

"She sent your dad to my mom's," he said. "All she wanted was help with her roses, not a boyfriend."

"You're saying it's my daddy's fault, too." Amber pointed a shaking finger. "I don't like you anymore."

"Calm down, everybody," Patsy said in a quiet voice.

"Calm down?" Julia raised her fist at her sister. "How can we possibly do that?"

"Girls." Matt tried to regain control.

"I want the hell outta here, Mom." Dex began to walk out of the room. "Let's go, Gordy."

"I've always thought your name was stupid." Julia smirked at Gordy

"You're just stupid," he said.

Gloria groaned. Matt looked as bewildered and sad as she felt. The kids resumed shouting insults at each other before either of them could say another word. Patsy fell to the sofa in a slump, crying.

Amber walked over to Gordy and pulled his arm. "Take it back. My daddy is not at fault."

Dex and Gordy finally stalked out.

"Get your stuff," Julia told her sisters. "We're going back to Mom's. I don't want to stay here one more minute."

When Patsy continued crying, Julia went over and slapped her on the arm. "Now."

The kids left the room, all of them furious or crying. Gloria glanced at Matt, feeling as if she'd been physically battered. Her whole body ached, especially around her chest area. She wanted to slump on the sofa and sob her eyes out as Patsy had. The kids' angry voices echoed around the room, though now silence reigned.

Matt put his arm around her. "That didn't go so well."

"You think?" She blinked to prevent tears, but she wasn't successful.

"Aw, Gloria." He pulled her into a tight embrace. "We'll find a way. We have to. I love you."

"I love you, too," she murmured against his broad chest. The whiff of his cologne and his nearness evoked sweet memories. After what had just transpired, maybe memories were all she'd ever have. "In this case, I'm not sure it's going to be enough."

"It will be," he said, his mouth near her ear. "These kids, our kids, were brought into this world with love and have been loved all their lives. They'll understand."

"I hope so."

He kissed her. In his kiss was the love he had for her, his want, and his need. Her heart swelled with love, but it also ached with pain for her sons, because the decision to remarry had driven a wedge between her and them, between Matt and his daughters. And at the moment, she saw no way this could be resolved.

****

"What are you doing back?" Angela demanded as soon as Matt walked through the door behind his daughters. His ex-wife glared at him. "I have plans tonight."

"That's okay, Mom. We'll be fine." Julia marched from the living room to her bedroom without saying good-bye to Matt.

Knowing how angry she was, he didn't try to stop her. At least Patsy and Amber told him good-bye, but they didn't hug him before they turned to leave. He couldn't allow it. His heart was already ripped to shreds by the scene at his house. Angela stood near him, impatient to know what had happened. He ignored her for the time being.

"Wait a minute." He held out his arms. "I need a hug from my favorite girls."

"I love you, Daddy." Amber threw herself into his arms.

"I hope so because I'll never stop loving you," he murmured against her hair.

Standing by the sofa, Patsy blinked. "Gloria is your favorite girl now." Her eyes filled with tears, and Matt's heart ached even more.

"Oh, so the bimbo...er..." Angela paused, probably because he'd told her countless times not to call Gloria names. "Your girlfriend caused this."

"Patsy, darling girl, you're my daughter, and no one will ever take that away from you."

He held out his other arm to her while still holding onto Amber. Patsy allowed him to engulf her in his arms. "I'll see you soon, girls. Go settle in. I have to talk to your mother."

Angela tapped her foot, encased in a four-inch, strapless red heel, as the girls left the room. He used to admire her legs, especially when she wore short skirts. Now he had to stop himself from criticizing her attire. She had teen daughters, for God's sake. Her blouse showed more cleavage than a woman her age should, too. He liked the way Gloria dressed—far more conservative, yet somehow still sexy.

"Well?" she asked when he didn't say a word.

"We had a bit of trouble."

"Obviously." She crossed her arms.

"Don't you think you should dress your age?" Matt blurted, wishing he hadn't said a word in the same instant.

"What?" She frowned at him and stopped pacing. Long, gold earrings dangled from her ears. "What business is it of yours? I'll dress the way I damn well please."

"You should set a better example. You have teenagers," he said against his better judgment.

"I know. I provide for them every day, but once in a while I like to go out, have some fun. Now the girls are back home way too early. What if I'd planned to entertain…later?"

She was trying to bait him. But he no longer cared what she did, hadn't for a long time, especially since he'd met Gloria.

"You're free to entertain whoever you want," he told her. "I don't care anymore as long as the girls aren't adversely affected."

"Look, I'd like to stay and chat, but Jorge is coming soon." She glanced at the front door.

"Don't tell me you're seeing that bum again."

She resumed her pacing. "He and I have a certain…connection."

"Yeah, well. The girls are back early because I asked Gloria to marry me. The girls…actually, none of the kids liked the idea. We had a big fight tonight."

21

"You and Gloria? Hey, this is worth making Jorge wait." Angela grinned.

"Not us. The kids."

"Hallelujah." Her grin widened.

"I'm glad you're so happy. I knew the story would make your day."

"My day, my night, my whole weekend. Serves you right. You can't bring in some woman and expect my girls to accept her. They know better. No one can replace me."

Her triumphant words grated on Matt's nerves. "I'm not trying to replace you, Angela. You'll always be the girls' mother. I fell in love."

"You fell out of love with me," she spat out, squinting. "What makes you think it'll last this time?"

"You killed my love for you when you had an affair."

"At the time you told me you'd never fall in love again. You wouldn't want to go through the pain again."

"I couldn't imagine love coming into my life again until I met Gloria."

"You can't marry her if the girls don't like her. They won't want to visit you, and I need a break sometimes." She walked to the closet and grabbed a thin red sweater.

"Don't worry. I'll always manage to spend time with my daughters." He watched his ex slip on the sweater.

"You'll have to get rid of Gloria. I don't want my girls unhappy," she said.

"You did so when you had the affair." He hated himself for bringing up the past again.

She shrugged. "I deserve happiness, too."

"And I don't?"

She motioned to the door. "You have to go. Jorge will be here soon."

"I need to talk to you about the girls on another subject. You seem to be angry all the time. Is something else going on?"

"Why should I be angry?" Her eyes widened in realization. "Patsy squealed, didn't she? She's so quiet, and she eats like a horse. She needs to be more like me, like Julia."

"Each of the girls is a person in her own right," he said, trying not to lecture her. "Leave them alone to develop their own identities."

"You never back me up, do you?" She waved her hands. "I just want Patsy to get out of her shell."

"You'll make the girls miserable pushing them to your tastes, Angela."

"I can take care of my girls."

Feeling tired all of a sudden, Matt ruffled his hair and sighed. "Sure you can. I have to go." His gaze lingered on the home he'd thought they'd made for their family. He didn't relish the thought of running into Jorge again. He would never forget the sight of the man in bed with his wife.

As he walked out, Angela said a clipped good-bye. He deserved happiness, too. He'd been alone for a long time. And he'd been content—until Gloria. He wasn't about to get rid of her, as his ex so glibly suggested. Somehow, he and Gloria would achieve happiness together. Wouldn't they?

****

"I'm going on a cruise, Gloria. To Europe. Can you

believe it? My husband just presented me with the tickets," Celeste Hinojosa, the bookstore owner, said as soon as Gloria entered the back office of Books and All.

"Oh…great." Gloria tried to sound enthusiastic, but she was still reeling from the events of the weekend. Her sons had gone to their room Saturday evening after they'd returned from Matt's house. They hadn't come out again. Sunday, quiet reigned throughout the day, her sons only speaking to her when necessary. Dex had perused the classifieds looking for an apartment. Matt had called last night, but they both had been distracted, thinking of their kids.

"Oh, I'm so excited. We're visiting fifteen cities, and I can't wait. You can be in charge of the bookstore while I'm gone. Normally, I'd have to close up, but with you here, I have another option." Celeste patted her on the arm.

Gloria swallowed hard. "When are you leaving?"

"Next week," Celeste said without batting an eyelash.

"What? But you can't. I'm not ready."

"Nonsense. You've been here six months, and I've been watching you. You're a natural."

"But we have those children's authors coming in for a book signing."

"Everything's ready. You just have to make sure the tables and books are set up, and plenty of coffee and cookies or whatever are available. You can do it. I know you can. Otherwise, I wouldn't leave."

"But, Celeste, there are still so many things I don't know." Gloria tried in vain to make her boss understand. She wasn't afraid of the challenge, but with things so chaotic in her personal life, she wasn't sure she could manage.

"You'll know what to do. I just know it. Besides, I'll have my cell on."

"But Europe is like a day ahead. I'd probably be calling you at night."

"I probably won't be sleeping." Celeste grinned and winked.

"For sure, you don't want to be disturbed then, do you?" Gloria couldn't resist grinning back, even though her heart felt heavy.

Would she and Matt ever go on a cruise? At the moment, she just wanted to be with him in his house, on his bed. And she wanted the kids to get along. Talking about cruises reminded her of her friend, Tanya Simmons. She was on a cruise at present, actually due to arrive back home this week.

Gordy had blamed Tanya for sending Matt to her. Did he really believe it, or had he been caught up in the emotion of the moment? Gordy was usually so easygoing. All kinds of things could be happening around him, but if he could still do what he wanted, his activities, video games, weight lifting, and no one bothered him, he was fine. The way Dex was feeling probably influenced him. Her sons were very close, not only brothers but also best friends.

Celeste was still talking. "Come into my office. I need to give you access to the accounting software and the online catalog so you can update it if you need to. You've been helping me, so that's familiar to you. Otherwise, I've shown you everything else you need to know."

Gloria couldn't believe it. Celeste wanted to leave

her in charge of the bookstore for the next three weeks. After an hour, her boss left in a bustle of activity, a wave of jasmine perfuming the back office. She had wanted to get started packing for her cruise.

How am I going to handle this? I'm so new.

Her body shook as she heard the bell from the front door. A customer. Okay, she'd dealt with those before. She still could, even without her boss present. She kept busy assisting the flow of customers and finding what they wanted. She was grateful Celeste had hired a cashier. On busy days it'd taken too much of her time to help everyone without asking them to wait longer than necessary. The cashier was scheduled to start this week. Another thing Celeste had left her to deal with.

Trepidation made her stomach flutter. Then she squared her shoulders. She could do this. Running a bookstore was something she'd aspired to do for some time now—her dream come true, aside from also owning one. And now she had a personal dream: to marry Matt.

Her excitement and wonder at the idea a man had actually proposed to her at this time of her life paled somewhat when she remembered the kids' reactions. Somehow, everything would settle into place.

****

Matt sat in his truck in front of the office complex where he had a meeting in twenty minutes. This was a huge contract, and he needed it, especially if he was going to plan a wedding. The events of the weekend still jarred inside him. He'd tried to talk to the girls, but Patsy and Amber sounded sad, and Julia refused to speak to him. *Totally unacceptable.*

When his marriage to Angela ended, he swore

nothing would ever come between his daughters and himself. He needed to be a part of every aspect of their lives. And he'd managed it—until now.

He didn't regret meeting Gloria. He had a future with her, and somehow they'd be able to achieve happiness together—along with their kids. He picked up his cell and punched in her number.

"Hey, beautiful," he said after she greeted him. "I'm working on getting a new contract."

"Is that good?"

"You bet. This is my big break. If I make, or I should say, when I make a success with this, I'll finally be on my way to grow my company in a new direction."

"I'm so happy for you, Matt. When does the job start?"

"Not sure. Today I meet with the owner of the property. I'm here right now. But I had to call you."

"I'm glad you did."

"He'll show me what he wants. I'll give him an estimate. Hopefully, he'll accept it, and I'll have a new contract. Thing is, I've heard he's very particular about what he wants. Apparently, the man has a reputation for terminating contracts after a couple of weeks if he's not satisfied."

"He'll like you," she said.

"I think you're biased." Matt fiddled with the steering wheel.

"Well, maybe, but you do good work. Do you want me to write up a testimonial for you?"

He heard Gloria's teasing voice, and he could imagine her smile. "I should have thought of it before I had my media kit designed."

"Yes, what could be a better ad than to say, 'With Matt's company, you find love among the roses'?"

"I think the ladies would appreciate it. I'm not so sure about the men, though." He grinned. He could always count on Gloria to make his day lighter.

"I miss you."

He heard her sigh, the wistfulness in her voice. "Me, too. We need to go out again."

"I know. I'm not sure…"

"How's it going?" he asked.

"They're looking for an apartment. I need to have a talk with them. This can't go on. We're a family, and we're barely speaking to each other."

"I tried to talk to the girls, but they're still upset and worried. Julia won't talk to me. And Angela is furious—and worried, too—because the girls won't want to visit me and she needs her space."

"My sons want to give me too much space." She laughed, but he knew she wasn't happy about her sons moving out. "Well, I mean, they're old enough to have their own place, but they're leaving for the wrong reasons."

"We can't let the kids bully us into giving up. We want to be together, right?"

"Right."

"So we'll work it out. I just wanted to hear your voice before I went in. Wish me luck."

"You know I do. Call later and let me know what happens."

"I love you," Matt said in a soft voice.

"I love you," Gloria said.

He smiled, liking that he could share his business with a woman. Angela had always believed his job as a landscaper was nothing more than a lawn man trying to make a few pennies for extra money. She'd always told him doing yardwork was something a schoolboy did. Gloria, on the other hand, made him feel his business was a real business. Only one of the many reasons he loved her.

For now, he had to go and get a contract. He had wedding plans.

Chapter Three

I can do this!

Her boss had been gone a little over a week now, and Gloria was determined not to let Celeste, or herself, down. Still, her stomach flip-flopped as she heard the bell from the front door. *A customer! No problem.* She set aside her sandwich and walked to the cashier's station, where Beatrice Lopez waited.

Gloria ran to her friend and hugged her. Some minutes were taken in exclaiming over how the other looked and how they'd missed each other.

"The agency isn't the same without you," Beatrice said, adjusting her purse strap on her shoulder, as she always did.

Gloria shook her head. Why didn't she just set her heavy purse down? "I miss seeing you every day, but I don't miss the office. I'm having so much fun working here with books, meeting people who love books. At least, I was having fun until now."

"What happened?" Beatrice wrinkled her brow.

"My boss left for a three-week cruise."

"Wow." Beatrice sighed. "I'd love to go on a cruise, but I'm afraid of the water."

Gloria laughed. "Oh, Beatrice. With Celeste gone, I'm in charge. I've only been working here six months."

Beatrice dismissed her misgivings with a wave of

her hand. "You can do it. You ought to be in my shoes. Now that's something hard to deal with."

"What? Or should I ask who? As if I didn't know." Gloria grinned.

"Chavo," they said the name together. Beatrice's husband.

"What happened?" Gloria asked.

"The stupid man tried to build the girls a tree house. They don't even want one. He treats them like boys sometimes. I told him the girls don't want to climb trees. But, of course, he insisted."

"And?"

"He fell out of the tree, broke both his right arm and right leg, and almost knocked himself out cold because the boards he was carrying up with him fell on him." Beatrice's eyes glittered with fury.

Gloria laughed. She couldn't help herself. "He tried to build a tree house, and all it cost him was an arm and a leg."

Beatrice smiled with no humor.

"I'm sorry." Gloria tried not to laugh again.

"I'm so angry with him. I want to break his other arm and leg, plus crack his dumb skull. He's driving me crazy. He's taking more of my time than the girls ever did, even when they were babies."

"How long will it take for him to heal?"

"It already seems to have taken forever, and it's been one week. But the doc said four to six weeks."

"I know it'll be hard for you to be patient." Gloria patted Beatrice's hand.

"It will. You know how he can be. That's why I had to come over to talk to you. I don't have to explain. You know how things are."

"I'm glad you stopped by. I'm always here for you, you know. As a matter of fact, I have a bit of news, too. Happier than yours, though."

"What?"

"I'm getting married." Gloria lifted her left hand.

"Really? Wow." Beatrice admired the ring and hugged her. "I'm so happy for you."

Gloria handed her friend a tissue after she released her and saw her teary eyes. Which made Gloria's eyes water as well—and made her remember all the ugly events of the weekend when they'd told the kids.

"When are you getting married?" Beatrice asked.

"We haven't set the date. We're having a few problems." She sniffled. "The kids had a big fight two weekends ago. They're not talking to us. Matt is trying to contract a new job. Celeste has left. It's a big mess."

"It'll work out. You guys love each other."

"Maybe we're just kidding ourselves. I mean, we can just continue as we are. The kids are happy with that, right? And that was hard enough to get them to accept. Why unbalance everything?"

"You sound as if you're trying to convince yourself. You need to marry Matt, share your life, his bed." Her friend finished with a wicked leer in her eyes.

"Oh you," Gloria said and laughed. "Though that is something to think about."

"Of course it is."

"It's so hard when you're older. You think too much about it. When I married Eddie, I eloped. I didn't even stop to think about anything. Of course, I was in my early twenties. When you're young and carefree, you don't think about families, who's going to like who, who won't like each other, what if it doesn't last.

32

What if he won't love me forever? All you think about is each other, about him, about the love you feel, and you want to be with him. You have to be with him."

Beatrice eyed her closely. "So...I don't see the problem."

"I have two sons who hate Matt. He has three daughters who don't like me. For sure, Julia doesn't."

"You're thinking of others again. Your sons will be okay. They're grown up. They're just not willing to share you. They've had you to themselves for all this time."

"You're right. Dex, especially. I think he feels usurped."

"He'll understand eventually. You can't let Matt get away."

"I'll send you a wedding invitation if everything is resolved."

"Once it's resolved," Beatrice said.

"Come on. Let me show you the store. Do you have time?"

Beatrice looked at her watch. "A little."

"I'll show you the children's section first. We received a new shipment of books from a couple of new children's authors you might like for your girls." She led Beatrice over to a corner with two shelves of books. In the middle was a small square table with four chairs.

"This is nice," Beatrice commented.

"Maybe you and your girls can come to the book signing. Those two writers will be here this Saturday morning at ten."

"You know Saturdays are hard for me, but I'll try. I do want to get the girls more interested in reading. But I'll see. I have to do my usual chores—laundry, mopping, changing bed linens. And now with Chavo laid up in bed… Oh, I get so mad every time I think of it."

"See! It's perfect. You can get away from your humdrum tasks."

Beatrice laughed. "I like the idea."

"If you can't make it, I'll save the books and have the writers sign them for your girls," Gloria said. She hugged Beatrice at the door.

Beatrice looked at her watch. "I'm going to be late."

"Tell your boss it's my fault," Gloria said with a grin.

She sobered up as soon as her friend left, remembering she wouldn't see Matt again this weekend. He was busy negotiating the new contract. They hadn't seen each other since the weekend with the kids. Talking on the phone was not the same. She wanted Matt to grow his business. He'd worked hard for several years now, and he deserved this new opportunity. But she missed him, not only his physical touch but the emotional sensations he brought to her life.

With Eddie, it'd been such a whirlwind romance. Now she wasn't so sure. Maybe it'd been all about sex. Eddie showed up, young, virile, exciting, thinking only of having fun. She'd become intoxicated with him and could think of nothing else. When the smoke cleared, she was married, and a baby, Dex, was on the way. Suddenly, Eddie's fun-loving ways weren't so exciting anymore. He still wanted to continue in the same way while her life had changed completely. A life grew inside her, and she wasn't ready. Her life with Eddie was one crisis after another, some of which could have been prevented if only he had manned up.

With Matt, the relationship evolved a little more slowly. Of course, now both of them had others to consider, their kids, who barely tolerated each other. Amber, though, was so sweet, thinking of Gordy as her big brother. He pretended to ignore her, but he had let her play video games with him.

Gloria was determined to make the relationship work, their marriage work. She needed to tell her sister Lynda so they could plan the wedding. This time she wanted to do everything right.

Matt was also more solicitous of her. He talked to her about his work, his daughters, and his ex. Eddie had, too, the times he was home, but more often, he would get home, eat, shower, and then want to have sex. Even then, at so young an age, she wanted more. She wanted to share a life with a man, not just a bed, although as Eddie loved to point out, the sex was great.

Now the sex was fabulous, and so was the man. Maybe she and Matt could get together next weekend.

****

"I will never like her," Julia yelled. "I don't like you anymore either."

Matt didn't know what to do with Julia. Admittedly, she'd always been a challenge. She was so much like her mother, stubborn and determined to get her own way. But then, he was like that, too. So maybe he was fighting a losing battle. They were too much alike. No one wanted to give way. He'd inveigled Angela to let him visit the girls after work this evening to try to patch things up. Since his ex had ulterior motives, she'd agreed.

"Julia, we have to find a way to work this out," he said.

"Never. I will never accept her as your wife. Mom is the only wife you should ever have had. And if you hadn't been so busy with work, she'd have never been lonely and looked for someone else."

"My God! What did your mother tell you?" He couldn't believe Angela told Julia about her affair, let alone tried to discuss it with her. *Loneliness, my foot.* She craved attention. What was she showing Julia? If your husband neglected you, it was acceptable to turn to someone else, forget your vows, the love you'd pledged. Sometimes he wished he'd never have to talk to Angela again, but he couldn't have her influencing his girls in such negative ways.

Patsy and Amber had remained silent.

"Do you girls feel the same way?"

Patsy opened her mouth, but before she could speak, Julia interrupted. "Yes, they do. So you can just leave. We're never going to visit you again."

She ran to her room. Patsy and Amber followed, waving to him, but neither of them gave him a hug.

Angela walked in from the hallway. "You sure have messed it up, haven't you? You'd better straighten it out. I can't have the girls here all the time. I need my space."

Matt clenched his fists at his side. He longed to hit something, but any damage he did he'd have to pay for. Angela would see to that. He willed himself not to yell. "Do you care about anything or anyone but yourself? Why did you tell Julia about your affair?"

"Julia is a woman. She has to know how the real world works," she said and sat on the recliner.

"If it weren't for the girls, I'd wish I'd never met you." He realized he meant it with his whole heart.

"I wonder what Gloria would say if she heard you right now."

"What do you mean?"

"You used to pledge your undying love for me, and now you don't want me in your life. The same could happen to her. What if she makes a mistake? Or gets lonely as I did? She'll lose you, too. You can't stand it when people make mistakes. Or when they get sick. You're full of issues, Matt. Bad issues." She stood and pointed at him. "You need help."

"The only help I need is with the girls. Help me. You can influence Julia, and she'll influence Patsy and Amber."

"Over my dead body, Matt. You fight your own damn battles."

****

Gloria let herself into the house. No one was home, and she hated it. Maybe because she'd seldom arrived to an unwelcoming, empty house. Now her sons were usually out looking for an apartment. She didn't even know in what part of town they were looking. Did they want to be near her or as far away as they could get? And, really, who knew where she and Matt would live? For her part, she wanted to start fresh in a house where no ex had set foot. She wasn't sure how Matt felt about moving, though. There were so many things they hadn't talked about yet, and they really should. Maybe they didn't know each other as well as they should.

She went around the house, turning on lights. She didn't like dark rooms. So it wasn't energy efficient, but she couldn't help it. She turned the TV on classic shows, reruns. Right now, she didn't want to watch. She just wanted accompanying noise.

Should she heat up a frozen dinner? She wasn't hungry. Her heart hurt. Her sons seemed allied against her, something so foreign to her. They'd always been a team, the three of them against the world and whatever it brought—happiness, sadness, or a good jolt to bring them to their senses. Maybe her sons needed a good jolt.

As she sat at the dining table contemplating dinner again, she heard the key turn in the lock on the front door. Lately, they'd come home and go straight to their room. Today, Dex walked to the dining table with food bags.

"What is this?" she asked.

"A peace offering," he said.

"We don't like what's been going on here," Gordy added.

Gloria's eyes filled with tears. "I'm so glad because I don't either. We're a family, and we always will be no matter what."

She stood to hug them, and they indulged in a long-overdue group hug. "I never want you to think I'd ever do anything to make you unhappy. We would work on it until we found a solution."

"I'm not sure how we can, Mom," Dex said.

"I don't know either," she confessed. "But it's not like we're going to get married—"

Both boys groaned.

"Things aren't going to change immediately. Do you think I could be happy if you two weren't? We all have to be somehow. We have to find a way. Haven't we always?" she asked. "But we've always done it together."

"We're sorry, Mom," Gordy said. "Well, I am. I don't know about Stupid."

Dex hit his brother. "I do apologize, Mom. I'll try to understand."

"Just try to accept. I myself don't understand why I want to take a chance with Matt, risk my heart again, but love defies explanation. So let's eat. What did you bring?"

She thoroughly enjoyed the burgers from a new place the boys found. Even if they'd been burnt and awful, she'd have liked them. She and her boys were sharing a meal again and talking. They still had work to do, but together she was sure they could achieve what they all wanted.

She hoped Matt would be as successful with his daughters. She was afraid Angela exerted too much influence on their feelings, especially on Julia's. She was thankful Eddie wasn't around to muddy the waters even more, though Dex had called him when he'd first found out about Matt's proposal. She didn't fear Eddie. He had no rights over her, and her sons were older now, not babies. They could think for themselves. However, she'd better be prepared for whatever his crazy devious mind would come up with.

****

"I got the contract, Gloria," Matt said into the phone without a greeting the next morning. He was so damned excited as he'd climbed into his truck parked in front of the office complex. And the first person he'd thought of calling was Gloria. He couldn't make out what she said. She was speaking so low. Or was it the connection?

"Gloria, I can't hear you."

"He's signing next month… What am I going to do? Celeste didn't tell me anything about this. I'm sorry…what? I didn't hear you," she muttered.

"I said I got the contract. Remember? The big one I was working on? I'm going to need to hire some more workers, which means more taxes and paperwork, but I can handle it." He couldn't believe how good this felt. Finally, all his hard work was about to pay off. But he was also a little scared. He'd never taken a job this big. "I'm a little worried."

He heard more mumbling. "Maybe I could…the publisher…man's books…Celeste…cruise…it's a fine time …"

This was unlike Gloria. She was always willing to hear news about his business and share in his excitement over his accomplishments. What was going on? Was someone in the office with her? Then she should just tell him, not keep him hanging on.

"Yeah," she said.

"I'm going to be very busy, but it's a great contract. We'll be able to go on a honeymoon." If that didn't get her attention, nothing would.

"The publisher is in Houston… That's right, isn't it? Who is this man, anyway?"

"Gloria? It's me. Matt. Who are you talking to?" Had she heard a single word he said?

"Yes, great contract… I'm…so…happy for you, Matt." Something clattered, and she mumbled a curse. "Where is the darn number?"

"Is something wrong?"

"There it is," she exclaimed.

This time he heard her clear as a bell, but she

wasn't talking to him. "Have you heard anything I've said?" He was beginning to feel hurt. He was telling her something important, and she couldn't care less.

"I'm sorry. I have a crisis here."

"Do you want to go on a honeymoon with me?" He heard her catch her breath. Finally, he had her full attention.

"More than anything."

Matt cleared his throat as her words reverberated throughout his body. He wanted to be with her at this moment, holding her. "For a minute there, I thought I was talking to the wrong Gloria."

Her laugh made his pulse race. "I'm just distracted. Too much has been happening lately."

"Tell me about it." He couldn't help a sigh.

"Oh, Matt, I have to take this call." She hung up on him without another word.

He stared at his cell. *What the hell?* For a split second, he was taken back to his marriage with Angela. She'd frequently hung up on him when he'd called her regarding his work. He was tempted to call Gloria back, but she was working, after all, and had apparently encountered some problem and was very busy. With this new contract, he was going to be ultrabusy himself for the next several months. He might not even be able to get away for a honeymoon, if all the wedding details were finalized in the next six months. As far as he knew, no plans had been made. They hadn't even set a date. He and Gloria were still trying to get the kids squared away on the issue.

If her sons moved to their own place, then at least he wouldn't have to run up against antagonistic boys in his own house. However, Gloria wouldn't be happy if her sons weren't. As for his daughters, Julia still wouldn't talk to him, and Patsy and Amber followed her example. Angela was no help at all. No surprise.

He'd call Gloria later, when she was home. They needed to go out. Too many things were happening, and they needed to stay in touch and on the same page.

Work had always helped him through rough spots. He knew really tough ones were in his future, not only with his job but with his personal life. For now, he was going back to work.

Chapter Four

Gloria stood at the checkout giving Judy Ann last-minute instructions for customers who bought the authors' books this morning.

The girl had been working for a few weeks now, and she caught on fast. She was young, in college, and had a good head on her shoulders. She also loved books and finding out about new authors. Gloria couldn't have asked for a better employee.

"I'm so excited, Gloria," she gushed. "I've never met real writers before. Have you?"

"A few at the chain bookstores. That's how I got the idea to invite authors here. Celeste hadn't even invited anyone. She was content to sell books. Which is good, but maybe we'll get more buyers this way. Especially since these are children's books. It's a great way to start kids on a reading track and another way for moms to keep their kids busy besides just the TV."

"I can help with babysitting. I take care of these two kids, and their attention span is like five minutes." Judy Ann emphasized with her spread-out hand.

She exaggerated, but not by much. Gloria remembered her boys as toddlers. Sometimes, it did seem that way. She tuned in to Judy Ann's words again.

"They love for me to read to them. I do the characters' voices, and they get a kick out of it," the girl said.

"I bet they do. I'm sure they'll gain a love of books with your help."

"I'm going to buy these books for them. Have the author sign them, too. They'll be surprised. They are sweet, even though they drive me nuts sometimes." She turned to wait on a customer who'd just walked in.

Gloria went to check the area she'd cleared off for the reading and book signing. She'd made coffee and set out doughnuts and muffins. The chairs were aligned in rows. The author table was ready with books and bookmarks. A sign announcing the event, which she'd placed on the window until today, was by the table.

She hoped it would go well. She needed success right about now. She'd tried to call Matt the last couple of days since he'd told her of his new contract, and his cell had gone straight to voice mail. She'd thought about texting an apology but decided it would be too impersonal. And her sons kept looking for an apartment in the evenings. Her life was completely awry, so today must be a triumph.

The authors would arrive in thirty minutes. The event began at ten. Before she knew it, the time passed, and she greeted the two children's authors, Yvette Salinas and Marjorie Green.

"Welcome to Books and All, ladies. Come look at where you'll be." Gloria led them to the reading area. "Is everything to your liking?"

"Oh yes." Marjorie picked up one of her books about trains told in picture-book style. The cover depicted a colorful train. The book was titled *A Train's History.*

Yvette looked around as if searching for something.

"How about you?" Gloria asked. "May I help you?"

The woman leaned toward Gloria. "I thought I would have a separate table," she whispered. You know, we don't know each other. Our books are totally different."

Oh no, a diva writer. Just what I need.

Yvette showed Gloria her book, which featured a doll wearing a pink lacy dress. Gloria hadn't paid it too much attention when she'd first seen it. Since she'd raised boys, her attention veered toward boyish things.

"I'm sorry, Yvette. The PR person at your publishing company didn't say anything. Both of you are published through them. I promise you'll get a chance to tell everyone about your book, and you do have plenty of room."

Yvette sighed. "I suppose it'll have to do. I'm going to have to talk to Nicole."

Apparently, Nicole was someone she knew at the publishing company. Well, more power to her. Gloria had things to do. People came in with their kids, the store resounded with parents' voices admonishing children, and either quiet or protesting ensued.

"Judy Ann, stay at the checkout, but keep an eye on wandering kids," she said.

For the occasion, Gloria had removed knickknacks enticing to kids, but they could still knock books off the shelves.

As she looked out at the crowd, she felt relief, but also pride. Future book signings depended on the outcome of this first one. Now if only the books sold, it'd be an unqualified success.

She cleared her throat and called the crowd to

attention. "Thank you, everyone, for coming. I'm so glad to see so many of you here, especially on a Saturday morning. Please help me welcome two up-and-coming children's authors, Yvette Salinas and Marjorie Green.

The audience clapped. Gloria introduced Yvette first. Maybe the woman would curb her diva tendencies. She stood, walked to the podium, and began to talk about her doll book.

"Mama, I don't want to hear about dolls. Those are for girls. I want the train book." A shrill voice interrupted Yvette, who frowned at the boy.

The mother hushed her son and apologized. Gloria motioned Yvette to continue. After she read a few pages of the book, Yvette got a bit long-winded, talking about her path to publication. Gloria had to walk up and thank her so Marjorie could have a turn.

Marjorie's easygoing attitude and big smile did much to endear her to the audience. She was brief and to the point. "I want you"—she pointed to the little boy who'd spoken out before—"to be the first in line to look at this book. What's your name?"

"Gerard." The boy hung his head.

"Come up here, Gerard, and you can look at the trains. Maybe your mom can come, too."

He ran up to Marjorie, and the audience clapped. Yvette pursed her lips and straightened her already-neat lacy collar.

Gloria stepped up to the podium. "Thank you, everyone. Please come up and meet the authors and get your book autographed before you purchase it." As she said this, she spotted Beatrice and her girls at the front of the store.

"Beatrice, you came." She greeted her friend with a smile. "Hi, girls."

"It was a hassle getting them dressed, and they were so noisy." Beatrice pushed back her tousled hair. "I didn't want Chavo to wake up, but he did. It took me forever to get out of the house."

"I'm glad you're here. Did you get to hear the authors speak?"

"The last one. I heard you tell the other one to shut up and sit down." Beatrice grinned.

"I hope I didn't sound rude."

"She deserved it if you had been." Beatrice lowered her voice. "I've a good mind to buy the train book because I like the lady better, but I know the girls will like the doll book."

"She is very unlikeable, isn't she? I hope she changes her attitude, or she won't sell many books. This event is a test for me. Celeste never holds book signings."

"You'll be fine." Beatrice waved off Gloria's concerns, as she always did.

"Go over and meet the writers." Gloria stood back and watched as Beatrice and other parents went up to the author table.

"Hey, beautiful."

She turned to see Matt, hair wet, jeans and boots with stray leaves and dirt on them. His rust-colored T-shirt was cut off at the sleeves, showing off his muscled brown arms.

"Matt, you came. But I thought you were busy…" Her voice wavered.

"I am, but we hadn't talked in a few days, and the last time wasn't our best conversation. I missed you."

She drank in the sight of him. Even dressed as he was, he still looked wonderful. She remembered how distracted she'd been the last time he'd called. "I'm sorry."

He bent down to kiss her. She leaned closer and lost herself in his embrace. But she stepped away quickly when she heard giggles.

"They're kissing," a loud boyish voice yelled.

"Oh, Matt…" she muttered.

"I'm sorry. Wrong time and place, huh?"

Gloria took his hand. "Let's go to my office. Excuse us," she told the crowd. "Please continue talking to the authors. Judy Ann will help you if you need anything." She turned to the cashier, and the girl nodded and grinned. "I'll be right back."

As she led Matt to her office, she noticed Yvette unbuttoning her lacy prim top and eyeing Matt. Gloria fought the urge to pick up one of her doll books and hit her on her ponytailed head.

Once in her office, he pulled her into his arms and kissed her thoroughly. The smell of grass and sun mixed with his spicy cologne filled her senses. Her body warmed to his touch, and she wished there were a bed nearby.

"I missed you," he murmured again against her ear.

"So did I." She laid her head on his chest. "I'm going to be covered with leaves, too."

Matt laughed, the sexy laugh that made her nerves tingle. "I'll dust them off." He proceeded to pat her all over her body.

The sensation made her ache even more to be in bed, naked with Matt. "Stop," she said, not because she really wanted him to, but because she needed to get back to work. "I'll do it myself later. Not as much fun, but…"

"I'd better go." He kissed her gently on the lips. "Let's go out tonight. Eat, movie, something, anything you want."

"Anything I want." She caressed his neck with her lips. "Umm…I like it."

"I'll pick you up at seven."

"Okay. You go first. I have to put my bookstore persona back on."

He grinned. "You look like a woman in love."

"Which is what I am with you, but not with a packed bookstore." She reached up to smooth her hair back.

"Too bad." He kissed her again. "See you soon."

As soon as he closed the door behind him, she looked at herself in the wall mirror by her desk. Her mouth looked a bit swollen. Her hair was a mess, but she could fix it.

Slowly, she opened the door and walked back into the store.

"The lady who was kissed is back, Mommy," the same little boy yelled. "She's back."

"I'm so sorry. He's so outspoken," the boy's mother said.

Gloria smiled and relaxed, remembering the times her sons had embarrassed her. "Don't worry about it. I have two sons."

"Oh my, Gloria." Yvette fanned herself with her hand. "Who was he? He was so…dirty…but yet so…" She stopped as she noticed parents looking at her.

"He's my fiancé," she said, relishing in telling Yvette.

"Oh?" Yvette wrinkled her brow. "Well...oh..." The woman slinked away.

Beatrice walked up. "I bought both books, though now I wish I hadn't bought the doll book. Never invite her again."

Gloria laughed. "I'm so glad you came. You always make things better."

"Matt made quite an impression, didn't he?" Beatrice asked with a grin. "

"Matt and I are going out tonight. We haven't done so in a while. The kids, my job, his job."

"Don't lose sight of your goal. You're going to marry this man. In spite of everything." Beatrice glared at Yvette, who, Gloria was relieved to see, hadn't noticed. "I'd better go see to my Prince Charming."

"Thanks for coming, Beatrice." Gloria patted the girls' heads. "Hope you like the books." Beatrice's daughters grinned and hung their heads, staying close to their mom.

Most of the customers had left by this time.

"I sold half my books," Marjorie said. "Thank you so much, Gloria. This was so much fun. The children were so sweet."

"Sweet? The stupid little boy spilled his punch. It almost got on me and my books. Next time, Gloria, I suggest you not serve red punch." Yvette fiddled with her collar, realized her sweater was unbuttoned, and remedied the situation.

Gloria restrained herself from rolling her eyes. Marjorie winked.

She helped both authors pack up. They left several autographed books for customers.

"I'll send you a check for your percentage in about

two weeks. Thank you so much," Gloria said.

Judy Ann gave her a thumbs-up as both authors walked out the door. "Celeste will let you have one of these again."

She forbore to tell Judy Ann that Celeste had herself set up a writer but hadn't followed up on everything, and now Gloria had several loose ends to tie up in two weeks.

But first things first. Tonight she had a date with Matt. And she couldn't wait.

****

Gloria arrived home euphoric over the success of the book signing. She still had the problem of that other author coming for a book signing in a couple of weeks, but after today, she knew she could handle it. For now, she couldn't wait to see Matt, spend some time with him, touch him, and kiss him. The attraction she felt for Matt continued to surprise her at times. When her sons were little boys, she'd gone out to clubs, danced, and met men. However, all she'd ever wanted to do with them was dance and then go home alone. Finally, she'd just stopped looking. Once in a while, she'd missed dancing. When she met Matt, she'd been content with her life. All she'd wanted was a blooming rose garden. Matt had given it to her—and so much more.

As she opened the door, she was happy to know her sons were home. Nowadays, they were always out looking for an apartment when they weren't in school or at work.

"Hi, boys." She stood at the entrance of their room, which was in total disarray. "What are you doing?"

"Oh, hi, Mom." Dex walked out of the closet. "We decided to throw out some stuff we don't want anymore. That way we don't have to haul so much junk."

"Where's Gordy?" Her throat closed up, knowing her sons hadn't changed their minds about moving out.

"He went to get us something to eat. You, too, Mom. I think he's getting pizza and wings."

"I'm going out with Matt tonight." She hated herself for sounding apologetic. She wasn't sorry she was going out with Matt. He was her fiancé. She loved him and wanted to spend time with him.

He turned around and went back into the closet. "You do your thing. We'll do ours."

"Where are you looking for an apartment? I mean, what area?" she asked, just to change the subject.

"Around here. Gordo still has high school, and he can't transfer out, or he shouldn't have to. Besides, he's still new at driving. If we stay around here, he won't have too far to go."

Gloria laughed. "Good thinking."

"I think I did learn some things from you," Dex said and laughed.

"Oh you. I didn't want you to move too far away from me."

He threw some T-shirts into a plastic bag. "We'll be around."

"You know you can always come back. You'll always have a home with me no matter what." She remembered the lesson her dad taught her. In spite of the mistakes she'd made, especially when she eloped with Eddie, he'd always welcomed her back. Once the boys moved their furniture out, she'd put a bed in there, make it a guest room, in case her boys needed it.

"Thanks, Mom. But I don't want to come crawling

back at the first sign of trouble. I really want this to work."

"Just remember I'm always here. No matter what."

A clatter at the door announced Gordy's arrival. "Hey, Stupid! Come help me."

"Weakling," Dex yelled. "You can do it yourself."

Gloria ran to the door and took the pizza from Gordy's arms. He carried two liter-sized sodas, one under each arm.

"I didn't want to make two trips." He gave her a mischievous grin.

"I hope you didn't drop my wings," Dex said.

"Yeah, I did," Gordy said. He bent over the sofa and let the sodas drop from under his arms.

She hoped they wouldn't spew out when they were opened.

"Sorry to tell you, man, but all the sauce spilled out," Gordy teased.

"Sauceless wings," Dex said. "Just what I wanted."

"Let's eat," Gordy said.

"Mom's going out." Dex sat at the table.

Gordy's smile faded.

"I'm sorry," she said. "I'd love to spend some time with you. We'll do it tomorrow night."

"I have a project I need to finish," Gordy said. "I'll probably have to stay up all night tonight and tomorrow night."

"So this is your only free slot." Her stomach sank. The distance growing between her and her sons reared its ugly head.

Gordy grinned. "Afraid so."

"Well, we'll have to find a time so we can have a farewell party or bon voyage or something when you move. This is a milestone—my sons moving out."

Dex bit into a wing and shook his hand. "Mom, we're not going to the moon."

"It sure feels like it. Like you're moving so far away."

"We'll stay in the neighborhood. We have a couple of leads."

"But don't just move because of this, before you're ready. I don't want you struggling out there if it's not necessary," Gloria said.

"We're not, Mom," Dex said. "I've been thinking about it for some time now. I guess I just needed the right motivation."

"I also want you boys to get along with Matt. I don't want fights all the time."

"It's hard, Mom," Dex said.

"How about you, Gordy?" she asked.

"It feels weird sometimes. And I can't go against Dex. But then I'm against you."

"No, we are not enemies," she said. "Just remember I'm not going to do anything unless I'm absolutely sure everything will be okay with you, with Matt's daughters, and between Matt and me. I mean, I know things won't be perfect, but I'd like all of us to at least be willing to work things out. Okay?"

Dex and Gordy didn't speak.

"Boys?"

"Okay," Dex said.

"We'll try," Gordy added.

"That's all I ask. Well, I'd better get ready. Matt will be here in about an hour." She shot to her feet. "Oh gosh, he's going to be here in one hour."

"We'll be in our room," Dex said.

She didn't have time to argue. She had to get ready. And she wanted so badly to see Matt. She just wished they'd be able to reach some kind of a compromise.

****

The doorbell sounded. Matt had arrived. Her heart hammered in her chest when she remembered his kisses in her office this morning. She yearned for more. She checked her appearance once more in the mirror and rushed to open the door.

"You're more beautiful than you were this morning," he said. He wore jeans and a black T-shirt, which showed off his brown, muscled arms.

"You clean up well." She pulled him close to kiss him on the lips, something she'd been waiting on since this morning.

"Dex and Gordy are here, right?" He pointed to Dex's truck, one Matt had helped him buy.

"Yes, but they're in their room, packing up stuff to take and stuff to give away. They're still adamant about moving out. Do you want to come in for a minute?"

"No, let's go. I don't want them to feel they have to stay in their room."

"They were a bit disappointed I was going out." She turned to grab her purse. "They'd bought pizza and wings. I guess they were a bit angry, too."

"With me?" Matt stepped back on the porch as she closed and locked the door.

"At the situation. They'll be okay. I talked to them. We'll work it out. How about you and your daughters?"

In the truck, he turned on the ignition. "Not so good. I went to see them last week, but they were still angry with me, especially Julia. Something's going on with her besides how she feels about us."

"I'm sorry, Matt." She patted his shoulder.

"For the first time since the divorce, they refused to visit me last weekend. But as you said, we'll work it out, right?" He grinned. "Now, where are we going? I'm just driving here."

"I'm happy. I want us to be together." She held onto his arm.

"Not fair, though. I drive. You touch."

"So let's go park somewhere."

"And neck?"

"Ummm…sounds delicious," she said.

"I'd like to walk around with you on the River Walk, but today is the first day of the annual downtown festival. Too crowded."

"Sounds nice, though. Walking around somewhere."

"Are you hungry?" he asked.

"A little." She glanced at him, his body, face, and hair. She'd much rather be cuddled next to him on a sofa somewhere, or in bed.

"Me, too."

She wondered if he meant he was a little hungry as well, or if he'd somehow read her thoughts and wanted to be alone with her. In the end, he stopped at a diner, and they ordered sandwiches to go.

"I know a park where we can walk around, and hopefully no one will be there," he said. "Everyone will be downtown."

He drove to the park, not too far from the diner, and stationed the truck overlooking a lake toward the east.

"This is beautiful," Gloria said. "It still amazes me

I haven't seen everything there is to see in San Antonio."

She and Matt enjoyed the sandwiches as the sun set behind them but still reflected in pinks, purples, and blues over the lake. Afterward, he pulled her close and kissed her.

"You know, I could get used to this." She sighed. "I called Lynda about planning our wedding. I haven't had a chance to go visit her. Things got a bit hectic at the bookstore since Celeste left and then the book signing last Saturday. However, this coming Wednesday is J.L.'s birthday, so we're going over and celebrating. Do you have any preferences for colors, food, and so forth?"

"My only preference is I want you walking up the aisle to me, where I'll be waiting at the altar." He kissed her again.

"I want it, too. Should we go walk around?" The last vestiges of the sun were still in the horizon, so it wasn't completely dark.

"If you want," he said.

"Just for a little while."

He climbed out of the truck and opened her door.

"You're such a gentleman," she said.

"Not so much." He pulled her close to his hard body. "I only agreed because I wanted to feel you much closer to me."

"Yes," Gloria whispered against his neck. "You smell so nice."

"It's the cologne," he murmured against her hair.

"Cologne mixed with you. There's no other scent like yours—woodsy, spicy, tasty..."

"Tasty?" He gave a low laugh. "Are you still

hungry, woman?"

She laughed, too. "Only for you."

They strolled along the lake. A few people were there, but in the playground area.

"Maybe it wasn't such a good idea to get out of the truck," Matt said. "I can't kiss you."

"Don't you have a mattress in the bed of your truck? We could lie there and look up at the stars."

He laughed, and his arm tightened around her as they walked slowly back to the truck, hand in hand. "Somehow I didn't figure you for the outdoorsy type."

"I'm not." She caressed his back, neck, and face. "Only with you. Do you mind if I mess up your hair?"

"No," Matt said and kissed her.

She sighed at the warmth of his lips on hers, his hands on her body. *Everybody stay at the festival. This park belongs to Matt and me.*

"Let's go home," he suggested, still holding her close.

"You're going to have to pick me up and put me back in the truck. I'm only standing because you're holding me."

He laughed. "I have that effect on you, huh?"

"Oh yes."

They made it back into the truck and to Matt's house. The anticipation of being in bed together was heightened by the magic of the night and the lake. The scent of flowers as Matt led her inside his house only added to the intense atmosphere.

She and Matt were meant to be.

She knew it. Somehow, the dreamlike quality of the night made her feel secure—for this one enchanted night.

Chapter Five

"Don't answer," Gloria said against Matt's lips when the phone rang.

He snuggled closer in the bed. "You got a point there."

The call went to the answering machine, which he had lowered so they couldn't hear it. But his cell rang next, as well as the landline again. He picked up the landline, saw the caller ID and the time, eleven on Saturday night.

"It's the girls." He sat up.

"Daddy. Mommy's fainted. We can't get her up. And Julia is not here," Amber screamed in his ear. She sounded hysterical.

He disentangled himself from Gloria and the bedcovers. "Amber, calm down, sweetheart." He tried to speak in a soothing voice. "Tell me what happened."

Gloria got up to dress. He pulled on his jeans with one hand; the other held the phone.

"I can't calm down. Mommy's dead. I just know she is. She won't move." Amber continued to scream. "Help us, Daddy."

"Where's Julia?"

"With her friends. Please come home, Daddy."

"I'll be right there, but call nine-one-one," Matt said.

"Oh my god." Gloria's exclamation penetrated his

reeling mind.

"Stay on the phone with me, Amber. Tell Patsy to call nine-one-one on the landline, okay?"

He heard Amber scream, "Patsy, call nine-one-one. Daddy said."

"I'm going to hang up, Amber. Are you listening to me? I'm going to call you right back on my cell. Okay?"

"Okay, Daddy," she said, and he could hear her sniffle. She'd been crying.

"I've got to go, Gloria," he said after he hung up. "Julia's out with friends." He grabbed his cell and dialed Patsy's cell phone number. "Amber, it's Daddy. Stay on the line."

"Okay, Daddy."

"What time does Julia get home when she's out with friends?" Gloria asked.

"Midnight is her curfew," he said.

"I'll wait for you at the girls' house. I'll tell Julia what happened, and then I'll call Dex to go pick me up, and I'll take her to the hospital."

"Thank you." He hugged Gloria. "You're the best."

"Our kids come first, don't they?"

"Let's go." He took Gloria's hand, and they ran to the truck. With the cell on speaker, he talked to Amber while he drove as fast as he dared. Thankfully, the house wasn't too faraway. He hadn't wanted to move too far from his daughters.

The ambulance was already there, its red lights swirling ominously in the night. The EMS techs were sliding the stretcher inside.

Matt jumped out of the truck. "I'm the girls' dad. She's my ex."

"Her BP was really low. She's dehydrated. It's the reason she fainted. We'll have to take her in so a doctor can check her," the EMT said.

"I'll follow you in my truck," Matt said.

"Daddy." Amber and Patsy ran out of the house and into his open arms.

"Everything will be okay, girls. Come on. We're going to follow the ambulance to the hospital."

Gloria walked up, concern in her eyes.

"Oh, Gloria." Amber took her hand. "Mommy's sick."

"She'll be fine, sweetie," Gloria said. "The doctors will know what to do."

"Are you sure?" Patsy wiped the tears from her eyes. "I don't want anything bad to happen to her. The last words I said to her were mean."

Matt exchanged a look with Gloria. He could only imagine what had occurred.

"You'll be able to talk to your mom, Patsy," he said. "Right now, get in the truck. We're going to the hospital."

"What about Julia?" Amber asked.

"I'm going to wait for her here. As soon as she gets here, I'll take her to the hospital," Gloria said.

"But you don't have a car," Amber protested.

"I'll call Dex," Gloria said.

"Come on, girls," Matt said. "The ambulance is leaving." He leaned over to kiss Gloria. "Thank you. I'll keep in touch."

He helped his daughters into the truck and jumped inside. Damn! He hated going to the hospital. However, he also needed to know Angela was going to be all right. What in hell had happened to her? And what a bad end to such a beautiful time with Gloria. His heart swelled with love as he remembered how she understood immediately what he had to do when Amber called. No hysterics. No clinging. Somehow, they could work things out and be able to make a life together with their respective kids.

****

Gloria stood on the sidewalk and watched the ambulance drive away, red light flashing and siren wailing. She didn't like Angela, but the woman was a mom and her daughters loved her. She hoped she'd be fine.

She fished her cell out of her purse, texted Dex, and walked inside. This was the house where Matt had lived with Angela as his wife. Suddenly, she wasn't sure she wanted to be there.

Angela's extreme way of dress didn't extend to the house, which was decorated in beige and black. Gaudy, red-velvet slipcovers draped over two armchairs, and a lamp with a yellow-fringed shade contrasted with the other furniture. But otherwise, she could envision Matt living in this place.

Her mind drifted back to their date. She and Matt could find so many things to talk about. After their whirlwind romance, she and Eddie didn't talk. Usually, they'd just argue because Gloria didn't see him all day, and after work he'd go anywhere but home. Then in the wee hours of the morning, he'd want sex.

She sighed and turned to the huge window overlooking the street. Small hedges grew right under the window. Matt's handiwork, she was sure. Being in his ex's house made her feel out of place, incongruous. But the unexpected had happened. What could possibly

62

be wrong with Angela? Gloria didn't know her well enough to even hazard a guess.

The door opened, and Julia walked in. Usually, the girl appeared so fashionable. Tonight her hair was messed up, and the knee of one pant leg was torn.

"What happened to you?" Gloria asked.

"What are you doing here?" Julia demanded. "Where are Mom and my sisters?"

"Julia, please sit down. I need to tell you something."

"I don't want to. Where is everyone? I'm going to call Mom." She punched numbers on her cell.

Gloria caught her hand. "I've texted Dex and Gordy…"

Julia wrenched her hand from Gloria's. "Why? I mean…"

"We have to go to the hospital," she said, wondering why Julia wouldn't meet her eyes.

"What?" Julia dropped to the couch as if her legs had given way.

"Your mom is sick."

"What happened?"

"I don't know. Your dad is there. He and your sisters followed the ambulance. We'll go as soon as the boys get here."

Julia's gaze drifted away again. "I think…they're here already… I saw them when my…er, my friends dropped me off."

She sensed Julia wasn't telling her something, but for now, she didn't have time to question her. Besides, she doubted the girl would confide in her.

She locked the door, gave Julia the key, and ran down the sidewalk to Dex's truck. "You got here so quickly. I'm glad, though I hope you weren't speeding, Dex."

Aw, Mom, you always nag," he said. "What's going on?"

She and Julia climbed in the backseat. Julia didn't say a word to her sons, but then, her sons didn't speak to Julia either.

"Angela is sick. She's at the hospital," Gloria explained.

"What's wrong with her?" Gordy asked, for once without his headphones in his ears.

"I don't know." She didn't want to even tell Julia her mom fainted. She appeared worried enough already, and she looked so unlike herself. "Comb your hair, Julia," Gloria said. "You don't want to worry your parents. You never answered my question about what happened to you."

"I don't have to either. You're not my mother." The girl's voice cracked.

"I know. But you look as if you fell down. Your pants are torn, too."

"It's just the wind." Julia smoothed her hair down and then rummaged in her purse for a brush.

Gloria decided not to aggravate her further by persisting. She caught a look between her sons, though, and saw Gordy shrug. Something was up, and she would find out sooner or later. The rest of the trip was made in relative silence, with only the sound of the music from the radio.

"Do you want me to go in with you?" Gloria asked Julia as Dex pulled into the ER entrance.

"No." Julia stepped out and with short, quick steps, walked toward the entrance. She looked back and hugged herself.

"I'll be right back, boys." Gloria ran to Julia and led her inside the building.

The place was crowded and noisy. People talking, intercoms pinging, and now and then the sound of coughing. People stood around, even though a seat here or there was available. Medical personnel wearing a variety of colorful scrubs walked around with charts, IV tubing, and other medical equipment.

Gloria went up to the admissions window. "I'm looking for Angela Cerda."

"Are you a family member?"

"Not me, but this is her daughter." She pointed to Julia.

The clerk checked the computer screen. "Number eight."

Gloria went around the area, looking at numbers above the glass sliding doors to the rooms. Some had the curtains drawn, drab colors like dark yellow and forest green. Matt stood outside a room as they rounded the nurses' station, where both nurses and doctors worked at the various computer screens linked to the patient rooms.

"Daddy." Julia ran to him.

He opened his arms and engulfed Julia, who cried and asked about her mother.

While he explained, Gloria waved to him and motioned she was leaving. This wasn't the time or place for her presence. He said something to Julia and the other two girls and walked to her.

"I'm sorry our date ended so badly." He ran his hand through his already-unruly hair.

"Don't worry. Some things can't be helped. We

had a great time, and we'll do it again. Are you okay?" He hated sickness and hospitals.

"For now, I think so." He hugged her.

She felt the hardness of his body but knew how vulnerable he was at times like these. "Call me whenever, whatever time, okay? Your daughters need you right now. And I need to go home."

Matt kissed her, a rather subdued ending to their wonderful evening. However, as she'd just told him, they would have another opportunity. She hoped. Matt joined his daughters, and Julia was the first one back in his arms. Something had happened to her tonight. Maybe she would tell Matt.

What did the future hold? And what on earth was the matter with Angela?

****

Matt wished he could leave the hospital with Gloria. But then, he had to be present for his girls. Julia needed comforting. She was practically in tears. He led all three of his daughters to the ER waiting room. They huddled on the vinyl chairs.

"Your mother will be fine, girls," he said.

Julia lifted her head from his chest. "How do you know, Dad? They haven't even talked to us."

He'd noticed her disheveled state, but she was already upset. He didn't want to add fuel to the fire and have her angry with him again.

"Mommy fainted, Daddy," Amber repeated.

The sight must have jarred his poor little girl. "We'll find out what went wrong, and we'll get your mom well, okay?" He pulled Amber toward him and placed her head on his shoulder. He held out his hand to Julia and Patsy.

As soon as he'd done so, the nurse waved them into Angela's room. The doctor was there. Angela was awake, with tubes attached to her everywhere. An IV pump was running, as well as a machine to monitor her vital signs like blood pressure and heart rate. Another machine assessed her breathing pattern. The thing seemed to be breathing on its own, the way it sucked air in and out.

Matt's ears buzzed, and the hospital sounds faded away. In a matter of seconds, he was taken back to when he'd seen his mother like this after her heart attack. An attack he'd blamed himself for. Even now, sometimes the guilt resurfaced.

"It doesn't look like Mommy." Amber's voice brought him back to reality.

"But it is Mommy. And she'll get better," he said, his voice husky.

The doctor finished checking the various machines and tubes and writing on papers he had on a clipboard. "Mr. Cerda, your wife will be just fine. However, I do recommend she see her primary doctor, even her gynecologist. Her lab work showed some abnormalities that should be further assessed."

Matt cleared his throat. There was no point in correcting his marital status. "What kind of abnormalities?" Why did doctors talk in such riddles? They should be able to explain to a patient and her family exactly what was wrong.

"I don't like to say, because we would need to run further tests." The doctor wrote something else on the chart.

"Well, run them," Matt shouted.

Angela moaned. She lifted her hand and waved at

Matt. "I'll see my own doctor, Matt," she rasped out. "I don't know this one. He doesn't know me like Dr. Arispe."

"Angela, we need to know what happened to you," he said. "What if it happens again?"

"She was dehydrated," the doctor said.

"What caused it?" Matt asked in spite of Angela's protest.

"She didn't get enough fluids."

The doctor's answer sounded too simple. Wasn't there a better answer to explain a person fainting? Did Angela know something already? Was that why she stopped the doctor from doing tests? The girls had talked about her mood swings—crying, then angry.

Man, make the diagnosis be something uncomplicated.

****

Gloria woke up on Sunday morning thinking about Matt and his family, including Angela. Once he'd gotten the girls to his house last night, he called to tell her Angela was staying at the hospital overnight for observation.

Laziness filled her. Couldn't she just stay in bed today? Admittedly, it'd be better if Matt were with her, like last night. They'd spent such a beautiful evening together. Too bad it'd ended so abruptly.

Telling herself she'd better get up and make breakfast and then start doing the million-and-one things she neglected during the week, she pushed the covers off. This weekend she only had today, as yesterday she'd been busy with the book signing—and with Matt. A feeling of accomplishment added to her well-being this morning. The book signing had been a success in spite of Diva Author.

After she dressed, she went to the kitchen and made waffles—the frozen kind, but the boys liked them. She cooked bacon as well.

Gordy was the first to wake. He walked in, his hair all mussed up, and grinned. "Waffles? I want some."

"Okay, they're ready."

Dex ambled in as she filled plates for Gordy and herself. She brewed tea, which she preferred over coffee. Her sons drank milk.

"What a night," she said. "I hope Angela is okay."

"Why, Mom? She's your rival," Gordy teased.

"I don't want anything bad to happen to her… Much."

"Was Julia okay?" Dex bit into a forkful of waffle covered in syrup.

"Yes. I got her to her dad. She was in tears, the poor girl. She hugged Matt. Maybe this means she's ready to make peace."

"She's involved with some bad people." Gordy threw up his hands as Dex shook his head at him. "What?"

"Shut up, Gordo," Dex said.

"What bad people?" She remembered her sons' behavior last night when Julia got in the truck.

"It's nothing, Mom." Dex pushed Gordy. "See what you started."

"Boys, if Julia is in trouble, you have to tell me. Matt has to know."

"She's in with a bad crowd, that's all," Dex said.

"How bad? What do you mean exactly?" Her heart fell to her stomach as she remembered Julia's appearance last night—tousled hair, torn pants. "Boys, what happened last night?"

"Me and Gordo had to go pick up a friend at the movie theater. His ride had left him. We saw Julia being pushed around by some guys, and then she fell. The girls she was with ran away and left her by herself," Dex said.

"Guys were pushing her around?" She leaned back in her chair, appetite gone.

"So Stupid walks up and asks what's going on," Gordy said. "I went with him, not sure what we were going to do. They might have been armed."

"Which movie theater was it?" she asked, ready to admonish her sons never to go there again.

"Aw, Mom, it happens at every theater," Dex said, not comforting her one bit. "I was scared stiff, sweating bullets. They were the kind of guys who bullied me relentlessly in middle school but probably would be worse nowadays."

She could not believe it. While she'd been in bed with Matt, her sons could have been killed.

"Come on, Mom. Everything's okay. We're here," Gordy said. "And Dex was pretty impressive."

"What did you do, Dex?"

"I just confronted them and told them Julia was our sister. Poor Julia. I'd never seen her look at us like she did, grateful we were there."

Gordy laughed. "Yeah, poor chick."

"I told them nobody messes with someone's sister, right?" Dex said. "They backed off immediately."

"Oh, boys." Gloria could not fathom what she was listening to. "What if they hadn't backed off?"

"No guy wants to hurt someone's sister, Mom," Dex said.

"Most every girl is someone's sister, and you still hear of horrendous crimes," she said.

"Not every girl is defended, though," Dex said. "We felt pretty good. Julia hugged us. She was bawling so hard she even hugged Gordo." Dex laughed. Gordy punched him on the arm, and Dex punched him back.

"Then we drove her home since she had no ride, and she didn't want to tell her mom what she'd done," Dex said. "It was weird when you texted me because we were going where you told me to go. I didn't tell Julia, though."

She hugged her sons. "I'll worry about you more than ever now."

"It's okay, Mom," Dex said.

"No, it's not okay. Don't they have security at the theaters?"

"If bad things are going to happen, they happen," he said. "Besides, they were on a coffee break, probably."

"You're full of good cheer, aren't you?" she told her son.

"Gordo was in love with Julia. That's why he argued with her so much," Dex teased.

"You better watch it, or I'll punch you out," Gordy said.

"But now he thinks of Julia as his sister," Dex said.

"It's better this way," Gordy said. "As a girlfriend, I think she'd be too demanding, but as a sister, I'm older than she is and I can boss her around." He grinned.

"Oh you," Gloria said. "I think I'm going to punch *you* out."

"You know, it's funny, but we felt like she was our

sister," Dex said.

"Yeah, it was weird," Gordy agreed.

Her heart lightened a little in spite of all the upheaval during the past twenty-four hours. Maybe there was hope, after all, for both of their families, Matt's and hers.

Chapter Six

Gloria unlocked the door to the bookstore. Celeste had returned from her cruise; she'd text Gloria last night. However, she'd said she wouldn't be in until the end of the week, for the Hispanic author's book signing. Today, Gloria felt all right about it. She'd handled the bookstore well. Besides, she needed peace and quiet after the turbulent weekend she'd just experienced, though she remembered the night by the lake with Matt. Nothing that happened afterward had changed the magic of the evening.

Matt texted her last night, too. Angela was home and seemed as good as ever—back to her old self, he said.

Her cell vibrated as she set her purse down in the desk drawer. Matt!

"Good morning," he said. "Wish I'd been with you this morning."

"Hi, Matt. Me, too. Everything okay?"

"Yeah. I went to visit the girls this morning, make sure they made it to school. Angela was whining, but I suggested she stay in bed while the girls were in school."

"I have something to tell you…about Saturday night," she said.

"About how much you enjoyed our date?"

She imagined his smile at his words. "Oh yes." She

sighed. "I did have a good time. We must go to the park again. Actually, it's about Julia."

"Julia? What about her?" Concern etched his voice.

"Julia got into some trouble."

"How do you know? Did she tell you something?"

"No, though I did wonder about her appearance. Her jeans were torn."

"I did notice something about her, but she's already angry with me—and then Angela's situation. I didn't want to push."

"You have to talk to her, Matt. Dex and Gordy told me she's in with a bad crowd."

"What? How do they know this? You know they don't like each other, especially Gordy and Julia."

"She went to the movies with some new friends, and they're not the kind of girls you'd want your daughter to be around. Or my sons to date." She tried to lighten the mood.

"What happened?"

"Dex and Gordy happened to be at the same theater Julia went to, and they rescued her." She told him the story her sons had told her.

"My god, Gloria. I can't believe this. She could have been hurt."

"I know. My sons could have been killed. Who knew what these guys had on their minds?"

"I have to talk to her. She's been withdrawn and angry lately. I have to find out what's going on with her."

"Don't tell her about Dex and Gordy. I think we've gained some ground here with our kids and how they feel about each other. I mean, the boys helped out Julia, and she was grateful. But if she finds out they told what happened, the trust will be gone."

"I know," he said. "It's a sticky situation."

"I felt you should know about it, though. You need to stop her from getting into something serious and potentially harmful."

"I'm already worried about a thing or two I've seen in her room. I'll bring it up. Then maybe she'll tell me more. Sometimes if I listen instead of talk, I get more out of them," Matt said. "Did our parents have such a hard time with us?"

Gloria could imagine him scratching his head in wonder. "I think so. Maybe more so. I know I wasn't an easy child."

He laughed. "I really cannot believe you."

"Oh yes. I got into trouble from the moment I enrolled in school. Back then, teachers could paddle students, and I got paddled a time or two."

"Yeah. I got hit more than a time or two, by both teachers and parents."

"Well, by the time kids are teenagers, we can't paddle them. They have to have reached a point where they respect us, or not," she said. "I think you have a special relationship with your daughters. Julia will listen to you."

"Thanks for telling me about Julia. One of these days I'll find a way to thank your sons. When I think of what could have happened if they hadn't been there…"

"I know, Matt. Have a good day today. I'll be thinking of you."

"Me, too, love. We'll have to have another date really soon."

"Yes, we do."

Once she hung up with Matt, she settled down at

her desk to work until ten, when she would unlock the front door for customers. Judy Ann would come in then. She smiled as she remembered how her sons had helped Julia and how they actually said she was their sister. The hope still flourished. Now if only Julia would tell Matt what was going on with her. And if only their wedding plans could go forward without a hitch. She looked forward to talking and planning with her sister. Which reminded her—she had to buy a present for her nephew J.L.

****

After Matt spoke with Gloria on Monday morning, he'd called Julia to tell her he would pick her up after his last job. She'd protested, but he'd insisted. Now they sat at an outside table at a Tex-Mex restaurant.

"This cheese dip is good, isn't it?" He took another chip and smothered it in the *queso*."

"I have homework." Julia pushed her salad around on the plate with her fork. "I'd better go and do it. It's math, and you know I have trouble with it."

"I have to talk to you about something."

She stared down at her food, her stiff stance telling him she was close to throwing a temper tantrum.

"Please. It's important." He smiled. "I'm not going to scold you. I just want to talk."

She squirmed in her seat. "About what?"

"Before you say it, I know you're seventeen and practically an adult, but I'll always be your dad, much, much older and wiser than you, okay?"

She shrugged. The sun was setting, and a little breeze blew. He should really sit and enjoy the outdoors more often. Usually when he was outside, he was working. He and Gloria had sat on patio chairs in her

76

backyard when he'd first met her.

"Dad?" Julia asked. "I thought you wanted to talk."

Matt brought his attention back to his daughter. "I enjoy being outside. My work is being outside with plants, trees, and flowers, but I never just sit."

She didn't say a word.

"Look, I'm worried about you."

"Why?" She wouldn't meet his eyes.

He wished he could just come out and ask about the movie incident, but he had to build up to it. "You used to have a pink room at my house. You've added black."

"I thought you liked it."

"I do. But it…just doesn't seem…your style."

"Really, Dad." She squirmed again in her chair. "I just wanted a change. I'll take it out. Anyway, my room at home is exactly the way I want it, and Mom doesn't mind." She finished with accusing eyes.

He frowned. "I just worry. If anything is bothering you, you can tell me. Are you worried about your mom?"

"Well, yes…but Mom seems to do okay, though it was scary with the ambulance and…everything. I'm glad things seem to be back to normal. I'm busy, you know, with school—and my groups."

"Are you still in the same groups?" he asked before he bit into a taco.

She didn't look at him. "Yes, drama and debate."

He nodded.

"I…have some new friends."

He concentrated on his meal, hoping if he didn't say anything, she'd say more.

"They're nice girls," Julia continued. "For the most

part. I mean…I thought they were. And they're different…"

"How so?"

"They're not in drama or debate. In fact, they'd laugh at me if I told them." She met his eyes. "They wear black clothes."

"Oh. What made you think they weren't as nice as you thought?"

"You're going to get angry with me," she said.

His heart beat faster in his chest. He clenched his fists and then slowly opened them. He already knew what she was going to tell him. He just wanted to hear her say it. And he wanted to hug her because he was so grateful she hadn't been harmed.

"Something happened at the movies the other night…" She told him the story he already knew from Gloria. At the end, she was in tears. "I'm so sorry, Dad. I was so scared and so glad Dex and Gordy appeared. I've never been so happy to see anyone as I was to see them the other night."

Matt moved to the chair next to his daughter and hugged her. Her tears continued. He held her and remembered when she was first born, so tiny and beautiful. Even nearing young adulthood, she was still his little girl, his first daughter, and he never wanted any harm to come to her.

When she'd cried herself out, she apologized again and grabbed napkins to dry her eyes and blow her nose. Thankfully, the place wasn't crowded on a Monday evening.

"Let me ask you something else," he said. "Why did you make friends with these girls?"

She didn't meet his glance again and remained

silent.

"Julia?"

"I don't want to be like Mom. I mean, I look like her, but I don't want to be her."

He waited. He might have known his ex had a hand in this.

"She's always saying I'm just like her. I behave like she does, I dress like she does, and boys are interested in me like they were in her. I guess I don't mind it so much, especially about the boys." She smiled.

He had to bite his tongue to keep from commenting. As far as he was concerned, boys could stay away from his daughter forever.

"I want to be me," Julia said. "And...I'm not sure I know what that is yet, but I want to find out. I love Mom, but she can be so insistent."

"I know. If it'll make you feel better, I've told her to let you, and your sisters, become who you're meant to be without being clones of her." He paused and took a drink. "I think you have to tell your mom how you feel."

"Oh, Dad, she'll kill me."

"And you need to tell her about what happened at the movies."

"No, Dad, please don't make do it." She crossed her arms. "She'll never understand. And then I'll have to tell her about Dex and Gordy. You know how she feels about all...that."

Matt stretched out his legs. "Yes, I know. But you can't keep things like this from your mother. She needs to know. Maybe it'll knock some sense into her. She'll realize what she's doing to you."

She smiled. "Thanks, Dad."

"For what?"

"For listening and not getting angry."

"You know I've always told you girls you can tell me anything, right?"

She nodded.

"I mean it." He pulled her into his arms and tousled her hair.

"Oh, Dad, not my hair." She began eating her salad with gusto.

Gloria had asked if it was okay if she messed up his hair. He grinned and turned to look out at the trees and bushes around the perimeter of the restaurant. In his mind, the scene turned into the lake where he'd been with Gloria a few days ago. He already missed her. They must get together again soon. She was making wedding plans with her sister, so maybe soon they could set a wedding date. He couldn't wait.

****

Gloria drove up to Lynda's house and parked at the curb. Dex and Gordy jumped out from the back, eager to go and greet their cousins.

"Wait a minute," she said. "Help me with the stuff." She'd brought not only gifts for her nephew J.L. on his fourteenth birthday but also the ice cream and napkins Linda asked her to pick up.

Lynda joined her by the truck. "Too late, sister. They're already in the boys' room. J.L. received some video games. I'll help."

Gloria hugged her sister before she handed her the grocery bags. "We need to see each other more often."

"I know," Lynda agreed. "But with work, kids, and John, who has time?"

Gloria closed the truck door, and they walked toward the house. At home, she'd put the birthday gifts in a trash bag. Now she slung it over her shoulder as if she carried Santa's bag.

"How's Matt?" Lynda asked.

She grinned. "The best. I still feel as if I'm in a dream world sometimes. I never thought I'd ever meet anyone like him."

"I'm so glad for you. Come on in. Excuse the mess. I live in constant fear the house is going to fall into itself with all the clutter and the commotion we make."

The living room had the overstuffed gray-and-black sofa and chair, the flat-screen TV, but newspaper stacks of various sizes were strewn along one end of the sofa. John loved to keep them for a time, aggravation for Lynda, but she'd stop fretting about a lost cause. The family dog greeted her, wagging its tail, and she patted his head. Then she set the trash bag on the floor, brought out the gifts, and set them on a card table Lynda had set up.

John, Lynda's husband, sat at the dining table. "Welcome to the chaos."

"I'm used to it," she said. "Besides, my house isn't any different, and I only have two kids."

"Kids, come down," Lynda shouted up the stairs. We're ready to start."

The clatter of feet resounded through the house as they marched down. Gloria hugged her nieces, Lisa and Yolanda, as well as her nephews, Abel and J.L., whom she gave an extra squeeze. "Happy birthday," she told him.

J.L. sat at the end of the table—the better to be able to take pictures of him as he blew out the fourteen candles on his cake, which Lynda had baked. Every year J.L. picked a theme. This year it was basketball, so the cake featured a basketball court. He cut the first slice of cake, and Lynda helped him cut enough pieces for everyone. Gloria served the vanilla ice cream, which Dex refused. He said it was too much sweet for him.

Gloria bit into the yellow cake slathered with chocolate frosting. "Yum."

As J.L. opened his gifts, she took picture after picture. So did Lynda.

"Aw, Mom," he protested after Lynda made him pose the same way again. "You and Aunt Gloria can share. I just want to open my presents. Hey, Gordo, thanks." He pulled out a jersey depicting his favorite basketball team.

Once her nephew finished opening the presents, John escaped to the garage, and the kids thundered back upstairs.

"Remember, you have homework," Lynda shouted to them. Sounds of grumbling ensued.

"Mine do, too," Gloria said. "We probably shouldn't stay too long."

"Well, just a little while. Come to the table. Let's have a glass of wine, relax, and talk about your upcoming wedding. Have you set a date?"

Gloria sat. "No, not yet." She told her sister about Angela's unexpected trip to the ER over the weekend.

"Is she okay now?" Lynda handed Gloria a goblet of white wine.

"I think so. The kids don't like each other or the fact we're getting married. "

"Yeah, I guess so." Lynda pulled a chair from under the table and stretched her legs over the seat.

"But you can't let them stop you. I mean, after all these years, you've finally met a man who can make you happy."

Gloria grinned. "Yes, he can. I love him, and he loves me. Sometimes, it just seems so complicated."

"Good things take time. Be patient. Now, what colors do you want? I had turquoise in my wedding. Let's say you get married in June. It's the month for roses. And isn't it so appropriate because you met because of roses?"

"You're right. I love the idea. We need to get married where there are lots of roses, a backyard wedding somewhere."

"How about your backyard?" Lynda suggested.

Gloria shook her head. "No, Eddie lived with me in that house, even if only a short while. I think we need to have a clean slate."

"Well, really, it can be any place. We can just decorate with roses. Red ones, for love," her sister said and took a drink of wine.

"Maybe I should have the bridesmaids wear red. Only, I don't think I want too many. Just you as my matron of honor. Matt will probably ask Wayne to be his best man."

Dex walked in and frowned. "I just came down for some drinks."

Lynda took his hand. "This is a good thing, Dex. Your mom deserves to be happy."

He opened the refrigerator door and grabbed three bottles of soda and three of water.

"Dex?" Gloria asked.

"I'm still working on this, Mom." He left without another word.

"See?" She blinked so she wouldn't cry. "They don't like this, and I don't know what to do about it."

"It's an adjustment," Lynda said. "You and the boys have been on your own for a long time. It'll take some time. But don't you give up on this. I like Matt, and I like the idea of you and him together."

Gloria laughed and finished her wine. "So do I. We had such a wonderful evening the other night by the lake."

Too soon, it was time to leave. Gloria could have talked about Matt all night. Actually, she'd wanted to be with Matt again as she'd told her sister about their magical evening. Things would work out. As Lynda had said, this was adjustment time, and they could work past it.

****

Matt's cell vibrated in his shirt pocket, and he ignored it. He finished telling his workers what needed to be done according to the plan he and the new client had drawn up. Today was the first day on the new contract. The client had requested extensive landscaping, with new plants and bushes. He also wanted a rock garden. He'd said he was tired of wasting so much water during the summer and the flowers still died. Someone from the water department had suggested he use native vegetation to conserve water. Matt had tried it on a small scale with other clients, and they'd been pleased. He hoped this client would be as well.

His phone buzzed again. He pulled it from his jacket packet. *Angela*. Not the person he wanted to talk to right now.

He punched the number in and waited.

"I'm dying," she shrieked. "I went to the doctor, and he suggested I get a biopsy right away. I went today. And I'm going to die." She sobbed.

He looked around him, the yard of the office complex where he was working and up at the blue sky. What was Angela saying? His heart lurched. Even after her betrayal, she was still the mother of his girls and he'd loved her once, very much.

"What did you have a biopsy for?" he asked, trying to make sense of her news.

"Isn't it just like you to get practical and not even console me? I told you I was dying."

He pictured her dark eyes glinting with anger as they had so many times during their married life. Sighing, he considered hanging up on her. "Angela, of course, I don't want you to die. Hell! I'm working. You can't just call me up and say you're dying and not give me more specifics."

"They want to cut my breasts off. Is that specific enough? I have cancer, damn you. Cancer." More sobs.

God, give me patience. "So what did the biopsy show? How bad is it? Don't they have other options nowadays besides surgery?"

"It's bad enough they want to make me ugly. I don't know about options. This quack of a doctor I saw doesn't know anything. It's just a damn lump. I'm going to get a second opinion. But I need money. I heard you got a big money-making contract."

"I'm just starting with it. But it sounds to me like you have to get this taken care of quickly. Why wait? It could get worse."

"Why? Why? How would you like to lose a vital part of your anatomy? And you know what I'm talking about. My body will be mutilated. I won't allow it to happen."

"Your life is at risk, Angela."

"I know, dammit. I'm so scared."

"Listen, I'm about to leave the job site," he said. "I'll go over there. We need to tell the girls as well."

"Oh God, I hadn't even thought of them."

Typical. She wouldn't think of anyone but herself at a time like this. But then again, would he? Well, maybe he would. Angela was different. She loved their daughters, but in this case she'd just been diagnosed with a life-threatening illness. Sickness and hospitals jarred him. He'd better psyche himself up. If Angela would indeed require surgery and chemo and who knew what else, he'd have to be there for the girls—and for her.

When would he and Gloria have time to plan their wedding? It seemed ages ago since he'd proposed, and they didn't see each other as much anymore. He'd enjoyed their date this past weekend, but the evening ended so badly with having to rush to the ER with Angela. Now she was really sick. Matt didn't want her to be sick. He and Angela were no longer together, but she was the mother of his girls.

He'd made another date with Gloria this weekend, but now he had to visit his daughters and tell them the bad news about their mom. Things had to smooth out so he and Gloria could make a life together. Was that so impossible to accomplish?

Chapter Seven

As Matt drove up to Angela's house on Saturday evening, he couldn't help but remember last Saturday at this time. He'd been on his way to Gloria's for a date, one which had turned out very nicely. Until Angela's trip to the ER—and the reason he was here tonight.

His ex opened the door, as usual wearing a low-cut blouse that appeared painted on her and a short skirt paired with high heels. He bit his tongue so as not to make a comment.

"I'm so glad you could take time from your busy schedule to spare us a few minutes," she said.

He sighed but again didn't comment. For once, he hoped conversation with her wouldn't end in argument. "Hello to you, too."

She walked to the living room. "I don't know how we're going to tell the girls. You have to tell them. I'm not sure what to say."

"I know it's hard. That's why I'm here."

She held on tightly to one of the sofa chairs. "It seems so unreal. One minute my life is normal, and the next everything is wrong."

"How did you find out something was wrong in the first place?"

"Jorge felt a lump."

Matt clenched his hands. "Spare me the details."

"Well, you asked." Angela smirked, but then she

sobered up. "I'm just so scared." She began to cry.

Julia, apparently overhearing, entered the living room. "Stop coming over here, Dad, and upsetting Mom."

"We have to talk about something..." he said. "Aren't you going to give me a hug?"

She hesitated, but after a few seconds she walked into his arms. Patsy and Amber ran into the room, and they indulged in a group hug. He looked above his daughters' heads at Angela. She held out her hands, palms up.

He let go of the girls. "Your mom and I have to tell you something."

"Tell us what?" Julia asked, a look of fear in her eyes.

He hated to see fright in his daughter's face. A feeling of dread filled him, the same anxiousness he'd tried so hard to keep at bay ever since he blamed himself for his mother's heart attack. He'd tried even more when Patsy had been ill and then after he'd met Gloria and found she had hypertension. Now his ex had been diagnosed with breast cancer. His daughters would be affected in a bad way. He had to fight these feelings.

"Might as well just say it," Angela said.

At her words, he returned to the present and nodded.

"Girls, I went to the doctor," she said.

"Are you sick, Mommy?" Amber rushed to Angela's side.

"Yes." Angela's voice broke.

"Let's sit down." He waited until everyone had taken a seat either on the sofas or on the floor. "Your mom is going in for surgery on Monday."

"Surgery?" Julia asked. "What kind of surgery?"

"The doctors found a lump in my breast," Angela said. "And it's…it's…"

"Malignant." He didn't want to say the *c* word, which seemed so ominous.

"Cancer," Julia said. "Mom has cancer."

Patsy began to cry. "Oh, Mom."

Angela became a heaving mass of sobs in the recliner. Patsy and Amber knelt by the chair and hugged her. He tried to think of something to say, but what words could he use? Nothing he could say could change the facts—and the fear.

"We'll be there at the hospital with your mom. We'll support each other, okay?" he finally said.

"Now you have to stay with us, Dad," Julia said. "You can't marry Gloria. You can't leave us and Mom alone."

A twinge of guilt filled Matt. However, he was not about to leave Gloria. After all these years, he'd finally met someone he could make a life with and be happy.

Angela stemmed her crying bout long enough to smile in triumph, her eyes gleaming. "I don't want the girls unhappier than they are already, Matt."

"I don't either, Angela. But I'm not leaving Gloria."

"You see how he is, girls," she said. "He doesn't really love you."

"The girls know it's not true, right?" he asked.

Patsy and Amber nodded, but Julia glared at him. "I'm beginning to think Mom is right about you," she said. "Everything and everyone is more important to you than we are." She ran to her room before he could stop her.

"Angela, I know you're sick," he said. "But please don't make this a drama."

"How do you expect me to be? I have cancer. I don't just have a cold, Matt. I have cancer." She emphasized each word.

"I know you do, and I'm here to help you with our daughters. Just don't make me out to be the bad guy. I have a separate life from you now, and I'm not going to change it because you're sick."

He hugged Patsy and Amber good-bye. Julia refused to come out from her room, and he left with a heavy heart.

He wasn't wrong. Gloria was a part of his life now, and she was there to stay. No matter what.

****

Gloria finished up at the bookstore and looked forward to tonight. After last Saturday with Matt, she'd wanted a repeat performance. She'd been so happy when he'd called to say they needed to go out again. She couldn't wait.

She'd just shut down her computer, go home, and get ready to spend time with him. They didn't even need to go anywhere. She wanted to be with him, in or out of bed. She enjoyed talking with him; hearing his voice was enough.

The phone rang. *Drat!* She'd forgotten to forward the calls to the answering service.

"Books and All," she said.

"Hey…" Matt said.

"Oh, hi, Matt. I'm glad it's you. I was afraid it'd be someone I didn't want to talk to. I was just leaving."

"I…listen…"

Oh no. I'm not going to like what he's going to say.

"Angela has been diagnosed with breast cancer."

"Oh no. I'm sorry." How sad for those poor girls.

"Yeah." He sighed. "She's going in for surgery Monday morning. I must be here for the girls."

And for Angela. Gloria's heart plummeted. "I understand." But she didn't. Her eyes filled with tears.

"I'm sorry, Gloria. The girls are really worried. I'll make it up to you really soon. Angela is...well, she's my girls' mother."

"We'll get together some other time," she managed to say.

"We have a wedding to plan, right?"

"Yes..." She switched her computer back on. Even though she agreed, she wondered if their plans would really materialize. So many problems had cropped up. One would be resolved, and another one would arise. She felt sorry for Angela, but somehow she feared her illness would put a huge obstacle between her, Matt, and their wedding.

"I'll call you tomorrow," he said.

"Okay. I hope everything goes well for Angela."

"I love you."

"Me, too." She placed the phone on its cradle, blinking back tears, and picked up a stack of papers, a project she'd set aside for tomorrow. Her sons weren't home. Tonight they'd gone out with friends. Tomorrow they'd continue their search for an apartment.

This empty-nest syndrome was really kicking her butt. She'd known it would happen sooner rather than later when Gordy entered high school. Now he was a senior, and Dex was in his last year of college. The time had arrived too quickly.

After she'd met Matt, she'd stopped thinking about

it because she'd felt so good with him, spending time together, falling in love, but now things had changed. Maybe she should never have accepted his marriage proposal. Since then, everything had gone awry with the kids and their relationship.

She shook these thoughts away. This was no time to feel sorry for herself. She and Matt would work things out. Dex and Gordy wouldn't live with her, but they were still a family and always would be.

Matt had his family, his daughters, and he had to be there for them at this time and with their mother. This didn't mean their romance was over. They still had the love. Challenges emerged, but with love, they would be able to overcome anything, right?

****

Matt bided his time in the waiting room. They'd just taken Angela into the operating room. *God!* He hated hospitals and wished for the hundredth time he were anywhere else.

His girls sat apart from each other, only Amber next to him. Last night had been harrowing with Angela whining and complaining and driving him crazy. He hadn't reacted well, and Julia had gotten angry with him and still was. Patsy had burst into tears. Even now, her eyes were swollen.

"Is Mommy going to get better?" Amber asked.

He felt her hand on his. "Yes, baby, she is." *I hope so.*

Over the speaker, someone called for a doctor. He heard the rolling wheels of hospital equipment as patients were taken to their destination in beds or wheelchairs.

Thank God, no one else was in the room. Some

people tended to talk too much.

"How do you know, Daddy?" Amber persisted.

"Oh, shut up, Amber." Julia curled up in her chair.

"The doctors will make her better." He wished he knew what to say to Julia to lessen her anger and fear. It all boiled down to those emotions. She was afraid. So was he. Not everybody pulled through.

His mother hadn't. She'd collapsed in her garden, and once she was at the hospital, nothing the doctors did could revive her. Surely, Angela's chances were better. His daughters needed their mother, even with all her flaws. God knew he wasn't perfect either.

"I'm going to get a snack. Anyone want anything?" He stood and got his wallet out.

Julia only curled more tightly into herself.

"I'm not hungry, Dad," Patsy said.

"I'll go with you, Daddy," Amber said.

He stared at Patsy. Was it his imagination, or had she been avoiding meals lately? Could it be due to the situation? Who could eat with all the drama? Still, Amber had told him Angela said Patsy was a big disappointment to her. He'd have to talk to her once Angela got out of surgery. Right now, he didn't want to add to Patsy's worries by confronting her about her eating habits.

"Come on, Amber. Let's go," he said.

Matt walked with Amber to the elevators. Somehow even the elevator buttons served as a reminder of that long ago time when his mother died. This was an area he had to resolve. He couldn't carry his teen guilt forever. But then, it'd been his fault, hadn't it? Even if the doctors said there was nothing further medically possible to do.

Once back in the waiting room, he ate his snack with Amber. The operation would take forty-five minutes. *Shouldn't be too long now.*

The doctor entered the room. "Mr. Cerda, your wife is in recovery. The surgery went well. She'll have to have chemo and radiation for several weeks afterward, but the oncologist will give you more information. You can see her for a few minutes. I'm sorry the kids can't go in."

"I want to see Mommy," Amber yelled.

Patsy jumped from her seat and stood by Matt. She wanted to see her mom as well. Only Julia sat without moving.

"I'm sorry," the doctor said. "Once she's in a room, you can visit. In about an hour or so."

"Wait for me here, girls. I'll be right back," he told his daughters.

He followed the doctor to a big room and an area curtained off. The doctor pulled the drape aside, and he saw Angela. She'd hate anyone to see her like this. Including him.

Her hair was a mess. Her face looked swollen and red. A white sheet covered her body. Tubes and needles came out of both arms. Machines whooshed and pinged as she received whatever medicines she needed.

He walked over and touched her hand. "Angela?"

Again, he was reminded of his mother. He'd seen her like this and screamed out "Mom." To this day he didn't remember doing so. His dad had told him later. Today, thank God, he didn't scream.

Angela moaned, opened her eyes. She tried to smile, raised her right hand, and found it almost immovable by the tubing.

"Lie still," he said.

"I must look a mess," she whispered.

"Don't worry about it. You've always been one of the most beautiful women I've met." And he really wasn't lying.

"Only one of, Matt?"

He laughed. "Now I know you'll be fine if you're already arguing with me." He held onto her hand. "The girls want to see you."

"Don't let them come in, Matt. If they see me like this, they'll worry."

He was touched, but then, she loved the girls, too, in her way. "They can see you later when you go to a room. You can get ready for them. Are you in pain?"

"I'm kinda hazy. The doctor said I can ask for something if I do have pain."

"Take it easy. Rest. I'm going to take the girls to eat, and then we'll return so they can visit with you a little."

"Don't let Patsy eat too much. She needs to lose weight."

"Angela, don't..." he began, remembering Patsy's refusal of a snack.

"I don't want her to get as big as a house. No one will like her... Boys, you know..."

Matt shook his head, but he wasn't about to argue with her. She'd just gotten out of surgery. The woman was incorrigible. He'd talk to her about Patsy later. He also needed to see Gloria, hold her, and make love to her. Most of all he needed reassurance, for her and for himself.

Chapter Eight

"Hi, Tanya. I'm so glad you're back. I want to hear all about your cruise," Gloria said.

"I'm divorcing Wayne," Tanya announced.

Gloria sighed. Tanya Simmons, her friend and wannabe matchmaker, always regaled her with the same refrain, but she never filed the papers. She was also the one who'd sent Matt to help her with her rose garden, so Gloria would love her forever—and also listen to whatever bee she had in her bonnet.

"What happened this time?" she asked.

"What do you mean 'this time'? This time is not like all the other times. This time he cheated on me."

She didn't want to remind Tanya she'd accused Wayne of cheating on her numerous times. Why was she so insecure? As far as Gloria could see, Wayne was faithful to Tanya and always tried to make their home a happy one.

"Since we returned from the cruise, I haven't seen him in two months. It's a good thing we made love morning, noon, and night because we haven't done so since we got back. Oh, I'm so angry I could spit. But I'm not spitting. I'm eating and getting as big as a house, and for sure, Wayne won't love me now. Last night I sat in front of the computer looking at the slide show from our trip. I got hungry, so I microwaved a box of spinach-and-cheese quiche and ate until I finished the whole box. They're so delicious, but they pack a powerful caloric punch, but I don't care." She sniffled, and her voice cracked.

"And I topped it off by drinking a whole bottle of wine, too. Wayne has put on some pounds. I mean, how long ago was it we were in high school? He was the star football player, and I was a cheerleader. On him, extra pounds look good. On me and my short self, I look like a football now!"

Gloria knew Tanya wouldn't calm down until she let out all her feelings. So she settled back in her chair and closed the file she was working on. "Okay, start from the beginning."

"You don't want to hear such a long story. Last Friday night is when I gorged myself. On a Friday night here by myself. The kids were out with friends. And where was Wayne? In Austin, of all god-awful places. I mean, sure it's the capital of Texas, but what in blazes was he doing over there on a Friday night? He called to say he had to get up very early to go talk to a potential customer, so he was staying in a motel. Yeah, I'm going to believe such crap. I'm sure he wasn't in the damned motel room by himself."

Gloria held the phone away from her ear, and she could still hear Tanya loud and clear.

"You should be glad you have Matt. He's loyal and true, not like this bum I married," Tanya said.

Yes. Matt was loyal and true. But he wasn't with her right now, and he broke a date. Maybe Tanya would give Gloria a chance to tell her what was going on in her world at some point during this call. But she knew her friend wouldn't ask until later in the conversation.

"We had so much fun at first. We took pictures at

the Parthenon in Greece," Tanya said. We shared a drink at a sidewalk café in Paris. We made love like we used to when we first met way back in high school. Then we get home, and he announces he wants to start a branch of the business in Austin. I asked him not to, even before we went on the cruise. I thought it was the end of it. He told me he'd decided, and then he disappeared. I haven't seen him in two months. I'm alone all the time, and I hate it."

Gloria took advantage of Tanya's pause to take a breath. "Have you talked to him about what you're feeling?"

"No, I refuse to talk to him. He went behind my back with this new business. I don't believe it for one minute. Well, maybe for one minute. He doesn't lie to me about his business. But I'm sure he has some floozy over there to make his nights a bit warmer. And here I am alone every single night, and on the weekends the kids take off. Junior is barely fifteen, and he thinks he's in love. What does he know about relationships? And Nikki is so rebellious. Was I like that when I was her age? Well, probably, but where the hell is Wayne to help me with these things?"

"Tanya, please talk to Wayne."

"I loved him from the first moment I saw him run in with the football team at a pep rally. He was the quarterback, and I was the newest cheerleader on the squad. But I set my sights on him, and he asked me to the prom. Of course, he thought I was some kind of slut, but I soon set him straight. I didn't blame him. All the other girls did throw themselves at him all the time. I mean he was the star of the team." Tanya sobbed.

"I know." Gloria paused. "Do you want me to go

over there after work? You don't sound so good."

"No, I'll be okay. I know you're busy with work and Matt," Tanya said, and her voice sounded a bit stronger. "How are things between you?"

Finally. Gloria smiled at the thought of her friend. She was always like this, full of her problems, and then she could turn it off and concentrate on someone else.

"Matt proposed." She waited for Tanya's reaction.

Where before she'd been in tears, now Tanya screamed with joy. "Oh my goodness. I knew Matt was the man for you. I am so happy for you. When's the wedding? Do you want me to help you with flowers or cake, anything? I'll do anything to help you."

"I hate to throw cold water on all this. Yes, it's exciting, and I'm in love with Matt, but the kids are angry about it and won't accept it. Of course, they're old enough, well, except for Patsy and Amber. They're still young teens. But Matt and I want everybody to get along. We want our families to be happy."

"Oh, Gloria. You can work it out. Kids will be kids. They're possessive of parents, but in the end they want us to be happy."

"I wish that was all of it." Gloria sighed.

"What else?"

"His ex is sick."

"Angela has always been sick, in the head," Tanya said. "I hate her."

"This time she really is sick. She has breast cancer."

Tanya didn't say a word.

"Tanya, did you hear what I said?"

"Yes. I'm counting to ten so I won't say something mean. I wouldn't wish that on my worst enemy. But really? What the hell?"

"Matt has had to spend a lot of time at her house to help with the girls."

Tanya screamed out a curse. "Oh for God's sake. Did I tell you I hate that woman? Well, now I despise her. She's milking this for all she's got, isn't she?"

"Matt loves his daughters."

"And she's using them to get to him. You know she is. Playing the 'helpless little me' card."

"Maybe we're just kidding ourselves. We met each other too late. Maybe if I'd eloped with Matt way back when. But then, I wouldn't have my beautiful sons."

"No, my friend. You are not kidding yourself. This is meant to be. How many men have I tried to set you up with? None of them affected you one bit, until Matt. It's in the stars."

Gloria laughed. "Oh you. Well, the star is a bit off kilter, but maybe…"

"No maybe about it. Now, between Wayne and me, it's a whole 'nother ballgame. I think our star has burnt out."

"Tanya, promise me you'll talk to Wayne."

"I'll talk to him. I'll tell him a thing or two…"

"I mean listen to him. Don't go off on a tangent. Please. He's a good guy, and you love him."

Tanya sniffled. "I do. I always have."

"Plus, you and Wayne have to go to my wedding. You helped us get together."

"Of course, tell me the time and place."

After she hung up with her friend, Gloria wondered if indeed wedding bells would ring over her and Matt's heads. Or had their star burned out, too, as Tanya believed hers and Wayne's had?

****

Matt drove Angela to her house. The girls were home already. Amber had wanted to have a welcome-home party. Patsy and Julia had been against it, but he had told them to help Amber when he realized how important it was to his baby girl.

"I just want to go to bed," Angela said.

He hoped she'd play along when she saw what the girls had done. Should he tell her? Prepare her? Before he could decide, he'd arrived and Amber rushed out.

Angela groaned. "I'm not ready for this."

He had to tell her. "They have a surprise for you."

"Why? Couldn't you have stopped them?"

"No. Put on a happy face."

"I just got out of the hospital."

"And they're scared. This is their way of celebrating your return and hoping everything will be okay now. Don't mess it up, Angela."

He opened the door, and Amber stopped at the passenger door. He touched her shoulder. "Let your mom get inside, baby, okay? She's still not feeling her best."

"Okay… But she will, right?"

"Yes, baby, she will." He helped Angela inside the house while Amber ran ahead of them. She leaned on him as if her legs couldn't hold her up. Was she really this weak? He hated himself for doubting her, but he couldn't trust her. He hadn't for a long time. Somehow, they would get through this, and he and Gloria could go on with their future.

Inside, the girls yelled, "Welcome home, Mom!"

"Oh. My," Angela said. "Thank you, girls."

He watched as they hugged her. Then he helped

her sit down on the recliner.

"Thank you, Matt."

Julia showed Angela the cake. "Patsy baked it, but I decorated it."

"Nice, honey," Angela said in a soft voice and smiled.

"Do you want a piece?"

"No…"

Matt motioned her to say yes.

"Well, maybe a small piece."

Patsy declined. "I'll just drink some punch."

"Good idea," Angela said. "Sweets are not a friend for someone like you."

"Just a small piece, Patsy?" he asked.

"Leave her alone, Matt," Angela said. "She needs to lose weight."

"It's okay, Dad. I don't want any."

He forced himself not to say one more word. But at some point, he needed to talk to both Patsy and Angela. This couldn't go on. Patsy had to eat.

"Mommy, I made you a card." Amber handed Angela a homemade card on green paper, the message, *I love you, Mommy* spelled out in multicolored glitter.

"Oh shit," Angela said. "Now I have glitter all over myself."

"I'm sorry, Mommy," Amber said. "I guess I put too much."

Matt glared at Angela.

"Well, I'm tired. I can't be sociable right now," she said.

"Go to bed, then," Julia snapped. "I didn't want to do anything anyway."

"What have you done to Julia? She's always been

on my side."

"There are no sides here," he said. "You're the parent, for God's sake."

Amber's and Patsy's eyes welled up with tears, and Julia stalked to her room.

"I'm sorry, Mommy." Amber took the card, which Angela had laid on the arm of the chair. "I'll take some of the glitter off."

"Welcome home, Mom." Patsy led Amber from the room.

He wanted to lash out at his ex. Knowing what she'd gone through stopped him, but it didn't lessen the anger.

She sat back on the recliner. "Go ahead and yell at me. I deserve it."

He sighed. "They sure as hell didn't deserve what you just did to them."

"Typical Matt. You can never empathize with me, can you?"

"I notice you're not so weak when you criticize me or the girls."

"What do you want from me, Matt?"

"Right now, I just want you to get well." He stacked the plates to carry them to the kitchen.

"So you can return to the bimbo, er, Gloria."

"I'm still with her, Angela. I'm not changing my life to suit you."

"Well, I'm going to need your help with the girls."

"I'm here for you." He wondered how much help she'd need.

"But, I mean, more than on weekends. Tomorrow I have an appointment with the oncologist. God knows what he'll tell me."

"I'll drive you to the appointment. The girls have school, right?"

"I can't handle it." She put her hands to her cheeks.

"What do you want me to do, Angela?"

"Take the girls with you."

"You can't displace the girls."

"Well, move in here and help me."

"You can't be serious."

"Just for the girls. I don't mean share a bed, for God's sake."

"The thought never crossed my mind. But you're crazy. You must have taken one too many pain pills."

"I won't be able to manage. They're so demanding."

"And you're not?"

Matt's mind was in a whirl. He couldn't possibly do what she asked. Gloria would never understand. How could they work it? The girls needed to get to and from school. He especially needed to watch out for Julia after she'd gotten into trouble with those kids. If Dex and Gordy hadn't intervened... He refused to think of what could have happened. Then, he had the new contract, now Angela's appointments. Maybe he could hire someone to help out.

"Don't worry yourself to a frazzle. I'll be fine. My girls will be fine, too." Her voice penetrated his fogged mind.

"I can take the girls to school, and I'll be here in the evenings."

"What about my appointments?"

"Maybe I can hire someone."

"Hire someone? I don't want some stranger knowing my business."

"Angela, you have to work with me here."

"You don't care about me. You never have," she said and soon was sobbing. "You always left me alone to take care of things. Well, thanks for nothing. Now I'm dying, and you can't spare me a few minutes out of your precious day."

"Oh for God's sake." He stormed out of the house. He yanked the truck door open, but Amber and Patsy yelled and ran to him.

"Are you leaving, Daddy?" Amber asked, close to tears.

"You didn't say bye," Patsy said.

"I just needed some fresh air, girls. Give me a little time."

"Why do you and mom fight all the time?" Patsy asked.

Because she drives me insane. "I'm not sure, darling girl. I'll try to do better, okay?" He put his arm around Patsy's shoulders.

"Mommy should, too," Amber said.

"I'll be right in," he said. "I promise. I'm not leaving you."

Both girls hugged him.

Hell! Being around Angela wasn't going to be easy. But he had to be there for his daughters. Taking her to doctors and hospitals and being around sick people was going to be damned difficult as well. Somehow, for his girls, he'd do it. He'd have to tell Gloria, too. God only knew how she'd react.

****

When Gloria left for her date with Matt, her sons were not home. She seldom saw them anymore. But at this point, she wasn't sure what she could do.

As he helped her into the truck, he suggested dining at a new Mexican restaurant. "A live band is scheduled to play at eight."

"We can dance. I don't think I've danced with you," she said once he'd climbed into the driver's seat.

"We have to remedy that tonight." He turned the key in the ignition.

She noticed he hadn't kiss her. Why? "No kiss?"

"I'm sorry." He gave her a quick kiss on the lips.

Something is wrong. Well, his ex-wife just had surgery.

The meal was delicious, but she didn't eat too much. Matt's mind wasn't solely on the present. He didn't initiate conversation, but then, his mind was probably on the upcoming ordeal with his ex's sickness and having to be at the hospital.

"I'm sorry about Angela. Are the girls okay?" she asked.

"They're fine. This is our night, though. We've been apart too long."

Without a doubt, he was avoiding saying something, but he was right. They hadn't been together in a while, and she didn't want to spoil it.

The band began playing. "Let's dance." He stood and held out his hand to her.

As he took her in his arms, she allowed herself to enjoy the moment and moved in tune to his body and the beat of the ballad, the lyrics about love lost and found again. She hoped it wasn't an omen. The music swirled around them like fairy dust and encircled them in a magical movement of the song.

She felt Matt's heartbeat, his hard body against hers, and realized she'd missed him, physically.

"Let's go home," he whispered in her ear.

In the truck, he pulled her close and kissed her. She sighed and gave herself up to the pleasure of the feel of his lips against hers and the feel of his body underneath her fingertips. His hand moved to caress her hips.

"Matt, I want you"—she attempted to speak coherently—"but not in the truck."

He stopped kissing her but still held her close and laughed, catching his breath. She laughed, too.

"Let's go," he said.

When they arrived at his house, they ran inside and kissed again. Matt led her to the bedroom. He pulled off her blouse and bra. He took off his shirt, and their naked bodies touched.

She sighed. "Ummm…"

They flung off their pants and fell on the bed. Matt caressed every inch of her and kissed her lips, breasts, down her body. She lay under him, exploring the hardness and smoothness of his back and hips, and wrapped her legs around him.

When they climaxed, they held on, lethargy and warmness engulfing them. He lifted his head and kissed her. Then he rolled them onto their sides, but still held on.

She caressed his chest. "I missed you…"

"So did I," he said.

Much later, Gloria could finally bring herself to get up and dress. Matt did the same. In the living room, he asked if she wanted anything.

"Just you." She smiled and kissed him on the lips.

He grinned. "I mean to drink."

"Just you."

"I love you," he said.

"Me, too."

"Listen, I have to tell you something."

"All evening, I've thought you weren't quite yourself."

"All evening?" He held her close.

"Well, not the last part."

"This is something I have to do, Gloria. I don't see another way. Tomorrow I'm moving in with the girls."

"What about Angela?" This was going to affect their relationship in a bad way.

"She'll be there, too," he said, turning away from her.

"What did you say?" She could not believe her ears. She must have heard wrong. He couldn't possibly...

"She needs my help with the girls. I don't see how else to do it without disrupting the girls' lives." His eyes beseeched her to understand.

"What about the disruption to our lives? What does this mean for us?" she asked, feeling he was ending their relationship.

"Nothing has changed between us. And nothing will."

"Are you sure? Because I have this sinking sensation in my stomach that things will change."

Matt pulled her close. "Nothing will change. I'm doing this for my daughters, not for Angela. I love you."

"Oh, Matt. I love you, too. And I know you love your girls, and you have to make it as easy as you can for them."

"This situation won't last forever. Okay?" He kissed her, melted her insides.

Everything was right with the world once again, for the moment anyway.

****

Matt walked into the house he'd thought he'd live in with his wife and daughters until he was old and gray. Now he felt as if he were entering a stranger's house. But what he saw as soon as he arrived in the living room and dropped his bags on the floor was a reminder of an all-too-vivid nightmare, one that had replayed itself in his mind for months afterward. Jorge held Angela in his arms. Thankfully, this time they were fully clothed and not on his bed.

"Maybe I should come back at a more convenient time." He forced himself to remain calm. Even though he didn't love Angela anymore, the sight of the man who had helped to ruin his marriage made him see red. For him to be present the day he was moving in, totally against his wishes, irked him to the point he wanted to kick his butt out of the house.

"Oh, Matt." Angela disentangled herself from Jorge and wiped her eyes.

Tears. Of course. She always knew what strings to pull. Hadn't he always fallen for it, too? He should feel sorry for the SOB, but somehow he didn't. Sooner or later, he'd find out what kind of woman Angela really was.

"Jorge just came by to visit. I hadn't seen him since the surgery," she said.

Matt walked into the room, and Jorge stepped back. As well he should. Last time they'd seen each other, Matt had wanted to throw him across the room. "Let's get one thing straight, Angela. If you want me to help you with the girls—and I'm still not sure this is the best way, but for now we'll do it your way—I don't want this bum in my house at all. Do you understand me?"

"I'm sorry, man," Jorge said. "I just wanted to—"

Matt held up his hand. "Do not say one word to me." He turned to Angela. "I'm going to go drive around. Say your good-byes, roll in the hay, for all I care, but until I'm out of this house, this man will not come in here." He turned toward the front door.

"Matt, wait," Angela said.

She'd called out to him back then, too. But that time, it was before he'd clipped Jorge on the jaw.

"Jorge was leaving." She took the man by the elbow. "I'll see you out."

He heard murmuring at the front door. Only the thought of his daughters and how much they needed him now kept him where he was. He longed to walk out the door and leave Angela behind with Jorge, or any other bum she wanted to take up with. The only woman he desired now was Gloria, and this situation with Angela was driving a wedge between them. He wasn't sure he could forgive her, even if she was sick.

"You could have been a little bit civil," Angela said. "He's a guest in my house. My house, by the way, not yours."

"I was civil to the bum. I do apologize for my remark about the house. This is the girls' and your house. He just makes me see red, brings back ugly memories."

She grinned. "You must still care."

"Of course, I care. You're the mother of my girls. But that's the only reason. Don't get any ideas."

"Shit. Look who has a big head."

"Where are the girls?"

"They're out with friends." She walked toward the kitchen. "Do you want something to drink?"

"No, thanks." He picked up his bags. "Where can I set up? The den? Is there still a sofa bed in there?"

"Yes. You could sleep in the guest room."

"No." The guest room was next door to Angela's room. He didn't want to be so near to her. "I'm not going to be here too long."

"How do you know? I haven't even started chemo. I'm going tomorrow. Who knows what'll happen to me? I may not even be able to walk or do anything for myself. I talked with Bessie, you know, one of the few women I can stand. She said her mother had breast cancer, and the chemo seemed worse than the cancer."

Matt patted her on the shoulder. "Calm down, Angela. Take it one day at a time. You'll go crazy otherwise."

"That's the nicest thing you've said to me in a long time."

"Well, I'm not going to make a habit of it." He strolled away to the den.

All he wanted was to be in his house with Gloria. He hoped this would work out. He wasn't sure how, but he hoped so. At least he and Angela hadn't argued too much this time. He needed to be with Gloria. He remembered last night, and the thought made him smile—and ache to be in bed once more with her.

If they made it through all these obstacles, they'd be stronger at the end.

Chapter Nine

"It's not like we're moving across town," Gordy said.

Gloria grabbed his hand and pulled him toward her in a bear hug. He allowed it, although he didn't always. What eighteen-year-old wanted his mom holding him like a child?

"Gordo, let's go," Dex shouted from the front door.

"I'm coming," Gordy yelled back. "Let's go, Mom."

With another glance at the empty room, which made her stomach do a flip-flop and tears burn in her eyes, Gloria said, "Okay."

Dex drove away in the U-Haul, with Gordy following in Dex's truck. He'd get his car later. She waved to them. Dex kept his eyes on the road, without a backward glance. Gordy turned to her, grinned, and waved. She climbed into her pickup, heaved a sigh, and followed her sons to their new place.

How was Matt faring with his family? At least his family was together in one place. He was even living with them, his ex and his daughters. *How cozy.* She didn't want to be spiteful. He loved his girls and would do anything for them, including putting up with Angela. And now Angela was sick, which put an additional stress on him since he hated illness and all it entailed.

Tears filled her eyes—and infuriated her. She'd

always been such a crybaby. But for once, she allowed herself a pity party. Her life was in a mess. Her sons were moving out from under her wing. The empty-nest syndrome loomed before her. Matt was with Angela, although only temporarily.

Near the apartment complex, Port Ranch, she pulled a tissue out of her purse, dried her eyes, and blew her nose. Her sons must not see her in such a state. Gordy would be upset. Dex seemed angry, and she wondered why. She'd believed they'd made their peace.

As she parked, the boys carried some furniture into the apartment on the first floor. Gordy had pointed out that upper floor apartments were safer.

"We're not girls, man," Dex had retorted. "Besides, I'm not hauling furniture upstairs."

Gloria scanned the apartment. The carpet was clean. The living room had big windows. The dining room and kitchen were to the left of it, and the two bedrooms were down a small hall, one on each side. The bathroom was located in between the two rooms. The place reminded her of the first house she and Eddie had bought. *Good heavens. Why am I thinking about Eddie?*

"You're going to need a sofa and chair," she said.

"We're getting those." Dex peered outside. They'd left the door open.

She stared in the same direction and saw Eddie climb out of a truck on the passenger side. In the bed of the truck was a black leather sofa and chair.

"What's he doing here?" she muttered. She could see what he was doing, but he was the last person she wanted to see right now.

"I told him about our new place. He said he could

help us," Dex said, a worried expression in his eyes.

Her heart lurched. No matter how she felt about Eddie, her sons, especially Dex, wanted him in their lives. It wasn't her place to damage the relationship.

"Hey, guys, I've got the sofa. Where do you want it?" Eddie asked.

She watched him swagger in, and then he saw her.

"Gloria, I didn't expect to see you here." He grinned. "But I'm sure glad you are." He walked closer as if to hug her.

She stepped back and knocked over a TV table. He moved to help her, and she jumped away. "Why shouldn't I be here? They're my sons," she said. She wanted to tell him to unload the sofa and leave.

"It amazes me how you always manage to leave me out of the equation. You did have help in getting your sons, you know?"

She ignored his statement. "This is not a good time for you to be here."

"Mom, it's my apartment. I can invite anyone I want," Dex said.

"Why are you so angry, son?" she asked. "I thought we'd made our peace."

Dex turned away to go back outside. "We have. Now I've left your house. You're free to do as you like. So am I."

Even Eddie's brow furrowed at Dex's attitude. He'd always been easygoing, especially with her. Both her sons had.

"Eddie, I have to talk to my sons. Unload the stuff and leave," she said.

"I'll go get the sofa." He walked to the front door but glanced back before he stepped outside.

Dex waved him to go ahead. "Maybe you should leave, Mom, since you and Dad can't get along."

Gloria stared at Dex. What was going on? What was he angry about?

"You knew I was going to help you today. Eddie should have come another day." She picked up the broom and swept the clean carpet. In moments of stress, she did housework.

Dex sighed. "He insisted on today. I know you're unhappy about Matt spending so much time around his ex because she's sick, but it just proves he wasn't right for you, doesn't it?"

"And you're angry?"

"Yes. For a man who told me and Gordy both he'd loved you no matter what, he sure changed his tune quickly, didn't he?"

To her chagrin, Eddie chose that moment to reenter the apartment and heard Dex's words.

The man who'd driven him over helped him carry the sofa in. "What's this? Trouble in paradise?" Eddie asked when he'd unloaded his burden. He waved the man outside. "I'll be right out, man."

"Stay out of this, Eddie," she said.

He laughed. "How soon the rose shrivels."

She glared at her ex. Her hand itched to slap the grin off his stupid face, so she kept a tight grip on the broom. He'd always managed to bring out the worst in her.

"I'm sorry, Mom," Dex said before he left the room.

"Eddie, leave," she repeated. "And if you have any ideas about making a nuisance of yourself here in the boys' apartment, think again. I don't want you interfering."

"But it's okay if you do?"

"If I'd really wanted to interfere, I would have forbidden them to move out of my house," she shouted. She hated this. Eddie was the only man who could make her lose her calm. A psychiatrist would probably say she had untapped anger regarding him.

"They're grown men, not babies."

"I realize that. I'm not stupid."

"So what's wrong?"

She refused to answer him and turned away, taking the broom with her into the kitchen

He followed her. "Gloria, answer me." He got so close she swept at his feet before he grabbed the broom.

"We're just working out some issues."

"Like what?"

"I don't want to talk to you about this. I don't want to talk to you at all." She yanked the broom from his hand and began sweeping again.

"You look very sad. You've been crying."

She was amazed at his perception, something he'd seldom shown during their turbulent marriage. "My sons left my house. Isn't that reason enough?"

"I suppose, but now I've learned about this other thing. I'm so sorry, baby." He stopped her from sweeping and pulled her into his arms.

She dropped her hold on the broom and brought her hands up to push him away. "Eddie, please. I don't need this."

He wouldn't release her. The scent of his cologne suffocated her. "Let me go." She lifted her foot and stepped on Eddie's—hard.

He yelled, "Ow." But he released her.

"Dad, thanks for the stuff." Dex stood in the hallway. "We can handle it now."

Gordy entered the kitchen. He'd been in his room all this time. He wasn't as comfortable with his dad around as Dex was. "Yeah, Dad. Thanks."

Eddie released his hold on Gloria. "I'm just trying to help your mom."

"She's fine. We're here, like always," Dex said.

"Always" hung over them like a rebuke. She knew Dex, even now, had issues of abandonment. He'd never worked those out. Did a child ever forget?

"Okay, I'll leave. But if you guys need anything, you call me, okay?"

Dex walked up to Eddie and patted him on the back. "We will, Dad. Thanks."

"I'm sorry, Mom," he said when Eddie finally left.

"I'm fine, Dex. He's your dad. He just gets to me every time I see him. I guess I'm still angry."

"Me, too."

"I know."

"Not only about Dad. Matt, too," he admitted.

"Is this why you're so angry lately?"

"Yeah. I hate it. He said he loved you."

"He still does." She hugged Dex with one arm, waved Gordy over, and put her other arm around him. "I love him. We'll work it out. But in the meantime, we're a family like we've always been, and I don't want us to be angry with one another."

"I'm fine." Gordy leaned over and gave Dex a punch on the chest. "It's Dexie who keeps messing up."

Of course Dex punched Gordy back, and pretty soon they were having a punching bout. Gloria laughed. Things were back to normal, at least with her family, even though her sons had moved out and would be on their own. They were embarking on a new chapter in their lives just as she and Matt were.

****

Matt woke up and for a second didn't know where he was. His gaze searched the room, the den in his old house, the house Angela lived in with his daughters. He closed his eyes, wishing he were anywhere but here. But then he flung off the covers. He was here for a reason and one reason only, for his daughters. He didn't wish Angela any harm. He wanted her to get well, but he wanted her to hurry up and do it, as unreasonable as he knew he was being.

"Matt, are you awake?" Angela tapped at his door.

God! Here I go. "I'll be right there, Angela."

"You know my appointment is at nine. It's seven fifteen. We have to go. I'll be late. The doctor wants me there an hour early. Probably to fill out paperwork. You'd think they'd have all my information already."

He grabbed his jeans and pulled them on. He grabbed a T-shirt. Now he was glad he'd showered last night. Angela wouldn't have the patience for him to shower this morning. He opened the door, and she stood in the entryway, dressed in a long black skirt and navy top that covered her arms and up to her neck. She seemed so unlike herself. He'd told her to dress according to her age, but for some reason, seeing her like this saddened him.

"If you say anything about how I'm dressed, I'll...so help me, I'll throw something at you," she said.

Amber's voice prevented his response. "The bus will pick up Patsy and me. You just have to take Julia to school."

"Is she ready?" Angela trotted down the hall to the bedrooms. "Julia…"

"Did you have breakfast?" Matt asked Amber.

"I did. I ate a breakfast bar and some milk. I don't like milk, but I want good bones. We're studying nutrition in health class. I don't want to be stooped when I'm old."

"Good, baby." He walked to the kitchen with Amber beside him, talking nonstop. "Where's your sister Patsy? Did she eat?"

"I don't think so, Dad." She ran ahead to rinse her dishes.

Patsy wasn't in the kitchen. He found her by the front door, adjusting her backpack over her shoulder.

"Did you eat breakfast?" he asked.

"I'm not hungry, Dad." She didn't meet his eyes.

"Patsy…"

Angela stormed in. "Let's go. I'm going to be late. You girls get to the bus stop." She air-kissed them.

Amber threw herself in his arms. "I'm so glad you're here in the morning, Daddy."

"Bye, Dad," Patsy said and hugged him.

Julia rushed by with her backpack. "Let's go. I don't understand the big rush."

"I have a doctor's appointment," Angela said. "Have you forgotten? What's the matter with you lately?"

Julia didn't answer and walked outside. Angela followed, still yelling at her.

Once in the truck, Matt drove off. No one spoke. Angela held some papers she flipped through.

He pulled up to the high school. "Bye, sweetheart. Have a good day."

"Oh…bye…" Angela said.

"Good luck at the doctor's, Mom," Julia said. Matt thought she'd been crying.

"I'll need more than luck, but thanks," Angela said. "Oh, Julia, that get-up is so…ugly for you."

Matt couldn't see anything wrong with the jeans and blouse Julia wore.

"You have curves," Angela said. "Show them off. Who knows when you'll lose them?"

"Angela, for Pete's sake," he said.

"You're not dressed to show off either," Julia said. "Bye." She ran from the truck and was soon lost in the throng of students waiting outside for the bell to ring.

"Do you have to be so critical?" he asked. "And another thing. This harping you've been doing with Patsy about her weight and eating habits has her missing meals. I don't think I've seen her eat in several weeks."

"Hah! You're not around all the time. She's constantly putting something in her big mouth."

"Lay off her. She's a young, growing girl. She needs to eat." He slowly drove out of the school parking lot.

"Isn't this just like you? I'm on my way to an oncologist, a cancer doctor, to start chemo because I have cancer and I'm dying, and you're criticizing me and judging how good of a mother I am." Sobs filled the truck.

"Hell. I'm sorry. I'm worried about Patsy. And lately, there's never a good time to talk to you about the girls."

"You don't have to worry about her." She sniffled. "Are you even the least bit worried about me?"

"Of course, I am," he said and entered the freeway. Thankfully, traffic seemed to be moving faster than usual for this time of the morning.

Angela didn't say a word for a few miles, for which he was grateful. The morning hadn't been as quiet as he was used to, but he had enjoyed seeing his daughters off to school. He realized he'd missed it.

"You're just worried my illness will destroy your happiness with your girlfriend. Well, I am so sorry I inconvenienced you," she said as if there hadn't been a pause in the conversation. She dissolved into tears again.

"Angela." He sighed. It didn't help he'd just turned into the medical center. To this day, a panic attack hit him whenever he drove near this place, let alone drove right into the middle of it. He glanced at the heart hospital where his mom died. Then he drove by the children's hospital where Patsy had been so sick he'd choked with the fear and anxiety.

She continued to sob. His heart constricted as he looked at her, face in her hands. Now his ex was sick with a life-threatening illness.

"I'm sorry," he said. "I know this isn't easy for you." It wasn't easy for him either. He had to get over this phobia. He had to have his wits about him.

He parked at the Medical Plaza building where Angela's doctor was. He helped her out of the truck, and they took the elevator up to the doctor's office. A cheery receptionist greeted them and gave Angela a ream of papers to fill out while he found them seats in the uncrowded waiting room.

She started the paperwork but became flustered, then angry. "I've already answered all these questions.

Don't they have this on record already?"

In the end, Matt asked her the questions and filled in the answers. He just had her sign.

"I thought offices were working toward becoming paperless," she said.

He didn't comment. He took the papers up to the girl, who said there would be a short wait, and returned to his seat.

"I hope we won't have to wait forever," Angela said.

I hope so, too. Matt looked at the magazines on the little table next to his chair—mostly women's magazines and a few health journals. Thankfully, after a few minutes, Angela was called. He picked up a magazine.

She took his hand. "Come with me, Matt."

"I'll wait here."

"Come with me. I'm so scared."

For once, he knew she wasn't acting, trying to get a certain reaction from him. He stood and kept his hand in hers. They walked into an exam room, and she let go of his hand.

The nurse came in to draw blood and ask more medical questions. "Is this your husband?"

"My ex," Angela said.

"Do you want him to have access to your health information?" the nurse asked.

"Yes, everything. We have three daughters. He has to be aware of what's going on with me at all times."

"Okay." The nurse filled out another form. "Sign here, please. Take everything off from the waist up and put on this gown. The doctor will be in soon."

Angela took the gown, and Matt stepped out while

she changed. Then they waited for the doctor.

The doctor explained the stages of breast cancer. Angela was at stage two. "This is the protocol we'll follow. We'll start the first dose today and will continue this medicine through sixty days, once a week. Mondays are good. Will that work for you?"

Angela nodded. As the doctor spoke, Matt's ears buzzed. This happened to him whenever doctors spewed medical terminology. *What did it all mean? Gibberish.* All he wanted to know was what was going to be done, in clear words.

"So every Monday morning at nine, be here," the doctor said. "I'm going to prescribe certain medications for side effects you might get—preventatives. Do you understand?

Angela nodded again.

He heard only bits and pieces now. *Antibiotics... Pepcid... Upset stomach...*

When the doctor asked if there were any questions, Matt tried to focus. Angela didn't speak, rare for her.

He cleared his throat. "You said through sixty days, then what?" His voice sounded hoarse.

"The first phase is for six months. We'll run more blood tests and do CT scans to assure the cancer remains in remission," the doctor explained.

"Will I lose my hair?" Angela asked.

Matt couldn't help a small smile. She must be feeling better if she was thinking of her looks again.

"Not right away," the doctor said. "Though some patients do. Sometimes it can't be avoided. I'm sorry. Anything else?"

When neither Matt nor Angela said anything, the doctor stood. "I'll send the nurse in to start an IV.

She'll take you to a backroom. You can sit in the recliner and get infused. Should take about an hour or so."

An hour? He was going to have to leave her. He braced himself for the tirade. "I have a meeting at ten. But I'll be back to pick you up," he said.

"I'll be here." She gave him a small smile.

"Do you have someone you want me to call to stay with you?" He really hated to leave her alone.

"I guess it would be nice, Matt, but no. I've never had close women friends. I know you wouldn't call Jorge."

His ire at the mention of the man surfaced. "Why don't you have him bring you to these appointments?"

She shuddered. "I just wanted to make you angry. Jorge's not important to me."

Did she mean he was still significant to her? He knew she regretted cheating on him. But he couldn't forgive her. He'd loved her with all his heart, and then she'd betrayed him. Maybe he should work on the anger issues due to his ex-wife's cheating.

"I'll be back. I'll make sure the receptionist has my cell phone." He patted Angela's hand.

She grabbed it. "Thanks, Matt."

"You're the girls' mom. I'll always be here for you because of them."

"Don't forget where I am."

He waved to her and left the exam room. He confirmed that the receptionist had his cell number and walked out of the doctor's office and the building, breathing a sigh of relief. He hated the smell of medical buildings—disinfectant and heartache.

It was time to get to work with his plants and trees

for his client. He had to see Gloria. Saturday was ages ago, and their time hadn't ended on a high note since he'd told her he was moving in with the girls—and Angela. He needed to see her again, to hold her and touch her. To tell her he loved her and wanted to spend the rest of his life with her. Challenges would always come, but with love, anything was possible.

Matt reached his truck and drove away. Work always helped him iron things out.

****

"Hi, Gordy." Gloria entered the apartment with bags of groceries. A delicious whiff of pinto beans cooking assailed her nostrils. She'd been going to cook spaghetti and meatballs for her sons. Dex would make the meatballs; he was good at that. However, at the last minute they'd decided they'd rather have crispy beef tacos with rice and beans. Dex loved pinto beans cooked in the crockpot.

"Hey, Mom." Gordy took three bags from her hands. "Dex went to get some drinks. He forgot earlier."

"Okay." She set her two bags down, grabbed Gordy, and hugged and kissed him before he could get away.

"Aww, Mom," he said, but grinned.

"I'll make the rice first. It'll take longer than the meat. I see the beans are cooking away."

"Yeah, they've been in the crockpot since this morning." He unpacked some of the bags on the dining table, then proceeded to store items in the cupboards and the fridge, except for the ones they'd need for the meal.

"Smells great." Gloria gathered the ingredients she

125

needed from the table and the cupboards. She sautéed the rice in vegetable oil, then added spices, diced tomato, and sliced onion. Once the rice boiled, she lowered the heat, covered the pan, and let it simmer. As she worked, she wondered how Angela's chemo treatment had gone. How was Matt? She hated not seeing him on a regular basis.

"So how's it going, Gordy?"

"Okay. I'm glad school's nearly over." He plopped down at the dining table.

"You don't sound like it's okay." She rinsed a skillet for the meat.

He sighed and squirmed in his seat, facing her. "I have to do a poetry notebook. Why? Not everybody is a writer. Dex likes to write. Not me."

"What kinds of poems do you have to write?"

He left the room, and she put the ground beef in a pan on the stove to cook, added spices, but not onions. Dex hated them, flatly refused to eat them. He thought the meal was ruined if he glimpsed an onion on his plate. He didn't like rice, and Gordy would just pick out the onion. His battle with the vegetable was not as intense as Dex's.

Gordy returned with the assignment sheet. "I have to write certain types of poems—prose poems, haiku. I don't even know what some of these are."

Gloria sat down across from him and glanced at the sheet. "Well, it tells you right there, Gordy. It shouldn't be too hard."

"What do I write about?"

"Poems are usually about feelings. How you feel about something. What you feel about something."

"About what?" He stared at the paper as if several

poems would appear.

"Anything. Like about graduation or your brother, Dex. You have a great relationship. Or even your feelings about Matt and me." She hoped she wasn't opening up a can of worms.

"How do I put it in a poem?" He stood again.

"Well, how about 'I was happy in my home with Mom and bro and me. Then this monster came and disrupted everthang'?"

Gordy laughed. "Matt isn't so bad."

"Well, I'm glad to hear it." She got up to stir the beef and check on the rice. The smell of meat, garlic, and pepper filled the kitchen.

"I thought poems had to rhyme."

"Not necessarily."

He picked up a pen and wrote.

The front door opened, and Dex grumbled, "You'd think getting a couple of sodas wouldn't be so hard. I hate traffic."

"Dex is here and not happy." Gloria raced to greet him, then stopped at the sight of Eddie behind him. "Or you could write a poem about how you feel about your dad. I know I could fill a book," she muttered to Gordy.

"Dad and I are okay, Mom," Gordy said, standing near her. "Be good."

Dex walked up to Gloria and hugged her with one arm. The other hand held sodas in plastic bags. "I didn't invite him," he whispered. "He just showed up."

Eddie swaggered in, as usual in jeans and boots. "What a nice surprise, Gloria." He grinned.

"I wish I could say the same," she said. "The boys and I planned this supper. Couldn't you come another night?"

"Mom," both boys bellowed.

"Well, I want to enjoy my time with my sons, and you tend to ruin everything."

"I just got a job with a construction company out of town. I'll be leaving for Seguin tomorrow morning, and I'll be there a few months. I won't be able to see the boys, so I came today," Eddie said.

"Great, Dad," Dex said. "You can stay and eat. Can't he, Mom? There's plenty of food. I made beans."

The last thing Gloria wanted was to eat with Eddie, but it was important to her sons. This was the boys' apartment. So she agreed Eddie could stay. What choice did she have? Matt, too, was having more contact with Angela than he wanted. She was confident things would settle soon.

She finished with the food, heated up taco shells, and the boys set the table. Eddie brought out a six-pack of beer, and Gloria drank one with her meal. She smiled as Gordy broke up his tacos into a salad along with the rice. For once, she and Eddie didn't argue. She remembered happier times, but all that was over. Eddie hadn't changed. She could tell. She wished him well with his new job. Maybe he could keep this one for the duration.

After she helped the boys clean up, she decided to leave before Eddie did. He'd brought out a second six-pack. Was he spending the night?

"Let's do this again, boys," she said at the front door. The boys had walked her up to it. Eddie stayed on the sofa in front of the TV.

"It was fun, Mom," Dex said. "Sorry about Dad."

"That's okay. It wasn't so bad. For once. Bye, Gordy. I'll be by in the morning to take you to school.

Call me if you need help with your poems."

Eddie sauntered up. "I'll take Gordy to school."

She didn't like it one bit. Gordy's car was in the shop for maintenance, and Dex had an early class.

"Trust me," Eddie told her.

"That went out the window years ago."

"I have to leave early. I'll take Gordy to school and take off in plenty of time," he said.

"See that you do."

"Aren't you going to kiss me 'bye'?" Eddie grinned like a fool after all the beer he'd drunk.

Gloria glared at him. "And here I thought you'd behaved for once."

"Can't blame a man for trying."

She adjusted her purse strap. "Bye, boys." She hugged and kissed them again.

"You break my heart, Gloria." Eddie touched his chest and hung his head.

"You broke mine, too, Eddie. But it's mended now and has actually regenerated."

He looked up. "With Matt?"

"Yes. You go to bed and get some sleep. If I hear you didn't get Gordy to school on time, I'll drive to Seguin and beat you up. I'll call tomorrow, boys."

"Bye, Mom," they said, and Dex closed the door after waving to her one more time.

Gloria ran to her truck. She didn't feel altogether right leaving with Eddie still at the apartment—and drinking. But her sons were young adults. She had to let go, as hard as that was. She had a new life with Matt, and so did her sons, out of her house. Adjustments still had to be made. Angela had just started chemo. Her sons had decided to be independent of her. She and

Matt would soon begin their life together.

****

On Saturday morning, Matt stood outside the Starr Offices complex and inspected his men's handiwork. *So far so good.* Most of the plants and bushes were in place. The rock garden was next. Ben Starr, his client, was scheduled to arrive in a few minutes and give his approval, or not, on the work done thus far. To Matt, a lot of progress had been made, and they were within the deadline. But to Starr, who was known for being hard to please and stubborn, it was another matter.

Matt already met with the man several times, and there was always something. He figured it was the man's money to spend as he chose. But he loved plants, and uprooting them because of the whims of a rich man was a waste and a shame.

He walked around the front areas, where most of the native plants were placed. They were thriving, here and there a hint of color. Perhaps he should try these in an area at his house. He liked the flower bushes, but he could add to his garden. On the other hand, he probably should wait until he and Gloria decided where they were going to live.

He strolled around the circular parking area, which had embankments of more plants and bushes. The rock garden was to be erected at the entrance to the office complex.

He recognized Starr's big, heavy-duty black truck. *Here we go.*

"Hey, Matt." The man took his Stetson off. "Glad to see you here. I have a few matters I want to talk to you about."

What was Starr about to tell him now? He mentally

crossed his fingers.

"I like the plants and stuff there at the front, but I don't like these bushes. They're too big, too tall. Those grackles will fly in there and shit all over the cars," Starr said while walking and making a racket with the cowboy boots he wore. "That's why I've never planted trees in the parking lot, even though more times than I can count people have suggested it. Provide shade for the cars so they won't be so hot when the employees leave, they say. Isn't it the most aggravating thing to see bird shit all over your vehicle, though?"

Matt could think of worse things—an ex diagnosed with cancer, being unable to spend enough time with the woman he loved—but Starr was the client, so he agreed. "I can get smaller bushes, sir. But I can't guarantee we'll have them by your deadline." His cell vibrated in his shirt pocket. He let it go to voice mail.

"You pay whatever you have to, son. I've got plenty of money, and I'm not afraid to use it."

"Also, if I might suggest," Matt said. "About the big bushes, I could put them on the perimeters, away from parking spaces. I'd hate to throw them away."

"Yes, all right." Starr hit his leg with his hat. "Now about this rock garden..." He walked to the entrance to the complex.

Matt followed. The man clearly did feel he could throw money around, as well as good trees. But he only said, "The men are already working. The materials arrived a few minutes ago."

"You know I like these." Starr pointed to the area where Matt's workers began to form the rock garden. "I want another one at the back entrance, not as big. Can you do it?"

"Sure thing," Matt said, relieved he'd ordered extra materials.

"Looking good. I should have hired you years ago." Starr guffawed. "After this I'd like you to work on a couple of my houses, and I also have some rental houses. Though at those, I don't want to spend too much. Tenants don't take care of things like an owner would. Maybe you could use some of those big bushes there." The man laughed. "I know how you landscapers are, lovers of nature. Me, I don't care. I just want things to look nice."

Matt felt the vibration of his phone again. It had to be Angela. She was the only one who'd be so persistent. He finished with Starr and waited until the man drove off before he picked up his phone.

"What, Angela? I'm busy," he said.

"I'm sorry if I'm interrupting."

"Oh, Gloria love, I'm the one who's sorry. I'm so glad to hear your voice."

"I wanted to hear your voice, too. Actually, I want more. Can we get together? I know how busy you are, but maybe tea and dessert somewhere?"

Matt grinned. "I'm all for dessert."

"I mean, real dessert, like lemon pie."

"Me, too." He wished he could meet Gloria right now. "I can't. Angela received her first chemo on Monday. No side effects, but she's sure something's going to happen. I have to be there if only so she won't make the girls' lives miserable."

"Okay." She sighed.

"Maybe one of these days I can escape to the bookstore, and we can indulge in some heavy necking in your office."

"I'd love it. Listen, I want to tell you something."

"What? You love me? Because I love you and miss you."

"Me, too, definitely. However, I wanted you to know I had supper with the boys last night, kind of a housewarming."

"Sounds nice. Are they doing okay?"

"I think so. We made crispy beef tacos with rice and beans." Should she tell him about her ex?

"Invite me next time."

"Eddie showed up.

"How cozy," he said before he could stop himself.

"What about you and Angela in the same house?" she snapped.

"It can't be helped. My girls need me."

"My sons want their dad in their lives. I can't control his comings and goings in their apartment like I could in my house. Besides, he left for Seguin today."

He exhaled. "Good."

"Do you not trust me, Matt? I'm not Angela."

"Of course I do," he said. But did he really?

"If you really trusted me, you wouldn't say 'of course.' You'd just say 'I trust you.' "

"Do you trust me?"

"Yes…" she said. "It's Angela I don't trust."

"I don't trust Eddie. He still loves you." How had they'd ended up having this stupid conversation?

"Angela has always wanted you back."

"Why are we arguing?"

"I don't know." She coughed.

Was she crying?

"But I don't like it," she finished.

"Me either. I'm going to go visit you soon. We

must see each other."

"I can't wait."

"I love you." He wished he could get away right now.

"I love you," Gloria said. "Bye."

As he hung up, his phone buzzed. Angela again.

"What is it, Angela?" he asked, still wondering why he and Gloria had argued. To his knowledge, they hadn't argued since they'd almost broken up when he'd thought he couldn't handle her high blood pressure, a symptom of what had killed his mother.

"I think my skin is getting red," she screamed in his ear. "It's one of the side effects of the chemo. My arms and cheeks are beet red."

"Do you have a fever?" He rolled his eyes up to the blue sky.

"A fever? My God, Matt. You do have the best bedside manner in the world. Why are you saying such things? But wait. I do have a fever. Wherever I'm red, it's hot. I'm going to die!"

He sighed. What could he say to her? He'd no idea. He'd just argued with Gloria. That hadn't happened in a long time. Why now? "Why don't you lie down? The girls will be there soon. Have you eaten?"

"Who can eat? You'd better not be late. I need some peace and quiet. The girls are so noisy, especially Amber. She's such a child still. She really needs to grow up. She's already a teenager."

"I'll be there as soon as I can."

He stood staring out to where his men worked on the rock garden.

He was losing control over his life. He needed his wits about him, especially now with the new contract

and all the challenges he was up against lately.
He had to see Gloria.
He couldn't lose her.

Chapter Ten

Gloria sat at a table at the Chinese restaurant, one of her favorites with its subdued lighting, tinkling fountains, and Oriental music emitting from the speakers. Plus, the food was delicious. Beatrice was opposite her, eating lemon chicken and chow mein. Gloria always ordered beef and broccoli and fried wonton. She shouldn't eat it because of her high blood pressure, but once in a while she liked to indulge. Especially today. She'd argued with Matt over the weekend.

"I'm so glad you called. I can't stand it at the office," Beatrice said after the waiter left. "The boss is on a rampage because the auditor is due any day, and everyone keeps calling in sick, and I wind up with the phones."

"Sounds stressful." Gloria bit into a wonton. She remembered her job at the home health agency and almost cringed. Now she had different worries.

"Man, I'm under so much stress I think I'm going to have a heart attack. And here I am eating greasy food. I don't care. I have to find pleasure somewhere." Beatrice dug into the chow mein.

"Of course, you do." Gloria bit into crisp broccoli in brown sauce. "Yummy."

"I'll be so glad when the auditor comes and leaves. Then the boss will go back home and not bother about us until the next time. And Chavo is still laid up. I think he's better, but he's deliberately lying around moaning and groaning."

"Can he walk?"

"Yes, but he screams in agony the whole time. It frustrates me, and I refuse to help him. He practically sobs because he says I don't care. Of course, the girls are on his side. They see their dad in pain and accuse me of being mean. *Mean*? I'll show them mean. I'll throw Chavo out of the house until he's better and can go to work and I can be alone." Beatrice nearly knocked her tea over with the fork she waved about.

"Calm down, Beatrice. At least while you eat. Once I was so mad at the boys—I forget why—I sat down to eat, and I got upper gastric pain. My doctor said so. To me, my upper back hurt and I couldn't understand why."

"My upper back, lower back, and head hurt. Everything hurts when I'm home. I love Chavo, but he's hard to live with period and even more so when he's sick."

Gloria murmured in sympathy. Sometimes, that was all Beatrice needed.

"What about you? Wedding date set?"

"No." She took a sip of tea. "Matt's living with Angela."

"What?" Beatrice stared, her eyes wide and her brow creased.

"She was diagnosed with breast cancer, had surgery, and is now on chemo. She needs help with the girls, and she asked Matt to move in."

"And he did? Maybe he's not the man for you after all. I can't believe he did it. I wouldn't trust them together."

"I know. I don't trust Angela. But I can't do anything about it."

"Sure, you can. Tell him you'll break off the engagement if he doesn't move out. No, I don't like this one bit. How could you agree?" Beatrice didn't wait for an answer. "I wouldn't. Not with Chavo's ex. The woman is evil. Heck. I wouldn't trust Chavo."

"I don't have a choice. Matt will do anything for his daughters. Angela isn't the most nurturing mom at the best of times, and now with her sick…the girls need their dad."

Beatrice gulped her tea. "You're too trusting."

"We had an argument this past weekend. It didn't feel right arguing with Matt. Now, with my ex, that's practically all we ever did."

The water fountain tinkled nearby, and the music soothed her. Beatrice stopped eating and looked at Gloria.

"I had supper with the boys Friday night, and Eddie showed up. Matt wasn't too thrilled," Gloria said.

"Why did you tell him?" Beatrice waved her fork around again.

"I don't want to keep secrets from Matt."

"What purpose did it serve? Now he doesn't trust you."

Gloria admitted there was a grain of truth in what her friend said. She and Matt had argued because of it. Angela had cheated on him, a sore spot for him. "He's going to try to see me this week at the bookstore. We had a date a couple of Saturdays ago, and we had a great time. Until he told me of his plans to move in with Angela."

"Funny how you say he moved in with Angela and not the girls," Beatrice pointed out.

"Well, it's for the girls."

"Humph." Beatrice snorted. "He's a great catch, good looking, has his own business. Don't let her get her grubby paws on him again."

"She does want him back, I know. She immediately realized she'd made a mistake with the affair. I guess she thought Matt would forgive her."

"See? That's why it's not good he's there with her."

"Most of the time they're not alone. The girls are there." Gloria loved this meal, but today she wasn't enjoying it as much as she usually did. "Though he did take her to her first chemo appointment on Monday."

"Gloria, I think you need to talk to Matt about this now. I wish you'd called me when this first happened. I would have told you it's the wrong way to go."

"Actually, things haven't gone well since Matt proposed. Maybe we should just continue as we were— go out together, have fun, but not get married. It's too complicated."

"Dammit no," Beatrice said. "You're making all kinds of wrong decisions. You have to marry Matt. He's not only good looking and has a huge potential to make lots of money, but he's great in bed."

Gloria laughed, grateful to Beatrice. She always managed to lighten her load. "And how do you know he's good in bed?"

Beatrice giggled. "Well, you haven't said otherwise. Only good? I said 'great.' "

"And do you think I would tell you one way or the other?"

"Sure, you would." Beatrice grinned.

"Matt and I do need to see each other on a more regular basis, but it's almost impossible with our schedules."

Beatrice threw back her hair. "Well, make time for it. I know I complain about Chavo always underfoot, but the most terrible times we've had were when we were apart. And, of course, there was the time when he was up to no good with those wino friends of his. Man, was that ever an ordeal."

"You two have been through some hard times."

"Now's one of them. I wish he'd get better and get back to work."

"It's been a few weeks, hasn't it? Just don't let him stretch it out. You know he does," Gloria reminded Beatrice.

"And how!"

"I hope the auditor leaves soon, too," Gloria said.

"I'd better go back," Beatrice said.

After paying their bill, they stood at the entrance of the restaurant.

"And get Matt out of Angela's house, the sooner the better," Beatrice said.

Gloria hugged her friend. "It's so good to see you."

"Let's do this again," Beatrice said.

Gloria walked to her truck. She tried to ignore her friend's advice and warnings. Beatrice didn't trust men and women together, no matter the age or relationship. Things happened all the time. Was she seeing the situation through rose-colored glasses, as Dex always told her she did?

****

Matt stood at the front entrance of Starr Offices

and inspected the rock garden. Ben Starr had called him because one side of it had collapsed. The man had been furious, and Matt couldn't blame him. He quickly found the problem. Not enough mortar had been put in between the rocks. He'd instructed his crew on how to do it.

"Dammit," he muttered. He hoped Starr wouldn't terminate the contract. The man was known to end business relationships for smaller reasons than this, and this was big. Construction of the rock garden had been written out in detail.

He heard a honk. He stood and watched as his friend, Wayne, drove up in his work truck, Wayne's Landscaping on both doors. He walked over and shook Wayne's hand when he climbed out of the truck.

"How's it going?" Wayne asked and adjusted his cap.

"Shitty."

"Yeah, Tanya told me about Angela."

"I'm staying at her house to help with the girls."

"Not good, man," Wayne said. "I don't even have to look at a woman for Tanya to accuse me of cheating. What you're doing, man… I'd be toast by now, burnt to a crisp."

"How is Tanya?" Matt asked. He held a soft spot for her as she'd sent him to Gloria's house to take care of her roses.

"As usual, she wants a divorce." Wayne grinned, but he clenched his hands.

"What's the reason this time?"

"I branched out to Austin, as I told you, and I've had to spend a lot of time there. She thinks I have another woman over there."

At another time, Matt would have laughed, but now with things the way they were with Gloria, he couldn't.

"What's the matter? You usually have a good laugh at my expense," Wayne reminded him.

"It's hitting too close to home this time."

"What? Do you mean Gloria…"

"No, of course not." He remembered Gloria telling him if he'd really believed her, he wouldn't say *of course*. "No. But her damn ex is always in the picture nowadays."

"And you're living with Angela."

"I'm not 'living' with her. I made a mistake. I have to fix it."

"And quickly, man. You've been alone too long. Don't screw it up. How's it going with work?"

"Not too well either. My crew messed up on the rock garden, and the owner is furious. He should be here in a few to either let me fix it or fire me."

"Yeah, man," Wayne said. "He's a hard nut. Crazy, too. I worked with him a few years back. He pays well, but, man, he takes something I love and makes it a chore."

Matt grinned. "He does. Did he fire you?"

"More than once. Then he'd hire me back. I finally finished the job in twice the time it would usually take me."

"I guess we have to take the good with the bad."

"In love and work, man," Wayne said. "Let's have a drink sometime."

"Sure thing."

"I'd better get back to work. Just remembered you were nearby. I have a job a few miles up the road."

"Thanks, man," Matt said. "Call me. I could use a break."

His friend drove away. "The good with the bad." Life couldn't be perfect. Neither could jobs—or relationships. He and Gloria needed to see each other. They needed to stop arguing all the time.

Wayne was right. He needed to get out of Angela's house.

****

"I wanted to hear your voice," Gloria said when Matt answered the phone. "Are you busy?"

"A little, but I'm glad you called," he said.

Her body responded to the timbre of his tone, and she wished they were together, close, hugging, in bed. "I..." She couldn't bring up Angela again. They'd argue before. Maybe they would again. "How's everything?"

"Not good. I can't see you as often as I want." Voices intruded in the background, and Matt responded, "We need to finish today. I'm sorry, Gloria. It's intense at work with this rock garden."

"I'm sorry I interrupted your work day, but I'd like to see you, too."

"Maybe we can go out tonight. What do you say?" he asked. "I know it's a week night."

"I don't care. I want to see you. Maybe you can look at my roses. They're looking wilted. I think they miss you, too."

The sound of his laugh made her tremble with yearning. "I'd be happy to," he said. "What about you? How much do you miss me?"

"I miss you so much I can't concentrate. I can't do my work. I'm going to kill my roses..."

"I'll pick you up around seven. I think I'll be finished by then," Matt said.

"Okay." Gloria paused again, her heart in her throat. But she had to ask. Beatrice had put the idea in her head. And even though they'd talked about it, she wasn't sure she'd gotten her point across the last time since they'd ended up arguing. "I'm a little worried."

"About what?"

She fiddled with the computer keys. "You and Angela."

"What?" He didn't say another word for a few seconds. "There's no 'me and Angela.' "

"You're living with her and taking her to her doctor's appointments." She wished she'd kept quiet. But then, she didn't. She had to know what was really going on. Did she and Matt have a future together?

"I'm not living with her. I'm staying at her house to help with the girls. I keep trying to convince her to let me hire someone to drive her to where she needs to go. I don't have time to do it, and I really don't want the responsibility. Where is this coming from, Gloria?"

"I'm just worried, like I said. Angela has made no secret of the fact she wants you back."

"I don't want her back." He sighed, and she could hear the frustration. "What about you? You ate a home-cooked meal with your ex the other night?"

"Oh, Matt, really."

"Really? And he's made no secret he wants you back."

"I can't believe what you're saying." Tears filled her eyes. "You know Eddie always did the same thing when he was being unfaithful, turn it around and accuse me of something. I thought you were different."

144

"How do you think I feel? The woman cheated on me in my own house, in my own bed. It's taken me years to trust again. I thought I'd found it in you."

"You don't think you can trust me anymore?" She grabbed a tissue to wipe her tear-filled eyes.

"Eddie is always around on the pretense that he's helping with your sons. Where was he when you really needed him?"

As always when anyone criticized Eddie, even now, she felt she had to defend him. "He did the best he could. How dare you judge something you know nothing about?"

"Hell," he said.

Gloria couldn't believe she'd lost control of the conversation and she and Matt were arguing again. Her throat ached from holding back sobs. Apparently, their trust issues were so ingrained they couldn't work past them. She tried to speak but couldn't. She didn't want him to know she was at the point of tears.

"Listen, I have to get back to work," he said.

She cleared her throat. "Are we still seeing each other tonight?"

"I'll have to check and see if Angela needs me."

He was deliberately being mean. He always said "his girls," never Angela. Had she ruined everything quizzing him like this? "I'm sorry, Matt."

"Me, too. I'll call later." He hung up without another word.

They'd always said "I love you" at the end of every conversation. Gloria let the tears gush out and rested her head on the desk. When she'd cried herself out, she wished she hadn't said anything. She shouldn't have listened to Beatrice. But then, maybe this was for the best. What if she and Matt had gotten married soon after he'd proposed? Everybody would have accepted the union—the kids, the exes. What if a few months later this trust issue had erupted between them? They'd be married and not believe in each other. It would have been so sad—and too late to fix things. For the first time, she believed having a relationship with a man at this time in her life really was too late. At this fresh new thorn in her heart, she cried again.

****

Matt let himself into the house. God, he was tired. And frustrated. Sad. Empty. All emotions he hadn't felt since he'd met Gloria. Where had the distrust issue come in? He could never forget Angela's harsh betrayal. With Gloria, he'd learned to trust again. Now she didn't trust him—with Angela, of all people. Where had that come from? He hated to accuse her but wondered if something had happened with Eddie. Maybe there was something still there. She'd actually jumped to his defense.

Even though they'd argued, he really wanted to see her. This business of not seeing each other wasn't working. Too much stuff happened, pulling them in different directions.

"Daddy, you're home!" Amber rushed to hug him. "Mommy is lying down. She says she has a headache."

He ran a hand through his hair. *Just what I need now.* "I'll go see her."

"I need a snack for school tomorrow."

"Why didn't you text me before I got home?" He stifled a sigh.

"I forgot," she said in a low voice.

He patted her head. "Okay, I'll go to the store in a

146

minute."

"Patsy's crying," she shouted as she ran to the den.

Is there liquor in the house? He needed a shot of alcohol right about now.

Matt arrived at Angela's bedroom door, their room once. He ignored the thought and entered.

"Finally. Where have you been? The girls have been bothering me for hours," she whined.

"Where's Julia?" He really didn't want to tell his ex about his day. Lately, he was also concerned about his older daughter disappearing after dinner. Where did she go? Angela couldn't or wouldn't keep track of her comings and goings. She was too involved with her illness, and in a way, he didn't blame her. Much.

"She's the only one who hasn't come in," Angela said.

"Where is she?"

"I don't know. In her room probably... I have this terrible headache. It won't go away. I called the doctor, and he said it's a side effect. Well, duh. The pain medication isn't worth a damn."

"I'm here, Angela. I'll see no one bothers you."

"But..."

He closed the door on whatever protest she had. He didn't have time or inclination to listen to another of her dramas.

He walked to the room Patsy and Amber shared and knocked on the closed door. "Patsy?" He knocked again.

"I'm busy." Her voice sounded muffled.

"It's Dad. I have to talk to you." He opened the door.

Patsy sat in the middle of her unmade bed, hair

tousled and eyes red.

"Patsy, darling girl, what is the matter?"

She jumped out of the bed and ran into his arms, sobbing into his chest. "I was so…hungry, so…I ate…not too much…just a sandwich, but Mom got angry with me…. She wants me to eat only salads…" Patsy sobbed some more. "She told me I was too fat…and on my way to…becoming obese. Oh, Dad."

Matt's heart wrenched in pain. He let her cry herself out. When she calmed down, he said, "I want you to stop starving yourself."

"But Mom—"

He shook his head. "I'm going to talk to your mom. You're a growing girl, and you need to eat." He paused as a terrifying thought occurred to him. "You're not throwing up on purpose or wanting to be ultrathin, are you?"

"No, Dad. I'm only doing this because Mom wants me to. I watch my calories. Look…" She reached inside the drawer of her bedside table. "I keep a record. I'm only supposed to get so many calories for my height and age. I don't want to get fat, so I watch what I eat. Mom makes me feel as if I'm huge, though, so maybe I am."

"I'll put a stop to it. You continue keeping your records, and I promise I'll let you know if I think you're getting fat."

Patsy giggled. "Oh, Dad, you would never do it."

"No, I wouldn't because I think you always look beautiful, even now with your red nose and hair sticking out as if you stuck your finger in an electrical outlet."

"Oh, Dad, I love you." She hugged him.

"Me, too, darling girl. I'm going to the store to get a snack for school for Amber. Do you want some ice cream or something?"

"Do you know how many calories just one scoop of vanilla ice cream has?"

He laughed, kissed her forehead, and left. He walked back to Angela's room. She was on the phone, talking as if she didn't have a care in the world.

"Look, I have to hang up. Someone's come in," she said and hung up. "I thought you said I wouldn't be disturbed."

"By the girls." He pointed to his chest. "Me, I can disturb you whenever I want. Leave Patsy alone. She's been crying all evening long from the looks of her. She's not eating enough, and you're giving her a complex."

She glared at him. "What do you know about young girls and being fat and having no friends and no boy wants to look at you?"

He laughed. "What do you know about it? You always had boys after you as if they were ants and you were covered in maple syrup."

"Jealous, Matt?" She grinned.

"No, just stating facts."

"You managed to push your way through all those ants," she reminded him.

"A lifetime ago. It's in the past, never to be revived again. Understood?" He was determined to make his point.

"Don't worry. I've got other fish to fry."

"Okay," he said. "And leave the girls alone. I mean, you can advise them. You're their mother. But don't try to live their lives for them."

"What makes you such a damned expert?"

"I had parents who let me live my life, up to a point, and I'm very grateful." He stood at the end of the bed. "One more thing. I'm going to hire someone to drive you to your appointments. I don't have time, and I don't want to do it."

"I know you stopped caring about me a long time ago." Angela scrunched her face and burst into tears.

"Don't start. This isn't about caring about you or not. Living here has changed my life in a way I don't like. We made a bad decision, and we're going to make a better one."

"You can't abandon me," she yelled.

"I'm not, but I'm going to change things. So think about it. You can make your own arrangements. Or I'll set something up. I'll pay whatever's necessary. Whatever you want to do. But we are going to make adjustments."

"Your little girlfriend is jealous, isn't she? Is she threatening to break off the engagement if you don't move out?"

Matt's throat closed up. The thought hadn't even occurred to him. What if Gloria did come to the conclusion they couldn't work things out and broke it off? Would she really?

He heard Angela's laughter at the edge of his thoughts and brought his attention back to her. "I know a breakup between us would make you happy. But, no, this is my decision."

He didn't want to remember the conversation with Gloria yesterday. He wanted to find a way back to her and to the way things were before everything went wrong.

Chapter Eleven

Gloria sat at her desk updating the store's online catalog when she heard the bell on the front door tinkle. Judy Ann was at the cashier's desk, so she continued working.

"Gloria, I'm here." Celeste's voice sounded before she arrived at her office door.

The woman hadn't been at the bookstore on a regular basis since she'd returned from the cruise several weeks ago. What was going on?

"Hi, Celeste," Gloria said. "What did you bring?"

Celeste held several brown gift bags in her hands. "I hadn't given you the souvenirs I brought from the cruise. I finally got around to unpacking and found them. I'm sorry. I meant to give them to you sooner."

"Oh, how sweet of you."

Celeste sat on the chair and watched as Gloria lifted out item after item from one of the bags. Celeste had brought her something from every city she'd toured. Gloria couldn't help wondering what she was going to do with so many knickknacks. She had enough clutter at her house. In fact, she tried every day to reduce it. Maybe she could keep a few at the office. One could do only so much with miniature Eiffel Towers and Buckingham Palaces.

"This is for you, too." Celeste handed her another gift bag.

Gloria took it and drew out several T-shirts depicting Paris, London, practically all the cities Celeste had visited. "Thank you, Celeste. I love them." These, she could use. Sweats and T-shirts were the most comfortable attire for her.

"I love shopping—and spending. And my husband doesn't mind how much I spend."

"Lucky you."

"I'll be right back," Celeste said. "I have to give Judy Ann her gifts."

Gloria didn't like to go shopping. She shopped for necessities, whether they were groceries or clothes. Maybe if she had a bottomless wallet, she'd enjoy it more. Who knew? She'd always had to be practical. She remembered Beatrice's claim about Matt's potential to make lots of money. She never thought about it whenever she was with Matt. She was just happy to be with him, talk to him, be near him, make love with him.

Tears threatened to spill out of her eyes as she remembered their last conversation. They'd argued about their exes and trust issues. Where had it come from? She knew Matt didn't want to go back with Angela. The fact he moved into his ex's house bothered her. Knowing she'd spent an evening with Eddie had disturbed Matt. However, she couldn't have left. She rarely saw her sons anymore. She couldn't pass up the chance when she had it just because Eddie showed up. She'd never want her ex back. He'd hurt her too much and left her with two little boys to raise with very little financial help from him. Not to mention leaving her alone to deal with the anxiety and fear of rearing a family, sons who needed a male role model. She'd be grateful to John until her dying day for stepping in, especially when he had his family to deal with. He'd included her sons in his outstretched arms without blinking an eye.

The front door bell tinkled. Could it be Matt? No, he wouldn't visit her. They weren't even going out this weekend. He was busy with his family—and Angela. Tears threatened again, so she forced herself to concentrate on updating the book catalog.

Celeste returned to her office and sat. "I have to tell you something."

"What?" she asked. "You're not sick, are you? You haven't been at the bookstore much lately." She hoped she didn't sound accusatory. She'd become used to running the bookstore along with Judy Ann, and she'd found she could handle any problem that came up.

"No, I'm not sick. Thank God." Celeste shuddered. "I'm...I know this will probably shock you." She paused. "I'm selling the bookstore."

Gloria's stomach flip-flopped. "Never in a million years would I have guessed that's what you were going to say. How come?"

"I don't want the responsibility anymore. Being on the cruise and living a life of leisure helped me think about a lot of things, about my life. I've spent all my life working. My first job was when I was sixteen. I've been working nonstop since then, except for the few months I took off when I had my kids. My husband agrees with me. He's ready to retire, too. We decided we want to spend the remainder of whatever years we have left traveling, seeing the world, just being with each other, getting to know each other."

Being with each other. She and Matt were seldom

together anymore. Now not only was her relationship with him out of sync, but she was also about to be unemployed.

"I'm so sorry, Gloria," Celeste said when Gloria focused on her again. "I know you haven't been here very long."

"True. And I've enjoyed every minute of it."

"I've been in business for over twenty years. I love this store. But I love my husband, and there comes a time when you have to choose between being practical and what's really important. In my case, I've neglected my husband for too many years. I'm surprised he didn't leave long ago, but then, he had his own mountains to climb. And he feels like I do. Enough is enough."

"How soon will all this happen? Should I start looking for a job right away?"

"It's up to you. You could always apply for unemployment. It'll give you some extra time."

"I suppose," Gloria said. *Just when I thought I'd found the perfect job. The perfect man.* She blinked her eyes. Ever since her last conversation with Matt, she'd wept constantly.

"Things will work out. I'm going to list the bookstore with a realtor friend of mine. I really don't know how long it will take to sell, but I'm going to close the store by the end of September. I don't want to deal with holiday shoppers. I'm done."

"Okay. That gives me a few months. I'll start looking for another job."

"I'll write a letter of recommendation if you want to apply at another bookstore."

"Thank you." Gloria doubted she would find another job like this one at Books and All, but she could try. She'd never find another man like Matt. But he had to trust her again. And she had to trust him.

****

"You're fired," Ben Starr shouted. "Look at this crap." The man pointed to the collapsed side of the rock garden again. He poked and prodded and loosened the area even more.

How the hell had this happened again? The last time, Matt had managed to convince Starr he could get the job done. "I'm sorry, sir," he said. "But I can fix it."

"I don't have time for you to get your act together," Starr said. "I've already hired a new man. He'll even do it cheaper than you. Get off my property, Cerda. I wasted a lot of time and money with you. I'll send your final check by the end of the week."

Matt stifled the urge to argue with him, but the man had every right to hire and fire anyone, including him. As he walked to his truck, disappointment filled him, not only because of the loss of the money but also because this meant he'd have to start the process of looking for a big contract again. In the meantime, he'd work his smaller contracts. Maybe that's what he needed. Physical labor was always a good way to work out problems. And, man, did he have problems nowadays.

He picked up his cell to call Gloria, a reflexive action. Then he remembered their last conversation. He and Gloria had argued. He let his hands hang over the steering wheel and closed his eyes. If he were a man who wept, he'd probably be in tears. As it was, his throat ached, and his stomach didn't feel so good. He hadn't eaten breakfast, had only grabbed a cup of coffee before meeting Starr. But he wasn't hungry.

He dialed Wayne's number. The call went immediately to voice mail. His friend was at work, and he didn't need to bother him. Besides, what was he anyway? A kid? He could handle this on his own. He had other jobs to do, ones he'd neglected and left in the hands of his two supervisors. No time like the present to drive over and check out what they'd been doing. This crew had messed up with Starr. Who knew what was going on with the rest of his jobs? However, his supervisors would let him know about any problems. So far, he hadn't heard of any.

His cell buzzed. Wayne.

"Hey, man, what's up?" Wayne asked.

"Sorry," Matt said. "I know you're busy. I just got canned."

"It was a matter of time, dude. Don't get too busy with other jobs. He's going to call back. That's how he works. I think he just likes chaos in his life."

"What a way to live."

"Well, when you have a lot of money, you tend to want to make your own excitement," Wayne said and laughed.

Matt studied the rock garden. Starr had driven off. He knew he could repair the damned thing. He hated to leave things undone. Like with Gloria. He needed to do something. Would she agree? Or was she indeed thinking of breaking off the engagement? He hadn't been able to forget Angela's insinuation.

"Hey, Matt." Wayne's voice called him back to the present. "Are you there?"

"Yeah. Sorry, man. Just thinking."

"You're thinking too much. Have you seen Gloria?"

"About a week ago, and since then we've had two phone conversations, which both ended in an argument."

"Say you're wrong, and everything will settle down. That's what I do."

"I wish it was as simple as that." *She doesn't trust me. I'm not sure I trust her.*

"It is. I'd be divorced from Tanya since before Nikki was born if I'd tried to win every argument."

"It's not about winning. It's…well, trust. We don't trust each other."

Wayne laughed. "Tanya has spent all our married life not trusting me, man. I just convince her she has nothing to worry about, and I've never given her cause to think otherwise." He paused. "You need to get out of Angela's house. You made a bad move there, man."

Matt sighed. "I know. I felt I had to be there, physically present, with my girls. You know how I am with illness. I can't think straight."

"Who can, really? Especially when it's someone you care about. I know you have other issues, but…remember what's important."

"Thanks, man. I'm going to go check on some ongoing jobs with all this free time I have today." Somehow, the burdens he carried lightened after talking with his friend.

"Do it. Call me anytime. And remember the nut is going to call you back. Be ready."

This time Matt did laugh and closed his cell.

I have to talk to Gloria. He'd just told Wayne he had some free time. He'd go see Gloria, surprise her with a visit.

****

Gloria helped Judy Ann shelve the new arrival of children's books. She kept Marjorie Green's books on the shelf. She noticed six of Yvette Salinas's books and tossed them into the bargain-buy box with gusto, remembering how the diva author had eyed Matt.

"I didn't like her much either." Judy Ann grinned.

"I shouldn't do it, right? I'm allowing my personal feelings to get in the way of business."

"She was not very likeable. And remember how she was with the kids. How can someone who obviously doesn't like children write for them?"

"She probably has a lot of imagination." Gloria wondered herself. She'd listened to a lot of writers, and most said they wrote about what they liked or at least about something they'd always wanted to learn.

"She sure did let her imagination run wild when she saw your fiancé," Judy Ann said before she went to tend to a customer.

Gloria smiled and agreed. She remembered the day of the book signing. That was before everything had gone so wrong. Since then, she and Matt had argued so much. They had enjoyed the time at the lake, but it'd been marred when he'd confessed afterward he was moving in with the girls—and Angela. Somehow, she couldn't feel comfortable about the situation, even if he had no desire to return to his ex.

"Hello, everybody," Celeste greeted. She stopped to talk to the customer, a long-time friend of hers.

Gloria finished shelving the books and carried the box to the back, where she flattened it and put it in the recycle bin. Had Celeste come to tell her about the progress of the bookstore sale? At least she'd given her several months to look for another job. Gloria had just sat down at her computer to enter invoices when Celeste walked in.

"I listed the bookstore," Celeste said. "I'm so excited because the realtor actually told me she had a couple of prospective buyers. Can you believe it? I'd really like to sell before I close down or at the same time. Once I leave, I don't want to have to think about this place anymore."

Gloria could understand, but in her opinion, the bookstore could remain unsold until September. It'd be ideal for her. "If you sell before September, will you close?" she asked.

"No, I'll keep the bookstore open until September," Celeste said. "We're not planning another trip until mid-October. Don't worry."

She heaved a sigh of relief. "I'm sorry." Tears spilled from her eyes. "It's not your problem. It's mine. I'll work it out."

"Sure you will. I'm just so excited at the possibility. I imagined I'd have to wait years to sell, and my little store would be ruined. You know abandoned buildings tend to deteriorate faster. Somehow, the energy of people living and loving keeps structures upright."

"You may be right." Her body had undergone serious emotional damage during the past several days with things so bad between her and Matt.

"And the realtor only said she might know about some prospective buyers," Celeste said. "She's my friend, but she's a businesswoman, too. Of course, she's going to tell me what I want to hear, at least at the beginning, right?"

Celeste left, and Gloria continued with the

invoices. Music would soothe her. She turned on the CD player. Lately, she tended to listen to sad songs, because she was sad. And right now, she didn't know how she could be happy again.

****

Matt checked on the other jobs and found everything to his satisfaction. His supervisors knew their trade, and they knew how to get others to do the work. Both had been with him almost from the beginning. Now he was on his way to the bookstore to see Gloria. Should he call her? Maybe she wouldn't appreciate his just showing up unannounced, especially since they hadn't had too good a connection lately.

Because it was near rush-hour time, four in the afternoon, he got caught in a traffic jam on the freeway. He inserted a country-and-western CD and remembered he hadn't taught Gloria how to dance the two-step yet. He smiled; he must do so. It would be a good excuse to hold her close, too.

He pulled up to the bookstore at ten minutes to five, hoping Gloria was still there. He jumped out of his truck and jogged up to the bookstore entrance.

"Hi. May I help you?" Judy Ann asked. "Oh, you're him. Gloria's fiancée. It's nice to see you again."

He didn't remember the girl, but he was gratified to know she still believed he was Gloria's fiancée. "Is Gloria here?"

"Yes, in her office. You can go back there."

He walked to the back and remembered kissing Gloria in front of a crowd here. He smiled at the thought. Before he reached her office, she emerged.

"You're here," she said. "I thought I heard your voice. I'm…" Tears welled in her eyes.

He rushed to take her in his arms and hold her close. Her arms wrapped around him. Her heart beat against his. The faint tangy scent of her hair assailed his nostrils.

"Come into my office," she said.

Once there, he closed the door and pulled her into his arms again and kissed her. The feel of her lips against his shattered his already small self-control. He pushed her against a wall and slid his body over hers.

She sighed. "I wish I had a bed in here."

"Not as much as I do." He caressed her body, neck, back, hips. He wanted to make love to her right now. But she was at work. Anyone could come in or at least knock, and she'd have to answer.

"I missed you," she said.

He kissed her again, enjoying the feel of her soft curvy body against his.

"Matt, we'd better stop. Or we won't be able to stop."

"I know. Let's go somewhere. Are you about to leave?"

"Not for another hour or so."

"Damn. But we do need to go out, be together."

"I know. I haven't liked these last few days one bit."

"Neither have I," he said. "I don't like to argue with you."

"Me either. Brings back too many bad memories."

He stiffened. Eddie again. Was she always thinking about him? Comparing?

"I'm sorry," she said. "I didn't mean to bring up…anything."

He let her go. What could he say to her? He didn't

want to argue again. "Is this how our life together will be?" he asked before he could stop himself. "You're always going to be comparing me with your ex? Even if I'm the one who comes out looking better, I don't think I like it."

"I'm not comparing you. I don't think about Eddie when I'm with you."

Why couldn't they talk to each other without arguing? "Are you sure about that? How did he kiss? Am I better than he was? How about in the sack? How do I rate against him?"

"Now you're being ridiculous."

"Maybe I shouldn't have come here." He turned toward the door.

"Yes. Why don't you hurry back to your ex? The woman you're living with when you supposedly don't trust her."

"This was a mistake," he said. "Something's wrong between us, and I don't know how to fix it."

"Maybe you don't want to. Why did you move in with Angela? I'm sure there were other options. But you didn't see it. You saw the woman you love and the fact she'd been diagnosed with a life-threatening illness."

"She's not the woman I love." Matt fisted his hands on her desk.

She placed her fingers on her lips. "Please lower your voice. This is a place of business."

"Well, she's not. And I resent you saying it. I moved in because of my daughters."

"So you keep saying."

He pulled her into his arms and kissed her. Gloria struggled, but then she inched closer to him. He wanted things to go back to the way they were when they'd first met. He released her, and she heaved a deep breath as her eyes filled with tears. Was she remembering Eddie? He grabbed her again and kissed her. "Take that back to your ex. See how I compare."

"I hate you right now," she said. Tears trickled from her eyes.

"That makes two of us." He left without looking back.

He never should have gone to the bookstore. Another of his big mistakes, which he seemed to be making nonstop nowadays.

Chapter Twelve

After work, Gloria sat in front of the TV. A silly sit-com played on the screen. Maybe she should set it on the weather channel or a news station. This was irritating her. But then, it was a welcome change from the nonstop tears she'd indulged in since yesterday, after Matt left her office. Today, she was grateful Dex and Gordy weren't home. She'd never be able to pretend in front of them. Things were not good between her and Matt, and she feared everything was over. She looked at her finger. She still wore his ring, but did she still have his heart, his love?

The phone rang, and she saw on the TV caller ID it was Lynda. She stood to answer it.

"Dad's here, and he wants you and Matt to come over," her sister said. "He says it's time he met him." Lynda laughed. "Maybe this is a good time for Matt to ask for your hand."

"Lynda, I can't," Gloria said.

"Why not? Do you have to go back to work? You know working in retail is not a good idea. You'll never have free weekends."

"No. I mean, yes, you're right about the weekends, but this is not a good time."

"What do you mean?"

"Matt and I had an argument yesterday." *And we've been arguing every time we talk.*

"Well, take some time to make up and get over here," Lynda said, and from the tone of her voice, Gloria knew she was grinning.

"I'll see. Maybe Matt is working and can't get away."

"Get here. You know how Dad is." Her sister hung up.

She knew. Her dad wouldn't rest until he found out what was going on. Maybe she should break off the engagement. Her heart ached at the thought. She loved Matt. Why couldn't they resolve this issue? Maybe he wanted to break it off. She punched his number on the phone before she could think too much about it. She was about to hang up when she heard his voice. She couldn't say a word.

"Gloria? Is this you?"

"Yes." She picked up the remote, switched on the guide, and arrowed up and down on the channels.

"What is it?"

"My sister, Lynda, called me." She shouldn't have called him. They were angry. She'd told him she hated him.

"And?" he asked, now a bit irritated.

"I…well…my dad is at Lynda's. Last year he went on a senior citizens' cruise. I think I told you, didn't I?" She stopped and fiddled with the remote again. Matt didn't care to know so much about her dad. Maybe he didn't care about her anymore either. "And…and afterward, he traveled to West Texas to catch up with his cousins…and other relatives. Anyway…" She heard him sigh. "Anyway, he's finally back in San Antonio, and he wants to meet you."

"Do you want me to meet him?"

"I did." The TV had frozen. She couldn't move any button now. "I mean, I do." *God, now I sound as if I'm saying the marriage vows.* "I'll just say you're busy with work. It's okay."

"Gloria, what is going on?"

"My dad wants to meet you. We're supposedly getting married."

"Yeah," he said.

She heard music in the background.

"What time?"

"I guess now. He just arrived at my sister's."

"I'll meet you over there. Where does Lynda live?"

Gloria told him and hung up. Why were they doing this? They weren't even going to go together. But then, if they didn't go, it would require an explanation. Was she ready? Was he? He'd never sounded so distant. Her throat ached with the need to sob. She had to get ready to see her dad—and Matt.

Before she backed out of the driveway, she texted Dex and Gordy that their grandpa was at Lynda's, to go and say hello. She inserted a CD, rock music, to avoid thinking about what was going to happen in the next couple of hours.

Matt waited for her at the curb. She climbed out of the truck and joined him, her heart hammering against her chest. She was so glad to see him. He wore dark slacks and slate-gray dress shirt and tie. He was such a handsome man. What woman wouldn't want him?

"You…didn't have to dress up," she said. "It's just my dad."

"I've got daughters. I know I'd want any man who supposedly wanted to marry one of them to show me some respect by dressing appropriately."

They'd started arguing again. What was wrong with them? "Thank you." She turned to walk up the sidewalk to Lynda's front door. He didn't touch her, and that hurt more than the distant look in his eyes.

"Let's tell them." She rang the doorbell.

"Tell them what?"

"We're not supposedly getting married."

Lynda opened the door and grinned from ear to ear before he could respond. "Oh, how cute. The lovebirds are here."

"Stop it, Lynda," Gloria said. "We're not teenagers."

"Thank God," Lynda said. "I've got plenty of those running around here. Are Dex and Gordy coming? Hi, Matt."

"I think so," Gloria said. "I texted them. I'm not sure where they are. I think Gordy might be working."

"Maybe they're with their dad," Matt said.

"Oh, really, Matt," Lynda said. "That man disappears like quicksand every few months. Isn't he in Seguin, Gloria?"

"I don't know, Lynda." She didn't look at Matt. "I don't keep track of him."

"Well, you should have," Lynda said. "Especially when the boys were little so he could pay you child support."

"Lynda, will you please put a sock in it?" she said. And again she sounded as if she was defending Eddie, just adding more fuel to the angry fire already burning in Matt's heart. "Where's Dad?"

"He's with John in the garage. Drinking a beer. They think I don't know what they're doing. I'll go get him." Before she went to the garage, Lynda shouted upstairs, "Kids, get down here. Your aunt is here."

"Meet the parents—and kids," Matt muttered.

Gloria didn't respond. "Do you want something to drink?" she asked instead.

"Sure."

She walked to the kitchen, grabbed a can of beer from the fridge. Standing by the sink, she downed two gulps. Tears threatened again, but she blinked them away. When Lynda called to her, she poured the last of the beer down the drain and returned to the living room.

She handed Matt a beer and hugged her dad. "Hi, Dad. I'm so glad to see you." She wanted to cry in his arms like a little girl and tell him all her troubles. But he'd only worry. So she let him go and turned to Matt. "Dad, Dexter Mora, I want you to meet Matt Cerda."

Her dad examined Matt from head to toe. "I thought you were a gardener. What are you doing wearing good pants? Day off today? You know my daughter's ex frequently took days off."

"Dad…" Now her dad was bringing Eddie up.

"No, sir, not a day off." Matt held out his hand to her dad. "Just wanted to look presentable. It's an honor to meet you."

"Very good, son." Her dad took Matt's hand. "I like a man who knows his etiquette. What else do you have to tell me?"

What did her dad mean? *Oh for heaven's sake*. He wanted Matt to ask his permission to marry her. *What timing!*

"Dad, don't make Matt do it here," she said. "He can do so later."

"What's wrong with right now?" Her dad placed his hand on Matt's shoulder.

Matt glanced at her, a question in his eyes.

"He wants you to ask for my hand," she whispered.

"What?" Matt asked, almost as loudly as her dad.

"You don't have to. Not right now, especially since…"

The front door opened, and Dex and Gordy trooped in. She was never gladder for the interruption. They eyed Matt but didn't say anything, only nodded to him, then went to her dad and hugged him. Lynda's kids stomped down the stairs, and a madhouse ensued for a few minutes as everyone talked at once.

"Come join me, Matt. They'll do better without us here." John pulled Matt away toward the garage.

"You'd better clean up in there and not just be drinking," Lynda told him.

"Stop nagging." John gave her a kiss before he left. "I've got Matt and your dad to help me now."

Once Matt was out of the room, Gloria allowed herself to relax. But then sadness engulfed her. This should be a happy time—introducing her fiancé to her dad, being among the family. But neither she nor Matt was happy. She feared they were on the brink of calling everything off, and it hurt so much, especially because she'd thought she'd finally found someone to share her life with. Now it seemed it was too late.

After dinner, Gloria decided to leave. Her sons stayed to play video games. Outside, she stood with Matt. "Thank you for coming."

"This must be homecoming weekend," he said. "My dad texted to invite us over for Sunday dinner tomorrow."

"You can just say no."

"I can't. Or do you want to have to explain?"

"At some point, we'll have to talk about this. About what's going on."

"Well, be sure and let me know what that is," he said, "because I sure as hell don't." He walked away from her without touching her, kissing her, or even saying good-bye.

She ran to her truck and let the tears come as she watched Matt drive away.

****

Matt stood on Gloria's porch, but this time he didn't admire her appearance, kiss her, or even smile. He wanted to. She did look nice, as always, but he couldn't bring himself to say anything. "Are you ready? Let's get this over with."

"Why don't I just follow you in my truck?" she suggested. "Isn't this like an hour's drive away? We can pretend we're out on a Sunday drive, by ourselves."

"Don't be difficult."

"Who are you comparing me to?" she snapped, and locked the front door.

He didn't help her into his truck. "I'll put music on so we won't have to talk," he said when she climbed in.

"Fine."

In spite of the silence, the trip didn't take long, or so it seemed. He drove up an unpaved road and through a wooden gate to a long one-story house. Chicken coops and other cages were off to the side of the house. The horse, old Emiliano, galloped in a corral.

"The girls are here," he said.

"Is Angela here, too?"

An older man walked out of the house, leaning on a cane, before he could respond. "Come in, come in," he said.

His dad. Did he look thinner? He should visit more often.

Gloria climbed out of the truck without Matt's assistance.

"Didn't I teach you to be a gentleman, *hijo*?" His dad smiled.

She returned the smile and blinked, something she did when she didn't want to cry. He was acting like a heel, but lately he couldn't help himself.

Matt put his arm around her waist, and she trembled. "Dad, Alfredo Cerda, this is Gloria Amaya."

"It's nice to meet you, sir." She held out her hand.

"You're going to be my family," his dad said. "Come here and give me a hug." He held Gloria close. Matt hadn't done so in a long time.

"Thank you." She averted her face from Matt.

"Come inside. Some of the kids are here," his dad said. "Not all of them. Gloria can meet part of the family today."

They walked into a huge living room decorated in russet browns and forest greens. Two giant chandeliers hung from the ceiling, sending soft light into the area.

Matt spotted his little brothers, Freddy and Frankie. "Hey, you crazy F and F." He launched himself at his siblings, who quickly two-teamed him, and they fell on the floor in a heap.

Gloria laughed, the sound making his heavy heart lighten a little.

"Oh dear," a woman said. "I'm sorry, Gloria. I'm Matt's older sister, Minerva. Will you behave yourselves, guys? We have company." She slapped Matt on the butt.

"Don't worry about it. I raised two sons. If they

didn't engage in a wrestling match every day, I'd take their temperatures, make sure they didn't have a fever." Gloria's laughter resounded in the room again.

Matt stood and hugged his sister. Then he grabbed her around her neck.

"Let go of me, you big lug. Show some manners."

"Do you want something to drink?" his dad asked. "Carmelita, bring some sodas. Do you want a soda, Gloria? Or would you prefer some wine?"

"I'll take some wine," she said.

"I know what you want, Matt," his dad said. "Bring us a couple of beers, Carmelita."

Matt hugged the woman who had been his dad's housekeeper and friend ever since his mom died. Now she was more his dad's girlfriend. He introduced her to Gloria.

"Daddy," Amber yelled as she erupted into the room. "I'm so glad you're here. I love being at Grandpa's. We're going to go ride Emiliano."

Patsy and Julia walked up, and he was happy that for once Julia seemed relaxed. He smiled. "Good idea." He turned to Gloria. "Have you ever ridden a horse?"

She glanced up in surprise. And no wonder. He hadn't talked to her during the drive over. "No. Well, actually, I think I did when I was little. My aunt took us to a ranch. It's a hazy memory."

"You go ahead and go ride," his dad said. "Gloria can stay here with Minerva and me and talk."

Was that fear on Gloria's face, as if what could his dad want to talk to her about? But he was trapped. He had to go with his daughters and his brothers, who attacked him again as they walked to the door.

He stood by the corral and watched his daughters

take turns riding Emiliano. They'd all ridden him before, but since they didn't visit too often, the activity always seemed a new thing. He wished things were better between him and Gloria. Maybe they could have ridden Emiliano together into the sunset, like in the movies.

Using his cane and leaning on Minerva, his dad walked up. Gloria was with them.

He ran over to help. "Dad, are you sure you should be outside? You could fall."

"And I could drop dead in the next few seconds. I can't live my life with *what ifs*." He inched up to the corral and grabbed a rail. "Gloria and I had a nice chat. Nice lady. Unlike some I could mention."

Matt glanced at Gloria, but she wasn't looking at him. She was looking at his Patsy, the one riding Emiliano now.

"Let me take a picture," Gloria said.

He smiled. She liked to take pictures. Somehow, it gladdened his heart that she wanted to take photos of his family.

"Let's go inside," his dad said. "It's time to eat."

Carmelita was a good cook, and Matt enjoyed his meal. He glanced at Gloria, who was talking to Patsy. He heard snippets of the conversation, something about being overweight.

"I can't believe you ever had to lose weight," Patsy said.

Gloria met Matt's eyes but looked away quickly. "I think every woman has that problem at one time or another. The thing is don't let it overwhelm you."

"I like you, Gloria," Patsy said.

"So do I," Amber exclaimed.

Only Julia kept quiet, but at least she didn't say anything derogatory, for which he was grateful.

I like you, Gloria. Matt's eyes kept returning to her as she continued to talk to his daughters. What was going on with the two of them? At the beginning, they seemed to agree about everything, talk about anything, but now they couldn't even look at each other.

After the meal, he decided they shouldn't stay much longer. His daughters would spend the night since Monday was some kind of in-service day and there was no school. He'd pick them up in the afternoon.

"Good to meet you, Gloria," his dad said. "I think you're just the right lady for my son. Come back soon." His dad kissed her.

"Thank you, Mr. Cerda."

Matt hugged his sister and, of course, had to tussle with his little brothers once more before he left.

Back in the truck, he turned on the ignition and the music. It blared out, and Gloria started. "Sorry," he said.

The sun was setting. He couldn't help remembering the sunset at the lake, the last time he and Gloria went anywhere without arguing. Today they hadn't really argued, but they hadn't really talked.

"Do you want something to drink?" he asked. "I can stop at a convenience store."

"No, thank you. It's late. It's time I was home. I have to work tomorrow."

"Yeah." He gave a last wave to his family.

Maybe next time we come, you can ride the horse. He wanted to say it, but he didn't. It didn't seem appropriate somehow. Were they ever coming back together? The end of the day seemed to signal the end of their relationship. They didn't speak until he drove up Gloria's driveway.

"Well, goodnight," she said and opened the truck door. "This was...kind of a funky weekend."

"Yeah. Thanks for going." He wanted to ask what she and his dad had talked about, but then, maybe it wasn't any of his business.

"Your dad said he liked me," she said as if she'd heard his unspoken question. "He said he'd always had doubts about Angela from the moment he met her. But I guess you don't want to hear about comparisons. I mean, I don't want to be compared either. I'm just me. I guess we all want to be ourselves." She sighed.

He wanted to say he'd call her, but he wasn't sure she'd want to hear it.

"I'd better go inside," she said.

He stared at her but didn't say anything.

"Bye." She walked toward her front door, her head down.

Matt jumped out of his truck. Gloria was the woman he'd fallen in love with. He'd proposed to her and wanted to spend the rest of his life with her. He reached her and pulled her into his arms. She let out a cry, but her arms encircled him. For his part, the feel of her body against his felt right, as it had from the moment he'd kissed her in her backyard among her dead roses. Her body trembled with her sobs.

"I'm sorry, Gloria," he said. "I'm going to fix this. I don't want us to be like this."

"I...don't...either..." she mumbled against his chest. "It hurts so much."

"I love you."

She sobbed some more. "I...never...thought I'd

hear…you…say those words again. I love you."

He kissed her as they stood on the porch. The sky was clear, but the wan moon was no match for the blackness of the night. "I made a mistake with Angela. I'll fix it."

"Okay. I'll stop talking about Eddie."

Matt laughed and kissed her again. As he drove away, Gloria waved to him, and he felt better than he had in days.

Now to go talk to Angela.

****

Gloria's mood was lighter on Monday since she and Matt had made up. He'd kissed her last night. They'd apologized to each other. He loved her. She loved him. The world was once more in balance. He'd told her he was going to talk to Angela about moving out. She believed him. And he admitted he'd made a mistake by moving in. Sickness affected him in a bad way. And his first priority was always his daughters.

Her head understood all this, but not her heart. She didn't want to share him, especially with Angela, a woman who'd known him longer than she had and had his children. Which was probably how Matt felt about Eddie. She'd have to work on not comparing the two men. Matt was a stark contrast to Eddie, but what man wanted to keep hearing about the ex?

Her day at Books and All had been a good one. Celeste wanted to sell the bookstore, but now it didn't seem the end of her world. She could always find another job. She'd always worked to provide for herself and her sons. Her eyes were dry, no tears today.

Now she was on her way to Lynda's. They had wedding plans to make.

Her sister appeared in the doorway. "The kids are upstairs. Well, two of them are—J.L. and Yolanda. Lisa and Abel are out somewhere, though I told them to be back early. Tomorrow's a school day. Today wasn't, so the house is in an even bigger shambles. Wade your way through and come to the kitchen."

Gloria hung her purse over a chair and sat at her sister's dining room table, where she'd set out some spiral notebooks and bridal magazines.

"You look happy," Lynda commented. "On Saturday, I sensed something…"

Gloria smiled. "I thought you might have. I told you Matt and I argued, remember? We were still angry when we came."

"But he seemed so nice to Dad and everything."

"It's because he has daughters." She told her sister what Matt had said about respect.

"He's a good guy. Do you want something to drink?"

"I'll take water. I've been drinking too much caffeine." After her sister poured the drinks and joined her at the table, she said, "Matt and I are happy again."

"What did you argue about for heaven's sake?"

"Our exes."

"Exes? You mean you risked losing the best man you've ever met in your life over that Dumb Eddie?"

She laughed at her sister's familiar phrase for her ex. "He thought I was comparing him to Eddie. He didn't like it. You know how I am. I've always defended Eddie, and I did with Matt. I can't believe I did it. But he made me angry. Especially because…"

"Because?"

"Did I tell you Angela was diagnosed with breast

cancer?"

"I think so." Linda sipped her tea.

"He moved into Angela's house to take care of his daughters, and he takes Angela to her doctor's appointments."

"What?" Lynda wrinkled her brow. "That's wrong."

"At first, I thought, well, his daughters are his first priority. I can't interfere. But the more I thought about it, the more I didn't like it."

"Who would? I know I wouldn't like John seeing one of his exes on a regular basis even if they were never married."

"That's what Beatrice told me, too. Why didn't I immediately see it?"

"Probably because you were thinking like a mom instead of a girlfriend," Lynda said. "You've been a single mom for a long time, so kids are your first priority. But Matt is your fiancé. You can't let another woman see him on a daily basis. Especially not his ex-wife."

"That's what brought all these trust issues to the forefront. You know how Eddie cheated on me. The more I thought about Matt in Angela's house, the more I distrusted the situation, and then I began to distrust Matt."

"It was bound to happen. Is he moving out?"

"He's working on it."

"Well, he'd better do it quickly, or I'll tell him a thing or two."

Gloria laughed. "You would, too, wouldn't you?"

"And you have to set a date. We have to mail out the save-a-date cards," Lynda said. "Have you decided on your colors?"

"Well, we'd said red, but now I'm not sure."

She and her sister continued to talk about colors, dance bands or DJ's. Gloria took notes. Where could they hold the wedding? She was glad she'd told Lynda about her worries regarding Angela and Matt. And he would move out, she knew it.

She and Matt had to think about themselves. Yes, their kids were important, but their exes were in the past. It was time for them to move forward and begin a new life. However, no telling what wrench Angela could throw into the plans.

****

"I'm losing my hair," Angela screamed. She held out the wad of hair in her hand.

"Oh for God's sake, Angela. Buy a damn wig." Matt immediately felt like a heel. He knew his ex was going through chemo, but he also knew how vain she was. "I'm sorry."

True to form, she burst out crying. "You don't care about me. You never have. And now you're going to leave me here sick, scarred forever, and"—she gulped—"bald." Her crying turned to sobbing.

Julia glared at him. "I bet you never make *her* cry, do you?" She put an arm around Angela.

He'd made Gloria cry all weekend. His stomach churned.

"He's going to marry her, baby," Angela whimpered. "And leave us to suffer alone."

Julia held on to Angela and scowled at Matt. "I hate you."

In the last few days, two people he loved had said the phrase to him. Something was wrong here.

"Daddy, are you really going to leave us?" Amber asked. "Are you going to stop being my daddy and be daddy to Dex and Gordy?"

His heart clenched when his youngest daughter's eyes filled with tears. "Baby, I'll always be your daddy, no matter what, no matter who else comes into my life. Nothing will ever change that."

"But it has. You don't spend as much time with us anymore. Mommy says it's because you're always with Gloria."

"I like Gloria." Patsy spoke up.

Angela stopped crying and with a sniffle told Patsy, "You don't love me, do you? You never have. Well, go with Gloria. You might get your wish sooner than you think. I might not be around much longer."

"Oh, Mommy." Patsy ran from the room.

"Angela, I know you don't feel well, but please don't take it out on the girls." Matt frowned at his ex.

"It's your entire fault. Your damn fault. If you had just understood about Jorge and taken me back, none of this would have happened."

"So you're blaming me for the cancer? Dammit, Angela."

She resumed her bawling. He wished he felt more sympathy, but he didn't. At times he even felt she was exaggerating her symptoms, the tiredness, the lack of appetite, the nausea. He hated to feel this way, but he couldn't help it. She was keeping him from the woman he loved. People's innate goodness and wisdom emerged after a life-threatening diagnosis, or so he'd heard—not Angela's. In fact, her most undesirable traits had increased tenfold. Now he and Gloria were always arguing. He was relieved they'd been able to resolve the issue. However, it wouldn't be totally fixed until he moved out of Angela's house.

He turned to her. He must remember she was the mother of his girls. She deserved his help and support. "Have you taken your pills?"

"Yes," she said. "You don't want to be here anymore, do you?"

"No, I don't. Have you given any thought to other arrangements for your appointments? I can still drive Julia to school. I'll get up earlier and get over here."

"Are you going back to your house, Daddy?" Amber asked.

"Yes, baby, I have to. Moving in here was not a good idea. Your mom and I are no longer together. And Gloria and I are getting married."

"Go away. You don't love us," Julia said, her eyes shiny with unshed tears"

Matt pulled his daughter to her feet and hugged her close. "Julia, don't ever say that. You know it's not true."

"I'm so scared, Dad." She hung on tightly to him.

"I'm here for you, sweetheart, always." He kissed the top of her head. "For all you girls."

"But not Mom," Julia said.

He looked at Angela over Julia's head and motioned her with his eyes to say something to ease their daughter's fears.

Angela sighed. "Your dad's right. He shouldn't be here with us. I'll find someone to take me to the appointments. As much as I don't want some stranger around me."

Matt gave Julia one last squeeze and helped Angela to bed. This woman was mother to his daughters. In spite of her betrayal, he would always care about her. However, he didn't want to lose Gloria, and if he didn't make changes, he feared he would. The way they were this weekend scared him. They'd been like strangers among their families. He never wanted to be in that situation again. But they'd made up. He was ready to move out of Angela's house and make things up to Gloria, no matter what his ex took it into her head to do.

Chapter Thirteen

Gloria pulled the pan of roast with potatoes and carrots out of the oven. The appetizing smell of meat and veggies filled the air. She'd invited Dex and Gordy for supper tonight. She didn't care if it was a weeknight—Tuesday, of all nights. She didn't see her sons often enough to suit her. Besides, they were usually busy on weekends with friends and work. That's when they would work extra hours.

She heard sounds at the door. They were home. She ran to open the door, but by the time she got there, Dex had unlocked it.

She hugged them both. "It's so good to see you."

"We saw each other on the weekend, Mom," Dex said.

"I know, but it was at Lynda's, not here. Come and eat. I just took the meal out of the oven."

She served the plates, Gordy got the drinks, and they sat at the dining table. For a few minutes, the only sounds were of silverware against plates as they ate.

"What was up with Matt at Aunt Lynda's?" Gordy asked.

"Your grandpa wanted to meet him." She and Matt weren't on good terms that evening, or the next day when she'd gone to meet his dad. She smiled when she remembered how the day ended.

"So it's official?" Dex asked. "Meet the parents

and all that?"

Gloria pushed around a piece of roast. "Yes. It's going to happen, boys. I love Matt."

Both boys groaned. Dex muttered, so she knew he'd cursed.

"Well, I do, and I want to marry him." She lifted her hand and showed them the ring. "He gave me this. I want to spend the rest of my life with him."

"So Dad's out?" Dex asked.

"Dex, your dad has been 'out' for a long time now, and you know it. I would never return to him. I don't want to. Our married life was not good. I wasn't happy, and neither was he—or we would have tried to make it work. Maybe we didn't love each other enough. We were so young…"

"I guess I kept hoping," he said. "But I know how it is. I know how Dad is."

"What about you, Gordy?" she asked.

"It's weird," her son said. "But I guess I could get used to it. I don't remember you and Dad together."

"We divorced soon after you were born. I am sorry, Gordy. You never had your dad living with you."

"I'm okay with it," he said.

"I guess I have to accept it, too," Dex said. "I'm sure glad we've got our own place, though. It'd be more than odd to all live together."

"Yeah, it would never work," Gordy said.

The idea of her sons living apart was still very new, and unreal, but she could accept it. They were both older. Gordy was about to graduate from high school, Dex from college. They were old enough to spread their wings and fly. Still, she would worry.

"I know I have to let go of the apron strings," she

said. "You have to live your lives. I have to live mine. Okay?"

"Okay, Mom," Dex said. "I just don't want you to be hurt again, either. And Matt has done a couple of dubious things."

Gloria realized she'd never told her sons Matt had moved in with Angela. Maybe it'd been for the best. She'd had problems understanding it. The boys would never comprehend it.

"This is a delicious meal," Gordy said.

"Yeah, Mom," Dex agreed. "Gordo and I just eat eggs and sandwiches."

"You are always welcome here whenever you want."

"Even when Matt is with you?" Dex asked.

"Even then." She grinned. "But then the girls will be there, too."

"Aw, yeah," Gordy said. "On second thought, you can come to the apartment and cook for us there."

She laughed. After they finished the meal, the boys helped her clean up, and then she remembered Gordy's school project.

"Did you finish your poetry notebook?" she asked.

"Almost," Gordy said.

"Did you bring it with you? I can help you if you want."

He picked up his backpack from the floor. "Okay."

She sat at the table with her son, and they went over the remaining poems he needed to write. She also read some of the ones he'd already written. "These are pretty good."

"Really?" Gordy asked. "I thought most of them were lame, but if that's what I have to do…"

"Let me see, Gordo." Dex grabbed a sheet.

"No, give it back," Gordy said. "Come on, Dexie. Give me back my poem."

Gordy's nickname for Dex always riled him up, so they began punching each other. Gloria laughed in spite of herself. Her home welcomed the familiar grunts and guffaws of her sons, and so did she. After she married Matt, this had to continue somehow, at least until her sons were too old to wrestle around. Judging by Matt and his brothers, that time would be long in coming.

She hoped Matt would be able to set something up for Angela and move out of her house. The time was overdue, and they needed to finalize wedding plans. They hadn't even set a date. They needed to do it—and soon. When she thought about Matt, and just about him, she couldn't wait to be in his arms and in his life. It was only when other things surfaced that she began to have doubts. And her biggest doubt was Angela. Why did she feature so highly in Matt's life?

****

"You were right," Matt said. "I just got a call from the 'nut.' He wants to rehire me."

Wayne laughed. "Told you. So what now?"

"I'm on my way to meet him at his offices. You know I've enjoyed working on my other jobs. Maybe this big contract stuff isn't for me."

"I don't take many big ones myself," Wayne said. "Bigger issues, bigger problems. Not to mention bigger egos."

"The money's good." Matt drove into the complex. He stared at the rock garden—or where it should be. It was completely gone. What had happened?

"Weigh the pros and cons, man. I've made a good

186

living with the so-called smaller jobs. So can you."

Matt sighed. "I'll think about it. But it does sound a lot better than dealing with this idiot or others like him, right?"

"Right. Let me know what happens."

"Sure thing. Here he comes. Later."

"Hey, Matt." Starr climbed out of his truck with a huff. "Don't think I'm crazy, son. But the damned company I hired after I terminated the contract with you made such a huge mess I almost had to do physical violence to them. Did you see the rock garden? You're going to have to start over."

"What happened?"

"Who the hell knows?" Starr took off his Stetson and hit his thigh. "They were morons, all of them. I reported them to the Better Business Bureau and every other organization I could think of. I also told friends and other business owners never to use them."

Matt stared at the man. Did he think he was God? *Man!* Did he really want to work with this idiot? Wayne had said to weigh the good and bad of this job. Right now, there seemed to be more bad than good. Having to deal with Starr might outweigh everything else.

"So when can you start?" Starr asked, placing the hat back on his head.

Okay, he'd give it another try. But only one more. If he was fired a second time, he wasn't coming back. "I can call my crew back in today. They're ready to work. I've got some materials we can start with, but I'll have to order more."

The man nodded and patted Matt on the back. "Money's no object."

"I see the bushes are okay," Matt commented,

relieved. He'd have hated to think what happened to perfectly good shrubs.

"Good thing they only concentrated on the rock garden and left the plants alone."

Matt nodded. "Will you draw up another contract?"

"I'll do it as soon as I get to the office," Starr said. "I'll even add a little more money, just because of the inconvenience. No hard feelings?"

Matt took his outstretched hand. "No, sir. It's business."

"I like your attitude. Meet me in the office in about two hours. I'll have the paperwork ready. Welcome back, son."

Starr climbed into his truck, drove the short distance to the building, and parked right in front. Matt shook his head. More money, the man said. Well, he was getting married, so extra money would come in handy. And now he'd have to pay someone to drive Angela around. Who knew how much it would cost? But he was willing to pay it. He needed to get his life back in order, in balance. He needed Gloria to be happy, and that would make him happy. He and Angela were history, and though he wanted her to get well, he didn't have to live with her to support her.

His phone buzzed as he was about to call his crew.

"What's wrong, Angela?" he asked.

"Fine way to answer the phone. I bet you are all gushy and mushy when Gloria calls you."

Dammit! He could have told Angela the past few days had been anything but good with him and Gloria, but it was none of her business. "I'm busy. What's up?"

"I don't like any of these people who are coming over here."

"What people?" *What was the woman doing?*

"Well, I called one of those services who have people run errands for you and such. They can also drive you to places."

"So what? They sent you people to interview?" How much was this going to cost? But he'd told her he'd pay it. Leave it to Angela to choose the most expensive way.

"Yes," she said. "I don't like any of them."

"Don't be so quick to make a decision." He feared this could take forever with her in charge. He'd have to find a way himself. "Maybe you can do this on a trial basis."

"I don't like them. I'm going to cancel the rest of the interviews." She hung up.

Matt raised his hand to throw his cell through the windshield, but he managed to control his temper. *Dammit!* The woman was impossible. And, as usual, typical behavior, hanging up on him. Who would drive Angela to her appointments? He punched in the number for Angela's doctor. When the receptionist answered, he asked her if she knew of transportation services to and from doctors' offices. The girl gave him a couple of phone numbers.

Should he call them, or should he give them to Angela? He'd call the numbers himself. He'd tell Angela this was how it was to be. He was paying for it, after all.

****

Gloria's phone rang.

"I found someone to drive Angela to her appointments," Matt said.

"I'm glad. How often does she go?"

189

"Once a week now. But last night I had to take her to the ER. Apparently, the dosage of chemo was too strong and she became toxic. They've been hydrating her all night. I'm not sure how long she'll be at the hospital."

"Oh." She really didn't wish bad things to happen to Angela. She wanted her to get well. "What does this mean for you?"

"I can't leave the girls. It'll have to wait until after Angela gets back home and on a routine again. You can understand this, can't you?"

She stared at the computer screen, then at the picture on the wall—a rock on a blue background. Tears blinded her so she couldn't see the caption. "Of course, I understand. What kind of a person would I be if I didn't understand?"

He sighed. "Of course."

"You do what you have to do. Our kids come first. I've always said so, and I believe it."

"You're angry."

"Kind of, but not with you, at the situation." Before she thought too much about it, she added, "And you wouldn't be in this situation if you'd never moved in with your ex."

"Please, not again. We've been over this."

"No, we just let it go. We've never talked about it. I think you have a connection with Angela that will never go away. Besides your daughters. She cheated on you, so you hadn't given up on the marriage. She had. So now maybe you see this as a way to get back together."

"What the hell are you talking about? I don't want Angela back. How many times do I have to repeat it?"

"I don't want words from you, Matt. I want actions. And I think you've been doing what you really want to do. Otherwise, you'd have made changes a long time ago."

"What about you and Eddie?" he shouted.

"Well, you know, Eddie and I have the kind of relationship where he comes and goes, and while he's gone, I can have a little fun with someone else." It was way beyond the wrong thing to say. She was deliberately goading him.

"And when he returns, you can take up where you left off?" Matt asked, and Gloria could hear the anger in his voice.

"Of course. Just like every single time Angela crooks her little finger, you go running to her. Well, be happy with her."

"Are you going to hang up now?" he demanded.

"No, isn't that what Angela does? I'm not your ex. You hang up first."

"Gloria…"

Tears filled her eyes, and she couldn't talk anymore. She might have to hang up so he wouldn't hear her sobs.

"Are you still there?" he asked.

"Yes," she managed to say.

"I'm sorry. I told you I would take care of this situation. Only things keep coming up… Hell! I'm not putting this off on purpose."

"I already had a relationship where all we did was argue and there was no trust. I don't want another one."

"Shit," Matt said.

She shouldn't have brought up Eddie again, but she couldn't help it. Maybe her ex was too ingrained in her system. After all, they had two sons. Without him, she wouldn't have them, and they were her world. Or they'd been until she met Matt.

"I'll call later," he said.

"Bye." That was all she could say through the ache in her throat from withholding the tears.

She heard the click of his phone and turned off hers. Somewhere in her head, a bell tolled the ending of what could have been a good relationship. Maybe if they had met when they were younger and didn't have such huge responsibilities, the road would have been easier. They also had bad issues, too deep rooted to let go, apparently.

Matt should never have proposed. She should never have accepted. Why hadn't she remembered her plan to just find a male companion to go dancing with? She should have never gone beyond that. Emotions had gotten the best of her, as they had when she'd met Eddie. Back then, she'd at least had an excuse. She was in her early twenties, hadn't lived long enough to know what was the best thing to do for her future.

She finally dried her eyes. Celeste was out again, for which she was glad because she didn't want to make explanations. She went to the restroom and washed her face. In the storeroom, she pulled out the cartons of books that had arrived.

With Judy Ann's help, she spent the remaining afternoon shelving the books. Concentrating hard on what she was doing kept her mind away from her troubles. Judy Ann talked about her college and new boyfriend, and Gloria refused to think about Matt anymore. Today, at least.

****

"You sure you want to do this?" Matt asked.

Julia was in the passenger seat of his truck. She'd asked him last night if it would be okay to go with him on one or two of his jobs. She was working on a school project that involved researching careers. He was agreeable, although Angela had thrown a fit. Apparently, she was over the scary trip to the ER and ready to do battle again.

"She's a girl," she'd yelled. "What's the matter with you, Julia? I would never dirty my hands with plants and dirt. You'll break your fingernails."

"I'm sure, Dad." She smiled. For once in a long time, she seemed happy.

"Okay." He turned the key in the ignition and drove to a long-time customer's house, an elderly lady who needed her tiny lawn mowed and her flowers watered. As he drove, he couldn't help remembering the last conversation with Gloria, another argument featuring their exes. When would it end? Maybe never. At least that's what Gloria seemed to think.

He pulled up to the customer's house, an older home covered with siding instead of brick. Julia climbed out of the truck, a spiral notebook in her hand. Matt knocked at the door.

"Oh, Matt, dear boy." The elderly woman holding a pastel-blue robe close to her body slowly opened the front door, then even more slowly unhinged the screen door. Her hair was completely white and thinning.

He remembered when the woman would greet him with a cigarette in her mouth. "Hello, Mrs. Moreno. I hope you don't mind. I brought my daughter. This is Julia. She wants to learn a little about my work."

"Oh, how wonderful," the woman said in her raspy

voice, probably a result of years of smoking. "I always liked yard work, especially growing flowers. Did you see them as you walked by?"

"Yes, ma'am," Julia said. "They're pretty."

"Not as pretty as you, child. You're a lucky man, Matt. You'll have to fight off the boys."

His heart clenched at the thought. He didn't want to think about it. He just thanked his lucky stars Julia hadn't fallen seriously for a boy up to now.

"Anyway, I like yard work, but I can't do it anymore," the woman said. "That's why I'm so glad I found Matt. I used to mow my own lawn, too. Do you do that, child?"

"No, ma'am. But I'd like to grow flowers."

This was news to Matt. When did she decide this?

"I'd better get started, Mrs. Moreno," he said.

"Okay, let me know when you're finished. I'll wrap up some cookies I baked for you."

It didn't take Matt long to mow the small yard, both front and back. Julia took a turn for a few minutes. Then she watered the flowers. Soon they were on their way to the next job site, with a batch of chocolate chip cookies wrapped in foil.

"Wow, Dad," Julia said. "You even get goodies along with your fee."

"Can't beat it, huh? Now I'll take you to the complete opposite of a little old lady's yard. A contract job."

"He's the one who has given you problems, right?"

"How do you know?"

"Sometimes, I overhear you talking in the den to people. I didn't mean to eavesdrop."

"That's fine," Matt said and smiled. "My work is

not top secret."

"But that's how I became interested in your work. You sounded so knowledgeable and so in command. All my life I've heard Mom say your job is something boys do after school, not a real job. When I heard you, it seemed as if you were a corporate executive or something."

He grinned. He couldn't help himself. For his eldest daughter to feel pride in something that meant so much to him was priceless. For a minute he didn't think he had the words to comment. "Thank you. But it is just a job. However, it is something I love to do. This job we're going to, though, is fast becoming something else. Listen and observe. Tell me what you think afterward, okay?"

"I don't know enough, Dad."

"I want to know what you think." He drove into the parking lot of Starr Offices and parked at his usual spot by the curb, not too far from the entrance. The rock garden was taking shape again. He led Julia toward it.

After he inspected the work, he spoke with the supervisor. "Make sure you follow the specs. Don't lose the paper. I don't want to have to redo this again."

"Yes, sir," the supervisor said.

"This is the second time we've had to do this," he explained to his daughter. The sound of a vehicle alerted him to Ben Starr's arrival. He'd hoped he didn't have to talk to the man again.

"Well, Matt." Starr strolled over, hat in hand. "Who's this? You've got yourself a beautiful helper."

He didn't like the leer in the man's eyes. "This is my daughter Julia. She's working on a school project, so I brought her to the job site."

Starr grabbed Julia's hand, and the man ogled her—or so it seemed to Matt. He wanted to tell her to go back to the truck.

"It's nice to meet you, sir," she said.

He touched Starr on the shoulder and led him to the rock garden. He waved to Julia to stay where she was. "We're making progress. We should be finished by the middle of next week."

"Sure, sure." Starr sneaked a glance back at Julia.

Matt wanted to smash his teeth. He finished with him as soon as he could and led him back to his truck, not letting him get close to Julia again. Once Starr drove off, he walked back to her.

"What an ugly man," she said. "He was looking at me funny."

He didn't know what to say. Starr wasn't just an ugly man. He was a dirty old man. "He just thought you were pretty, and he's right. But watch out for those 'funny' looks. So besides putting a big black mark by the customer's name, what do you think of this job?"

"I like the small yards better. It seems more personal. This is more 'corporate.' "

"Exactly. But I do make more money with these. I was going to market to get more of these types."

"Sometimes money is not everything, though. Right?"

"Right. So should I give up on the big contracts?"

"You have yards like Gloria's, don't you?" she asked. "Those are a little bigger, more money there, and she also wanted help with the roses."

His mind took him back to when he'd first met Gloria in her wilting rose garden. She'd worn her hair up, and she'd appeared so happy, blushing and flirting with him—and he'd been attracted to her from the first minute. He hadn't been sure why. He had several women customers. A lot of them had done everything to get his attention except parade around nude in their backyards while he was mowing. But all Gloria had to do was walk out through her patio door wearing jeans and a T-shirt. And now what? Was it over between them?

"Dad?" Julia's voice penetrated his mind from far away.

He shook his head, focused. "Sorry, sweetheart. What did you ask me?"

"You have midsize yards like Gloria's. Not only small ones like the first lady we visited. I guess what I'm saying is you don't have to get those big jobs if you really don't like them."

"Yeah, I don't. I think I'm going to try one more. If I don't like it, then it's the job. This one, I think, has more to do with the customer than what I'm actually doing. What do you think?"

"Okay. But I still like the smaller yards."

He laughed and strolled to his truck. Julia followed.

"Thanks for letting me come with you, Dad," she said. "I want to tell you something else."

He stopped from turning on the ignition. His heart fell to his stomach.

"It's not bad. Don't worry."

"My idea and your idea of bad might not be the same thing."

"I've been doing something in secret," his daughter said.

"Oh yeah? Not making me feel better, you know."

"At the yard at home. I planted some flowers, and they're growing. I didn't want to tell you until I saw progress. This morning I went out there, and there's these tiny little green plants coming up."

His heart lifted at the smiling face of his daughter, and he hugged her. "I'm so proud of you."

"Do you think they'll grow into flowers?" she asked when he let her go.

"I wouldn't be surprised." He grinned.

"Do you want to see them?"

"I can't wait," he said.

After several days of bad stuff, today he was happy, at least until he was back at Angela's and wouldn't be able to keep the argument he'd had with Gloria from his mind. He put his arm around Julia and squeezed her shoulders. "I'm so proud of you. What do you think about Mateo and Daughter Landscaping?"

She laughed. "Hadn't you better wait until you see if I can grow flowers?"

"Oh yeah. You have to pass the test."

This was something so unexpected in his daughter, especially Julia. Now, Patsy he could see wanting to be outside digging in the dirt and weeds. But not his superfeminine beautiful daughter who took hours to get ready when she was going out with friends. The thought made him grin all the more.

The thought of Gloria and their argument sobered him up. Somehow he was going to change this. He had to. He loved her. Nothing had happened between them to alter his feelings.

Chapter Fourteen

"Mom, my face hurts," Gordy said.

Gloria looked at her son, then continued arranging the yellow roses in a vase. The color brightened the room, and she'd recently read in a decorator's magazine yellow was "in." A few hints of yellow—a pillow, an end table, some flowers—in a room made all the difference.

Gordy didn't agree by the look on his face. "Those are ugly, Mom."

"What do you mean? They're beautiful." These weren't her roses. Hers were red. She'd bought these at the store. The bright, sunny color called to her, especially since she was unhappy over her last argument with Matt. It didn't seem as if they were going to be able to find their way back to each other. Today was Friday, but she'd asked Celeste for the day off. She couldn't concentrate on work. Why even go?

"What's the matter with your face, again?" she asked Gordy.

"It hurts." He moved his mouth from side to side and grimaced.

"Is it dry?" she asked, still fiddling with the roses. "Maybe you need to put cream on it. You know, just because you're a boy doesn't mean you shouldn't take care of your skin."

"Aw, Mom." He touched his jaw. "It's not really

my face that hurts, but my mouth, inside."

She walked away from the flowers and reached up to touch his face. "It does feel swollen. I haven't taken you to the dentist in a while. You might have a cavity or something. I'll call the dentist and make an appointment."

The dentist couldn't see Gordy until the following week, so Gloria decided to call the family doctor. She'd taken her sons to him since they were babies, and he would see them whenever she needed him.

It proved to be the case this time, too. He saw Gordy later that afternoon.

"Well, Gordy, I haven't seen you in a long time," Dr. Cardenas said. "You're about ready to graduate from high school, aren't you?"

"Yeah." Gordy smiled. He liked the doctor.

"What's up with you today?"

"My mouth hurts," Gordy said.

The doctor turned to Gloria.

"I know what you're thinking," she said. "I tried to get him into the dentist, but he can't see him until next week. Something's going on with him. His face is swollen. Maybe you can just check him."

Dr. Cardenas nodded. "Okay, let's see, Gordy." He examined Gordy's mouth and face. "I'm going to run a blood test just to make sure he doesn't have an infection."

The nurse went in to draw blood from Gordy's arm. And then they waited. He played with a stuffed dinosaur, and Gloria laughed.

"You're still a little boy at heart."

He smiled, a mischievous twinkle in his eyes. She loved his grin. Since he was a baby, he'd had the ability to look at her—and people—as if he thought their antics were foolish and hilarious.

She picked up a magazine and leafed through it, then turned to the table of contents. She didn't want to think about Matt and their argument.

"Mom, what's 'leukemia'?" Gordy asked.

"What?" She had found an article on getting rid of clutter, something she'd been trying to do in her house for years.

"Dr. Cardenas said something about 'a minute chance it's leukemia.' Is he talking about me? Do I have it? What is it?"

"I don't know, Gordy," she said, still glancing at the magazine, admiring the clutter-free rooms. Then she put the magazine on her lap. Gordy stood at the door, peeking out. "Get away from the door. Don't be eavesdropping. They're not talking about you. The doctor will come in here and tell us what's wrong."

He closed the door and sat down, tapping the keys on his phone. Gloria went back to her magazine.

"It's cancer, Mom."

"Oh, Gordy. He's not talking about you."

"Blood cancer. Man, blood goes everywhere in the body. I'm full of cancer." He groaned and fell back on the chair.

"Gordy, that's not funny." She slapped him lightly on his shoulder with the magazine.

"I'm going to text Dex and tell him good-bye forever," he said and laughed.

"Gordy…" Then she heard him guffawing. "Be quiet. There are sick people here."

"He cursed at me and told me to stop being stupid." He texted something else, still laughing at his brother's responses.

"Leave your brother alone, too. Isn't he at work?"

Dr. Cardenas walked in then, face somber, and Gloria's heart gave a lurch. The word "cancer" floated in the air and zigzagged its way around the room.

"Gordy's white cell count is a little above normal," the doctor said. "He has an infection, and looking inside his mouth, I think it has to do with his wisdom teeth. They must come out."

"I hate the dentist." Gordy grimaced.

"I'm sorry, Gordy. Sometimes, you have to do things you don't like. I'm going to prescribe some antibiotics. You can't have the teeth pulled out with an infection. It should take about seven to ten days. In the meantime, go to the dentist and have him decide what he wants to do."

"Is that it? You seemed so serious when you first walked in," Gloria said.

"I'm sorry. Something else on my mind."

Her shoulders sagged. Then pain nipped at her back. She hadn't realized she'd been so stiff, wondering what the doctor's diagnosis would be. "Okay…it's an infection. And teeth have to be pulled."

"Or it could be mono," the doctor teased. "You know, the 'kissing disease'? Who have you been dating, Gordy?"

Gordy squirmed in his chair. "Nobody."

"We'll run a test on mono, too. Just to cover all the bases." Dr. Cardenas handed the prescription to Gloria. "After ten days, I want you to bring Gordy back, and we'll run another blood test." He patted Gordy's back. "Take care of yourself."

"Okay," he said.

"Congratulations again on your upcoming graduation," Dr. Cardenas said. "I expect big things from you. See you next time, Gloria."

She thanked him and followed Gordy out of the exam room. Outside in the sunshine, things looked brighter. Her son had an infection, that's all. All she had to do was schedule an appointment with his dentist.

"I'm going to take you to the dentist next week," she said.

"Does it hurt to get teeth pulled?"

"They deaden your nerves. Afterward, you might have pain. Your aunt Lynda almost fainted after her wisdom teeth were pulled."

"But then, she's a girl. I can take it."

"I don't know, Gordy. Mouth pain—now that's bad."

Gloria's worries abated. He was going to be okay.

****

When Matt arrived at Angela's, Julia took him to her little garden on the side of the house. He admired it and gave her a few pointers on watering and fertilizing. She wrote down his suggestions. With his arm around her shoulders, they walked inside.

"How did you like yard work?" Angela asked. She stood at the kitchen sink. Matt was surprised she was out of bed.

"I loved it," Julia said. "I want to be a gardener." She skipped out of the room.

"What?" Angela's mouth dropped open. "What have you done to my daughter?"

"She's discovered she likes my work. What's wrong with that?"

"Don't make me repeat it," his ex said. "You know

how I feel about it. For sure I don't want my daughter doing it."

"Stay out of it. Maybe it's a phase, but she loves it. Don't make her give it up until if and when she's ready."

Angela sat down at the dining room table, a cup of coffee in her hand.

"I'm surprised you're out of bed," he said. "I mean, I'm happy about it, just…"

"Surprised. The doctor told me I'd do better if I moved around. I'm not sure he knows what he's talking about because I feel weak. My legs feel rubbery." She sipped her coffee. "Do you want some?"

"No, thanks." He grabbed a glass from the cupboard and filled it with water from the tap. "Before you went into the ER, I'd found a place to drive you to your appointments, and they can also run errands for you, or they can take you."

Her eyes snapped. "Who is it? I told you I didn't like those people that one agency sent over."

"I got this number from your doctor." Matt finished his water and refilled his glass. "It's a private program, partly funded by the state, but for a fee they'll accept you. So I set it up. Next Monday someone will be here to pick you up and drive you to your appointment and anywhere else you want to go. I'll just pay a monthly fee."

"And you did this without consulting me?"

"I told you I was going to do this. Either you could do it, or I would. And I don't want this to be a long, drawn-out thing."

She rose, hands propped on either side of her waist. "If I don't like the person, I'm not going."

"If you don't like the person, then you'll miss your appointment. I will no longer take you."

"I'll call Jorge." Angela paced, her heels beating a staccato on the kitchen floor.

"Call the bum. Call a taxi, but you'll pay for that, not me. I am not taking you. Understood?"

"Okay." She waved her hand in the air. "I never thought you'd be the kind of man who was dictated to by a woman."

"What do you mean?"

"You're only doing this because of Gloria. She's probably throwing fits because you're living with me," she said and laughed.

"I made the wrong decision when I moved in. I was only thinking of the girls and how they'd feel on a daily basis with you being so sick and having to go to doctors. That's all."

"You keep telling yourself that, Matt. You married me for better or worse. I was the one who decided this marriage wasn't enough for me."

Gloria had used almost the same words. But they weren't true. Repeating them didn't make them so. "Yes, I married you, and I would have stayed married to you forever, but you were unfaithful to me and to our vows. I can't trust you. I've had a hard time trusting anyone, especially women, after what you did. But I'm ready to trust again with Gloria. We're over, Angela. And we have been for a long time."

"I'm sure you believe that. But you're still with me."

"I'm not with you," he said. "I'm here because of the girls, but just for tonight. Tomorrow I'm moving back home. I want to have a last dinner with the girls and tell them. I want things to get back to normal as soon as possible."

"Well, things won't get back to normal. I've got cancer, or have you forgotten?"

"No, I haven't forgotten. What I mean is I'll be in my own house. The girls can visit me whenever you want time to yourself. I'll drive Julia to school. But as far as you and I, that's over. There's no more 'Matt and Angela.' "

She laughed. "You're not really serious."

"Yes, I am. I've found a woman I want to spend the rest of my life with, and I'm finished with making bad decisions. You and I will only talk about the girls. I don't want you to call me about your personal stuff anymore. Or that you need more money. I'll provide for the girls. But not your needs. Understood?"

"So I can't call you anymore?"

"Only if it's about the girls." He poured the remainder of his water down the drain.

"If I'm not happy, the girls won't be happy," she said.

"If something is causing you unhappiness and you can't tend to the girls, then I'll take them to my house."

"Don't do this to me, Matt." She began to cry. "I need you. You've always been there for me."

"I shouldn't have been. I didn't realize how strong a connection we had until someone pointed it out to me."

"Gloria again." Angela sneered. "I hate her."

"Sometimes it takes new eyes to see what we can't see."

"Now you sound like some kind of poet. I'm sick. I need someone to help me."

"Look into getting someone to help you here. But get it through the insurance. I'm not made of money."

She frowned. "I'll be surrounded by strangers."

"Call your family."

"Those losers. I'd rather have strangers."

"I'll be right back," he said. "I'm going to get some groceries. I have to cook a special meal tonight." He strolled out of the dining room and out of the house.

Angela yelled out to him, but he ignored it. He needed to see Gloria. Tomorrow he'd visit her at the bookstore and ask for forgiveness once again.

****

Gloria sat at her desk. She'd almost called in sick to work again, but Celeste usually didn't go in on Saturdays. Judy Ann would be by herself. Gloria was sure she could handle it, but she was young and still needed guidance. So she updated the book catalog and entered invoices. Maybe Lynda was right. Working on weekends wasn't a good idea. Perhaps she would go back and work in the medical field, not home health, but something else. A place where she would only work weekdays.

She managed to concentrate on her work, trying to balance the receipts with what she'd entered in the computer. But the numbers wouldn't add up. Once in a while she would hear the bell at the entrance, but Judy Ann could handle the customers. Gloria had told her to call if she needed assistance.

"Hi, gorgeous." A man's voice.

She looked up from her desk and saw Eddie at the door. He was dressed in jeans and western shirt and boots. What on earth was he doing here? "I thought you were on a job in Seguin."

"I quit almost from the beginning," he said. "I like to be appreciated, and they weren't treating me right."

Typical Eddie. Always someone else's fault. But why had he come to the bookstore? How did he know where she worked? "I'm busy. You shouldn't be here." She stood, and Eddie walked nearer. She wrinkled her nose at the smell of alcohol on his breath. "It's ten in the morning, and you're already drinking."

"You sound like my wife again. I can do whatever I want."

"Why are you here? Go home."

"I needed to see you," he said. "I keep remembering the night we had supper with our sons in their apartment. Didn't it remind you of old times?"

She only remembered that telling Matt about the evening had resulted in an argument. "No, Eddie. The evening didn't remind me of old times. It was a celebration of the boys' new place, and I wanted to be alone with them. And you showed up."

"So now I can't visit my sons?"

"I can't tell you what to do." She wished she could.

"Oh, Gloria." He was suddenly too close to her, and alcohol gave him added strength.

She tried to step away, but he grabbed her and pulled her close. She struggled against him.

"Oh, baby," he moaned. "This is the way I remember you."

"Let me go." She tried to push him away. "I'm working."

"I want to hold you and kiss you," he murmured in her ear. "I know you want me, too. I can see it in your eyes."

Gloria tried to push him away again, but he twirled

her around and held her against the wall. He was so strong, and he wasn't thinking straight with so much alcohol in him. "Eddie, let me go."

He bent his head to kiss her, and she didn't know how she could avoid it.

Suddenly, he wasn't holding her. He was on the floor, nursing his jaw. Matt stood over him, his fists clenched. Then Matt pulled him up by his shirt and knocked him down again.

"Oh dear God. Matt, stop it." She grabbed Matt and placed herself between him and Eddie. "Stop it at once."

She looked down at Eddie. He held his jaw, and blood seeped through his fingers.

Judy Ann stood at the door, her eyes huge. "Do you want me to call the cops?"

Gloria shook her head. "No, this is my ex. It's okay. Just close the door and go back and see to the customers, if we have any in the store."

When the girl did as she said, she turned to Matt. "Get out of here."

"What?" he asked, a look of disbelief in his eyes.

"I'll take care of this," she said. "Just leave. Please."

"My mistake. I thought he was bothering you, but apparently not."

"I can handle this. You don't have to come in here like the cavalry and rescue me. I can take care of myself."

He unclenched his fist and stepped away from Eddie. "And you can take care of Eddie, right?"

"Yes," she said, not sure why she was defending Eddie, except that she always did.

"Okay, Mrs. Amaya. I get the message loud and clear. Excuse the intrusion."

He wrenched the door open and stalked out without a backward glance. *Wait. Don't leave.* But then Eddie grabbed her leg, nearly unbalancing her. She kicked him. "Get up and get out of here." Anger filled her, both at Matt and at Eddie. How dare they fight in her office?

"I'm hurt," he said. "I think I need a doctor. I'm going to file assault charges against him."

"Do whatever you want, Eddie. Just get out of my office. Get out of my life and never come back."

He stood and almost lost his balance. He was drunk. She'd have to call a taxi for him. He couldn't drive. How had he even gotten there? As far as she knew, he didn't have a car.

She didn't really care. She wanted him to go. In all probability, she'd alienated Matt for the final time. She left Eddie sitting on a chair and searched the store. Matt was nowhere in sight.

"He left. He was really angry," Judy Ann said.

"I know." Her voice broke. "I don't think he'll be my fiancé after today. Will you do me a favor and call a taxi?"

"Okay," Judy Ann said. "What happened?"

Gloria shook her head. "Maybe someday I'll tell you. Not today."

In the restroom, she wet some paper towels. Back in her office, she handed them to Eddie. "Clean yourself up," she said. "I've called a taxi for you."

He winced as he cleaned his face. "Don't think I'm kidding. I'm going to make a police report about your boyfriend hitting me."

"And I told you I don't care what you do." She really didn't want Matt to get into trouble for assault, but he could take care of himself. "I don't care what you do about anything. I want you to stay out of my life. You can be in your sons' lives, a bit late in the game, but it's your choice. I don't want you to behave as if there's a future for us. Because there's not. There will never be one. Do you understand me?"

"You don't really mean it." He dabbed at his face again.

"Yes, I do. I've just lost the best man I've ever met because I defended you. But it's over, too. I don't have to do it anymore. I actually never should have. You were my husband and father to our sons, and you didn't take your roles seriously. I enabled you to get away with your shortcomings by covering up for you, or trying to anyway."

"Gloria, baby…"

"Stop it. I admit we've had this connection between us."

He grinned. "You see?"

"But it's an unhealthy one. I guess through the years because I had two sons to raise—by myself—I allowed you to come in and out of our lives, and if you had a problem, I would help you. I think at the beginning I thought maybe at some point you would want to stay and be a family again. I don't know."

"We can now." He moved to take her in his arms.

She stepped back and put her hand out to stop him from getting any closer. "Do you know how ridiculous you sound? I don't need you anymore. I needed you when the boys were little. Now I want something else, but it's not with you. It's too late for us, Eddie." She remembered Matt's expression when she'd told him to leave. "It's too late, period."

"You're too beautiful to remain alone for the rest of your life," he said.

"I won't be alone. I have my sons, my family."

"You know it won't be enough."

No, it wouldn't be enough. Not after Matt. "That's not your concern."

A knock sounded on the door. She opened it to see Judy Ann.

"The taxi is here."

"Thank you," Gloria said. "It's time for you to leave." She grabbed her purse and gave Eddie some money. "Good-bye."

He stared at her. "You're making a mistake."

"I made a mistake earlier with Matt." She pointed to him. "This, with you, is not a mistake. It's closure. Please don't come back here again, or to my house. It's over."

Finally, he grabbed the money, and it seemed he was going to move to touch her again, but he turned and sauntered away. In her mind, she didn't see Eddie, but Matt walking away from her life, and she knew he'd never return.

She closed the door to her office, sank into her chair, and wept. It was over between her and Matt, and this time it was her fault. She could now see she wasn't ready for a relationship. Her epiphany regarding Eddie had arrived too late. Maybe someday she could have a relationship with another man. Her heart ached at the thought. She wanted Matt, but he would never return to her now. To him, today she'd chosen Eddie. That Dumb Eddie, as Lynda had called him.

She couldn't wait another hour to close the bookstore. She grabbed her purse and asked Judy Ann to close up. "I'll explain to Celeste on Monday. I have to go home."

"Okay." Judy Ann's eyes filled with concern. "Take care."

In the truck, Gloria wanted to indulge in a crying bout, but after a few tears, she turned on the ignition and told herself the sooner she got home, the better. Once there, she could crawl under the covers and cry for the rest of her life.

****

Matt arrived at Angela's house. He stayed in the truck a few minutes before getting out. Today he planned to move out. Today was the end of his relationship with Gloria. She'd chosen her ex, and he didn't know what to think. The man had been all over her. He'd helped her, and she'd gotten angry with him, not Eddie. Clearly, she and Eddie had a connection like the one he had with Angela. Funny, Gloria was the one who'd made him see it because she couldn't see the one she had with Eddie.

The plastic grocery bags reposed in the front seat of his truck. He'd planned the meal for his daughters so carefully, but now the last thing he wanted was to cook. The way he felt, the food probably wouldn't come out well. He wasn't the best cook to begin with. He'd just been going to barbecue some burgers and hot dogs. Maybe they should go out. He was exhausted. His fists hurt. And for what? Gloria hadn't wanted to be rescued. She hadn't fluttered her eyelashes and said "my hero." Not that he'd wanted her to, but he hadn't thought she'd mind so much.

He glanced toward the front door, where Amber waved to him. He managed a smile and waved back. *This is it. I have to get out.* He grabbed a few of the bags and opened the door.

"What are you going to make, Daddy?" she asked.

"How about some burgers on the grill?"

"Yummy."

"Girls, go get the rest of the bags, and I'll start the fire," he said as he entered the kitchen and saw Patsy and Julia sitting at the table.

He waited until they left the room, then opened the fridge to grab a beer. He walked to the garage and hauled the charcoal and lighter fluid out of there and outside. The evening wasn't too hot; a little breeze in the air helped. Well, it was still May. June would bring the hotter days, and the summer days would get blazing hot by August. He tipped back the bottle of beer.

"Drinking already," Angela said from the patio door. "You must have had quite a day."

"You can't imagine. I don't want to talk about it."

She walked closer. "You seem sad." She gazed up into his face.

He could take her into his arms, and she wouldn't resist. He bent down to put charcoal in the grill and wet it with the lighter fluid. Why was he thinking that way about Angela?

"I'll get you another beer," she said.

Matt breathed a sigh of relief. Gloria had jilted him, but he couldn't forget the pain by kissing Angela. Besides, he'd already set the record straight with her yesterday. He was moving out tonight. He was ready to be in his own house, doing his work, and forgetting the past several weeks and the woman he'd thought he was

214

going to marry. She still had his ring. It didn't matter. She could throw it away if she wanted. He didn't want it back. It'd be just a reminder of another failure in his life.

Angela returned with the beer and stayed close to him. He opened it and gulped half the bottle down. He was drinking too fast, and he needed to leave tonight. Otherwise, he might not do it, for whatever reason.

"You know you don't want to leave me," she said.

He leaned down toward his ex. She inched closer. Then he heard the sizzle of the charcoal and grabbed the beer again. "Yes, I do."

The girls' return smoothed things out and shifted his gears. He was here for his daughters, and he didn't need to complicate things with Angela. He turned on some music on the stereo and grilled the burgers and a few wieners. The girls cut up lettuce and tomatoes and set out the buns.

Before long, they sat down to eat at the stone bench.

Angela didn't join them. "Clearly, this is not a party for me," she said.

Matt stared at her, then down at his plate. "You can stay and eat."

"That's not enough, Matt."

"That's all there is," he said.

She waved. "It's been real."

"What's the matter with Mommy?" Amber asked.

He moved his food with his fork. "She's tired, I think."

Throughout the meal, he tried to think of something to say, but all he could think about was that he had to leave. His daughters stayed silent as well.

"Do you want some more?" he finally asked.

"No, Dad. I'm stuffed," Patsy said.

"I'm moving back to my house tonight, girls," he said.

"Oh, Daddy, why?" Amber asked.

"Because I have to. It was a mistake to move in. I wanted to be with you girls, but your mom and I divorced years ago, and once that happens, you shouldn't live together anymore especially…"

"Especially when you have someone else in your life?" Julia finished his thought.

He didn't answer for a few seconds. Well, he used to have someone. He wasn't sure anymore. "Yes, that's right."

"I understand, Dad," Julia said. "You've always been around. It was nice to see you every day and not have to leave the house."

"I know it's a chore sometimes to pack up and go visit me," he said.

"No, it's not," Amber said, and Patsy agreed.

"Yes, it is," he said. "But it can't be helped. What I can do is get duplicates of your things at my house. Maybe that way you'll only have to take clothes. What do you think?"

"Maybe," Julia said.

"And let's say you have plans with friends on a day you're supposed to go to my house. You don't have to change them. You can go ahead."

Julia smiled.

"However, don't make a habit of it, okay?" he added. "I really want you to visit me."

"I will, Dad. Now more than ever. I need help with my garden."

Matt laughed. "Always."

After the meal, they cleaned up. He packed up his bags, hugged his daughters, and left. He didn't see Angela again. That was for the best. He drove away feeling a sense of loss. But he had to go home.

When he entered his house, a hint of mustiness assailed him as if he'd been away a long time. He'd come home a few times to get away and to get clothes, but he hadn't stayed long.

Gloria had been in this house. Now she'd never return. He grabbed a few beers from his refrigerator, leaving his bags at the entrance. In his bedroom, he turned on the TV and fell asleep with an action flick. Which one it was, he couldn't have said later.

Chapter Fifteen

Gloria knocked on Matt's front door. She'd spent the night crying until she'd exhausted herself, and then decided to go to his house in the morning and explain things to him. Theirs was something special, and she couldn't lose it—or him. She called Angela's house first, in spite of her trepidation at having to talk to the woman. Julia had told her Matt moved out last night and was back at his house.

When he opened the door, he was unshaved and wore a white T-shirt and gray sleeping pants. Bloodshot eyes attested to the fact he hadn't slept well. But she didn't care. She hadn't slept well either.

"I'm surprised Eddie let you leave his side so early in the morning," he said, not moving aside to let her in.

She couldn't have heard him correctly. "What?"

"You told me you and him have this understanding where you can fool around with other people if you want. But then you return to each other."

Her throat ached, but she didn't want to cry. "You know I didn't mean to say it. I was angry with you because of all these problems we've had lately."

He stared at her in silence. "Congratulations," he finally said. He walked away and left her standing on his front porch.

Gloria couldn't believe her ears. Did he really not know her at all? She followed him inside the house.

"How can you think for one minute, especially after everything…" She stopped because her voice broke. *Ugh!* She hated that whenever she wanted to sound the most confident, her emotions took the best of her. "How can you believe I would return to Eddie after I'd been with you?"

"You chose who you wanted yesterday."

"I didn't want you to keep beating up on him. He was drunk. He couldn't defend himself."

"Why should he when he has you? Though he seemed pretty aware when he was pawing you. But I guess you didn't mind, after all." He ran his hands through his hair. "I think I'm still drunk."

Unshaven, hair tousled, and angry, he didn't look like the Matt she knew. Well, he'd just woken up, it seemed. Had he been drinking all night?

"I'm used to Eddie," she said. "I know how to deal with him."

He held up his hands. "As I said yesterday, I'm sorry I intruded."

"He says he's going to file assault charges against you. FYI."

"I doubt he'll remember what he did or what happened to him. But thanks for the warning."

She looked around the living room. Other times she'd been here, she and Matt had been happy. Now they weren't. She could almost see him fresh from the shower, as he'd been when she'd first visited. She'd walked up to him and kissed him. Would he respond if she did so now?

"I feel everything went wrong after you proposed and I accepted." She blinked. She must not cry. She had to explain things to him. When she cried, she couldn't talk. "Maybe we took on too much. I mean, we have kids, responsibilities. But maybe we could start over. Take it a little slower. Let the kids become used to the idea of us. We can spend more time together and not let…other people…distract us."

He laughed, but he glared at her. "Are you serious?"

"Don't you want to?"

He sat on a sofa chair and threw back his head. "Hell no. I'm tired of this. You're right. I completely agree with you. We had problems from the start with the kids, and then somehow it grew out of control."

"I guess it was a crazy dream," Gloria whispered, unsure if Matt heard. She cleared her throat and spoke more loudly. "Thinking we could have, I don't know, a new love in our lives, build a life together. But we've already lived our lives apart from one other, and we were kidding ourselves thinking we could make it work. We've been trying for several weeks now, and nothing works." Her heart was breaking. Maybe she'd believed he'd fight for her.

"Maybe if we'd kept it light, just weekend flings. What were we thinking, long-term stuff, right? How about we do that?" He stood and walked toward her and pulled her close. He caressed her back and then brought his hands up and held her face. "Do you want me to kiss you?"

She trembled at his touch. "No. You're just playing." Her heart ached that he could make a joke of their love. Maybe it hadn't been love, after all.

"Let's play together. We had fun doing this."

"Let me go." Being in his arms reminded her of how much she wanted him, and right now she could tell holding her meant nothing to him.

He released her, and she shivered with cold, even though the room was warm. She wished this were the first time she'd visited him, at the beginning of their relationship.

"You know I almost kissed Angela last night," he said. "She wanted it. I could feel it."

Gloria's stomach flip-flopped. "Why almost?"

"She's my ex. I finally realized it last night once and for all. I don't want her in my life as a woman. She's my girls' mother. Just wanted you to know. I'm not sure why. It doesn't matter anymore. But since you spent the night with Eddie, maybe I should have acted on my impulse and kissed her." He winked.

"I did not spend the night with Eddie. In fact, after you left the bookstore yesterday, I told him to leave and I didn't want to see him again for as long as I lived. I told him I was finished with having him come into my life whenever he felt like it and expect me to help him."

Matt laughed. "Yeah, right."

"Why don't you believe me?"

"I don't trust you. I'm still drunk. I did sleep, but I think I need more. This visit of yours has taken too much out of me. I'm going to bed. You can join me if you want."

"Why don't you just call Angela?" She snatched the ring from her finger and threw it on a table by the chair. It made a pinging sound and then spun around until it stopped.

He turned back to her and then stared at the ring on the table. She looked down at the engagement ring, too. Tears filled her eyes. So many dreams she'd had when he'd proposed to her. She remembered him kneeling by the coffee table and saying his knees hurt. Ages ago, it seemed.

He didn't say a word, not even to ask her to change her mind.

"Good-bye, Matt."

"So long," he said, waving. "If you need help with your roses, I know of a good gardener."

She wanted to laugh, but his reminder of how they'd met only made her want to cry more. "No, thank you. I can take care of things by myself. I've done it for a long time now."

Matt crossed his arms. "I guess there's nothing more to say, right?"

Gloria took a tissue from her purse and dried her eyes. How had they ended up like this? She'd really believed she'd found love after all this time. Now she realized, again, sometimes it really was too late.

She turned her back on him and left his house.

****

Matt woke up in his own bed, as he'd been doing all week. He still missed the sounds of his daughters getting ready in the mornings. The way he'd been feeling lately, though, it was better he was alone. He'd left the engagement ring where Gloria had thrown it. Maybe it'd fall to the floor and he'd vacuum it up and never have to see it again.

He rolled onto his side and tried to remember what jobs he had to do today. He was almost finished with the rock garden. Starr hadn't fired him a second time. However, he didn't want to work with the man again. If he ever called him, Matt was ready to say he was too busy to take the job, no matter how much Starr would pay. He still hadn't forgotten how the dirty old guy had eyed Julia. He smiled at the remembrance of her at his job sites. He hoped she'd keep the interest in gardening and landscaping, but he'd understand if she changed her mind. Maybe if she didn't make a career out of it, she could still grow a small garden as she was doing at her house.

Along with the rage that had boiled in his veins when he'd moved out of the house after Angela's infidelity, his heart had been pierced with anguish. He thought they'd be together for the rest of their lives. He couldn't diminish the pain he'd felt then. This time, however, upon losing Gloria, he'd lost his last chance. After all the challenges they'd faced with the kids and the arguments about their exes and trust, he wasn't up to going through that with anyone ever again.

From now on, he'd keep it light, as he'd try to do with Gloria when she broke up with him. He'd still been drunk. He'd even told her about Angela, somehow feeling he shouldn't keep secrets from her even then. Probably not a good idea. But as he'd said then and repeated now, it really didn't matter anymore.

He forced himself to get out of bed. *What in the hell do I have to do today?* He'd look in his calendar. He'd taken to writing things down. Sometimes he couldn't remember, and especially today. He wasn't engaged anymore. It was okay with him. He didn't want to be engaged. Stupid idea.

He stumbled into the shower. Afterward, he made himself some strong coffee and drank it black. The thought of food nauseated him. He opened his calendar to this month and to the job list for today. He flipped to June. Gordy was graduating on June sixth. The boy had invited him, and he'd received the invitation. He'd been put on the spot when he'd met Gloria's dad at Lynda's. He didn't have to go to the graduation. He was sure Gloria had told her sons she was no longer engaged. There was no reason he had to be present. Gordy had invited his daughters, too. But as he remembered, the boy had been forced to do it.

Still, maybe he should call Gloria, get her thoughts on the matter. No, he just wouldn't show up. It wasn't as if her sons weren't used to disappointment. Their dad had frequently let them down. Trouble was, he'd tried hard never to disappoint his daughters, and he'd succeeded for the most part. He sat at the dining table, pulled out his cell, and punched Gloria's number. The clock on the microwave indicated it was after eight. She was at work. He almost hung up.

"Hello?" She coughed.

"I'm sorry to bother you," he said without greeting. He flipped some pages in the calendar.

"It's fine. What…I mean, why…?"

He cleared his throat. "Your son Gordy invited me and my girls to his graduation, which is in about a week."

"Yes. What about it?"

He thought she blew her nose. Was she crying? Or was she sick? "Look, just tell your son, explain to him…I'm sure…ah…"

"They know," she said. "He'll understand if you don't go. It's not as if…"

"We didn't bond." He gave a bitter laugh. "It's not like he'll be hurt if we don't go. Again, I'm sorry for troubling you." He hung up, put an *x* over Gordy's graduation date, and closed the book.

He finished his coffee and left the house.

****

"What the hell's the matter with you, *amiga*?" Tanya yelled. And continued yelling.

Gloria held the phone away from her ear. She'd just gotten into her truck to drive home. Hearing Matt's voice on the phone this morning had jarred her. It'd been so unexpected. She thought she'd never hear from him again. He hadn't called to talk to her, though. He'd called about Gordy's graduation. He sounded hurt when she'd insinuated Gordy wouldn't miss him or his daughters if they didn't attend. It'd hurt her, too. She'd wanted it to matter to all of them from the moment they'd told the kids they were getting married. She remembered the kids' anger. That alone should have told her they were making a huge mistake. They were going outside the norm the kids were used to—and maybe even what she and Matt had been used to.

"Tanya, I'm going home," she interrupted her friend. "I'm tired, and I want to go to bed and cry."

"Well, if you hadn't been such a ninny, you'd be going to bed with Matt. Wayne told me you broke the engagement off. What's the matter with you?"

"You already asked me that, and I'm not going to answer you. In fact, I'm going to hang up on you à la Angela!"

"Don't you dare hang up on me. I'll just call back. And if you won't answer, I'll drive to your house and yell at you in person," her friend said, still screaming.

A pain jarred her between her eyes. She hadn't been sleeping well. Every time she closed her eyes, she saw Matt. But not the angry Matt. She saw Matt as he'd been in her backyard—so businesslike, pulling out his card and leaning on his mower. He'd looked at her as if he found her pretty. She hadn't felt pretty in such a long time.

"We made a mistake, Tanya." Tears gushed out of Gloria's eyes. "We should have kept it light. A fling, as he told me when I gave him his ring back. He wanted to go back to the beginning and just keep it light."

"Well, what the hell? Do it," Tanya yelled. "At least he'll still be in your life."

"It's too late. We made it serious or tried to, anyway, and it backfired. We can't go back in time, for heaven's sake."

"Anything is possible with love. Or did you fall out of love with him? I don't think that's possible. From the first time I saw you together, you couldn't keep your hands off each other."

"That's attraction, not love," Gloria said. "And it didn't last."

"Can you really sit there and tell me you don't love Matt anymore?"

"Well, of course, I love him." Gloria remembered telling Matt that if he really believed something he wouldn't say "of course."

"Then why did you break off the engagement?" Tanya asked.

"He beat up Eddie."

"Well, the bum deserved it, I'm sure. Someone should have kicked his dumb ass a long time ago."

Gloria raised her eyes to heaven. "That's not the point. Eddie was drunk, and it's really not why I broke it off. Matt doesn't trust me. I don't trust him."

"I understand why you couldn't trust him once he moved in with that slutty ex-wife of his. But why did he mistrust you?"

"I kept defending Eddie."

"*Maldicion.* Why in hell would you do that? The man ought to have been shot long ago. He left you with two little boys to raise without so much as a by-your-leave, and you stood there and defended the sleazeball to a good man like Matt? You deserve to spend the rest of your days alone."

"I couldn't help it. It became almost a reflex. I did it throughout our married life. I couldn't stop."

"Well, keep on defending him now," Tanya said.

"When I saw Matt hitting Eddie, I told him to leave. So he saw that as my choosing Eddie over him. Then, Eddie did have me in his arms when Matt walked in. That's what happened between him and Angela. He walked in on her in bed with another man. I've lost his trust in me."

"Well, explain it to him," Tanya suggested. "What are you waiting for?"

"I tried, but he won't listen to me. He's very angry. And he was still kind of drunk when I went to his house, so he wasn't ready to listen to anything I had to say."

"So you broke off the engagement. And I found this beautiful dress to wear to your wedding. Now where will I wear it?"

"You bought it?"

"Yes." Tanya giggled. "What's the point of seeing something beautiful and not buying it?"

"He called me."

"Aha! There is hope."

"Not really. He wanted to ask if he should attend Gordy's graduation. Gordy invited him after the family put him on the spot the day Matt met my dad."

"What did you say?" Tanya asked.

"I told him he didn't have to go. I was mean to him. I said he and Gordy, or Dex, hadn't bonded, so he wouldn't be hurt if he didn't go."

"Ouch."

"I know," Gloria admitted. "I'm hurt, so I want to hurt him."

"Do you want me to talk to him? I can, you know. I can knock some sense into him."

"No, please don't do that. After all, I was the one who broke off the engagement." She glanced at her bare ring finger. "He gave me such a beautiful ring, too. I never had an engagement ring before."

"*Ay chihuahua*," Tanya said.

"It's okay. My life is okay. I'm okay. I'll go back to my old life and forget about this little interlude." Her heart lurched in her chest at the thought of never seeing Matt again. She couldn't do anything about it, though.

"That's what's wrong with you," Tanya said, yelling again. "You're satisfied with *okay*. You could have had *fabulous*. I don't want to talk to you anymore. I'm going to go drive to your house and beat you up."

Gloria laughed. "Please don't. I'm tired. I'm just going to go home and go to bed."

"Alone, *amiga, sola*," Tanya reminded her. "And that's shitty."

****

Matt drove to a new job site with one of his workers. This customer was going to be on his employee's schedule. The woman needed yard work, including mowing, edging, and trimming trees. For the trees, he'd have to find a couple of more helpers.

When they arrived at the house, located in a new

subdivision, he stopped the truck. "Let's go."

A woman dressed in short pajamas answered the door.

"Hello, Mrs. Ellis. I'm Matt Cerda. This is Simon. He'll actually be doing the job after today."

The woman walked out onto the porch and sidled up to Matt. "I'd rather have you do it."

He stepped back. "Simon will do a good job for you. Here's the estimate. Please check it and let me know if you have any questions."

The woman batted her eyes. Matt stared at her, and all he could think of was she really should go back inside the house and let him and Simon get to work.

"I have a question," she said before he could turn away. "Do you want to go out dancing with me?"

"I don't dance, ma'am. But I'm sure you won't have a problem finding another dance partner. Excuse me."

Simon laughed. "Man, she'd have been happy if you went inside with her and forgot the lawn."

"It happens." He remembered Gloria. She'd come out to open the gate for him, and all he'd been able to do was stare at her. She'd been all business, looking at his card and asking if he could help her roses. But she'd smiled and blushed and had ensnared his heart in those few seconds. It was all over, though. Somehow, he had to stop thinking about her.

"Hey, Matt." Simon's voice brought him back to reality. "Having second thoughts about our new employer's invitation?"

"No, only some advice for you. This kind of thing happens from time to time. If you're going to work for me, you're going to have to keep it professional at all times. Understood?"

"Yes, sure," the guy said.

"Let's get to work." Matt lifted the mower from the back of his truck and walked to the backyard with Simon behind him. When Simon began mowing, Matt felt his phone buzzing.

It couldn't be Angela. She'd called a few times, but he'd quickly reminded her if the call didn't concern the girls, he didn't have time. The number on the caller ID was familiar, and he saw Julia's picture.

"Is something wrong, sweetheart?" His heart hammered in his chest. She had never called him at work.

"Yes, there is, Dad. Why did you tell Gloria we weren't going to Gordy's graduation? We've got plans."

What did she just say? Plans with Gordy? "What are you talking about?"

"You, me, Patsy, and Amber are going to Gordy's graduation and then to dinner. After that, us kids are going out to celebrate with him. Well, maybe not Amber, because she's such a child even if she is thirteen now."

"When did this happen?" He thought the kids didn't even talk anymore. He and Gloria hadn't had occasion to bring them together in a long time—first with Angela's diagnosis, then the arguments.

"Oh, Dad. If you don't want to go, I guess it's okay. But why not? This is a perfect opportunity for you to be with Gloria. I thought you guys were getting married."

"I thought you were against the idea." He realized he hadn't told his girls about the broken engagement.

"Well, it doesn't seem so bad now. You have to live your life. And when you were with us, with Mom and everything, you seemed sad all the time. I want you to be happy. We all do."

"Thank you, sweetheart, but…" He couldn't tell her over the phone, especially when she was giving him her blessing.

"We're going, right?" Julia asked.

"I guess so."

"Great. I'll call Gordy. Bye, Dad."

Matt closed his cell. *What the hell?* His daughters? Julia, of all of them, wanted to go to Gordy's graduation. Weren't they always at odds? Though both he and Dex had helped her out of a bad situation at the movies.

He hit his head with his hand. Kids and women—he'd never understand them.

Chapter Sixteen

Gloria stood in front of her dresser looking down at the boxes of earrings and trying to figure out which ones to wear. It didn't really matter. Today was her younger son's graduation. It was Gordy's day, and she was happy. She wished she wasn't so sad as well.

The pain of Matt's absence from her life overwhelmed her. She hadn't talked to him since he'd called about Gordy's graduation. And she'd hurt him. It didn't matter anymore, as he'd told her when she broke off the engagement. She held up her finger and missed her engagement ring. She missed the man who'd placed it on her finger. In her mind, she heard their happy voices, their laughter, and remembered their kisses as he'd proposed and talked later. Tears filled her eyes. She wiped them away, knocking off her glasses. *You'd think I'd have no more tears by now.*

"Mom?" Gordy tapped on her door. "I have to get going. They want us there early."

She opened the bedroom door. She had to smile at Gordy's appearance in his cap and gown. "You look so smart."

Her son grinned, but then he touched her on the shoulder. "Come into the living room. I have to tell you something."

"What?" She followed him.

Dex entered from their old bedroom. He didn't

smile and didn't meet her eyes.

"What's going on?" she asked.

"I think Matt may be at the graduation," Gordy said.

She shook her head. "He won't be. When he called me, I told him it was okay if he and the girls didn't go. I mean, it's not necessary now…"

"Well, he might be there because Julia and them are going," Gordy said.

"We made plans to celebrate," Dex added.

"Plans to celebrate?" Was she dreaming? Her sons and Matt's daughters didn't even like each other. Why would they celebrate together?

"At first, I didn't want to invite them," Gordy admitted. "But then, after they received the invitation, Julia called me and…we made plans."

"Well, we figured we might as well make the best of it," Dex said. "You and Matt wanted to get married. We couldn't go against you forever. Besides, it's your lives. We've got ours. I don't know…"

"I always knew my sons were intelligent people." Gloria smiled. "But now, Matt and I…"

"We know," Gordy said. "But we met Matt's daughters, and they're okay, for the most part. We were even going to tell you it was okay if you got married. We'd work it out."

"Since it meant so much to both of you," Dex said.

Tears welled up in her eyes. "Oh, *mijos*. It does. I mean, it did. Well…" She strove to pull herself together. "I understand. You can't turn your feelings off and on like a water tap. Just because Matt and I aren't getting married anymore…doesn't mean I stopped caring about him. And you can't stop how you feel

233

about his daughters." She cleared her throat. Her sons watched her, probably thinking she was going to throw a fit soon.

"It'll be okay," she said. "Matt and I are adults. We'll manage. I'll be there for your graduation. I mean, I've waited all this time for your special day."

"Yeah, Gordo," Dex said. "It took you long enough."

"If I wasn't dressed up, I'd wrestle you to the floor," Gordy said.

"And you keep your plans with the girls," Gloria said. "The only difference will be that Matt and I won't be at the dinner. Okay?"

"You're not mad?" Gordy asked.

"No. The breakup is between Matt and me, not between you and his daughters. I'm glad you have new friends. You can't ever have too many of those."

****

Matt dropped his daughters off at the coliseum, where the graduation ceremony would be held. "Wait for me at the entrance. I'll be right back." He drove off to find parking. After it seemed he and Gloria had worked things out, he'd wanted to attend Gordy's graduation. Now they weren't even engaged. He had no reason whatsoever to be here.

Parking was bad, but he found a spot not too faraway, climbed out of the truck, and walked back to the entrance. As he reached it, he saw Gloria and her sons greeting his daughters. The kids in harmony—what he and Gloria had wanted from the beginning—and it'd happened now when there was no future for them. He took a deep breath.

Julia hurried toward him with a smile. "Hi, Dad.

Gordy said we can sit together with Dex and Gloria. He already had to go in. He gave me these tickets."

Matt glanced at Gloria, who quickly looked away toward her sister, Lynda.

"Hey, Matt." John held out his hand.

He took John's hand and breathed more easily. He had no problem with the man. Maybe he could help him through this.

"Hi, Matt." Lynda grinned and waved.

They entered the building, and somehow he was next to Gloria. He put his hands in his pockets to keep from touching her. She'd probably jump out of her skin if he did. They climbed up to the middle of the section and found their seats

Lynda held John back. "Let Matt and Gloria go in first. They need to sit together."

Matt overheard the whispered words but didn't look back to see if Gloria followed him. When he sat down, he realized she was seated next to him.

She cleared her throat. "I'm sorry. I haven't told Lynda."

"My daughters don't know either." He leafed through the program. "Can you believe the kids are going out to celebrate?"

"No." She looked down at the ground floor where the seats for the graduates were placed. "I found out just before we left the house. Too late to do us any good, but as I told my sons, you can never have too many friends."

He shifted in his seat. Down the row, Dex sat next to Gloria, then Julia, Patsy and Amber, and then John and Lynda. "Where are your sister's kids?"

"They're sitting in the school section somewhere

down there," she said and pointed.

"Just wondered." He fiddled with the program. "Where's Eddie? Shouldn't he be here? It's his son's graduation."

She glared at him, then turned to Dex. "Where's your dad?"

"He had something to do, a job lead," he said. "He called Gordo last night and told him he couldn't be here. "

"And the only time he could do this was on Thursday, the night of his son's graduation?" Anger shook her body. But why should it surprise her? She'd known this about him for several years now, hadn't she?

"I yelled at him," Dex said.

"Oh, Dex, you know that never does any good. All it does is make you feel bad."

"I had to, Mom. It's a special day for Gordy." He pointed in Matt's direction. "Even Matt came, and there's no reason for him to be here except his daughters wanted to be here for my brother."

"My dad is a good dad," Amber piped up.

Gloria blinked, and Matt knew she was holding back tears. She grabbed a tissue from her purse.

"Don't you think so, Gloria?" Amber asked.

"Yes, sweetie." She blew her nose before turning to Dex. "Did you tell your father about the restaurant?"

"Yeah."

"I hope he doesn't show up," she said.

Matt wondered why she wouldn't want her ex to show up, but he didn't know what else to say. She didn't want to talk to him. He didn't really want to read a list of names off the graduation program, but there was nothing else to do. Well, he could put his arm around Gloria and have her put her head on his shoulder. They could be talking about their upcoming wedding. However, all that was over. Their last encounter had been when Gloria returned his ring. What else was there to say?

She opened her purse and pulled out another tissue. "I'm sure I'm going to cry." She sounded as if she was crying already, but he knew better than to comment.

"Here come the waterworks." Dex patted her hand.

The ceremony finally began—benedictions, speeches—and then the graduates filed up to receive their diplomas. Gordy was one of the first ones since his last name began with an *A*. Gloria clapped long and hard and used the tissue, then had to pull out another one. Several cheers went up, and Gordy's name was shouted out, even though the audience had been warned not to be noisy.

At the end of the ceremony, Gloria and the rest of the family slowly made their way out of the row, down the section, and outside.

Matt held out his hand to Gordy. "Congratulations."

The boy hugged him. "Thanks for coming, Matt."

"Sure."

Gordy knew he and Gloria had broken up. Why the hug? He put it to the fact that graduation was a time when feelings of euphoria filled a person. He remembered his graduation day.

Gloria hugged Gordy, and Dex punched him before he hugged him. Then his daughters were all around Gordy as well as Lynda and John's kids.

"I made you a card, Gordy," Amber said.

"I can't wait to see it." He put his arm around her shoulders.

Gloria and Lynda took pictures of Gordy with all the kids in various groupings.

"Come on. Let me take a picture of the new family," Lynda said. "Gloria and Matt with your kids, especially the graduate."

Gloria frowned.

But then Gordy said, "Come on, Mom. You know, for a memory." And he laughed.

She hugged him around the waist. "Only because it's your day." She stood by Gordy and Dex, Matt by his daughters, and Lynda snapped the picture.

Her sister aimed the camera again. "Gloria, you and Matt stand together behind the kids." For goodness' sake, you look as if you don't even want to touch each other. Did you have another fight?"

"Lynda…" Gloria stiffened.

Matt walked closer and stood next to her. He almost put his arm around her shoulders but decided he shouldn't. The kids grouped around them.

"Take the picture, Lynda," she said in a tight voice.

"Such a nice picture," Lynda said. "I'll send you a copy."

"Thanks," Gloria said.

Matt moved away from Gloria. When her gaze met his, he wanted to pull her even closer and kiss her. But it would be another bad idea.

"I…" she said. "I'd better go."

He watched her walk away. It was time to leave. He'd made an appearance.

Julia had other ideas. "Come on, Dad. We need to get to the restaurant, or they'll give our reservation away."

****

As Matt drove out of the crowded parking lot, he decided he'd better tell his daughters before they heard it from someone else.

"Listen, girls," he said. "I have something to tell you."

"What is it, Dad?" Julia asked. She sat in the front seat, Patsy and Amber in the back.

"It's about Gloria and me." He inched along behind the jammed-up cars. "We're not getting married, after all."

"What?" Julia asked.

"Why, Daddy?" Amber yelled. "I want Dex and Gordy to be my brothers."

Patsy didn't say a word.

"We broke up about a week ago," he said. "We couldn't work things out."

"What things?" Julia asked. "You always seemed happy to be with her. What happened?"

"Too many things."

"It was our fault, wasn't it? We made such a big deal about it," Patsy said.

"Partly," he said. "Mostly, Gloria and I have been on our own for too long, raising you kids, and when we tried to build a life together, we couldn't do it. It just didn't work."

"No wonder you didn't talk much," Julia said.

"It's so sad," Patsy said.

"Yeah," Amber agreed.

"I hadn't had time to tell you," he said. "I thought I'd tell you this weekend when you went to stay with me. I didn't know we'd be attending Gordy's

239

graduation until you called me, Julia."

"Maybe you just have to try harder, Dad," she said. "Haven't you always said you can accomplish whatever you want if you really work at it?"

Matt wished hard work was all it would take. But he and Gloria didn't trust each other. Their exes were too ingrained in their system. Or they'd been alone too long.

"Did Mom have anything to do with this?" Julia asked.

He swung into the freeway, finally out of the snarl of traffic at the coliseum. "Why would you think so? By the way, where are we going?"

Julia named a Mexican food place. "And don't change the subject, please."

"I don't think I should answer," he said.

"She did," Julia said. "What did she do?"

"Julia, this is between me and Gloria. Your mom had nothing to do with this." *Not much.* It was his fault. He hadn't been able to let go of Angela completely until it was too late.

"I think she did. I know how Mom is. She blamed you for the breakup of your marriage, but she's the one who had the affair."

"Julia…" he said.

"I'm not a child anymore, Dad. Patsy and Amber have to know these things, too, you know."

"I know," Patsy said.

"Me, too," Amber agreed.

He felt ancient. How did his little girls grow up so fast? "The fault is not your mom's only. I did neglect her."

"But you were working to provide for us," Julia

said. "It's like when soldiers go overseas. You have to remain loyal."

"I'm proud of you, Julia," he said. "You do have to stay loyal."

"I think you should try again with Gloria," Patsy said. "She still loves you."

His daughters agreed. He wasn't so sure. What if he and Gloria did start again? How long would it take before they were arguing because they couldn't trust each other? Once was enough. He didn't want to have a relationship with endless arguing. Both of them had lived through that already. He couldn't chance it either.

****

Gloria stood outside the restaurant with Dex and Gordy. They'd given their name to the hostess but had to wait for the others before they could be seated. Matt would be here soon. She had to get ready. Sitting next to him at the graduation had taken a toll on her emotions—and nerves. Her upper back hurt, and a headache would be coming along any minute. She must tell Lynda. She didn't want any more lovey-dovey pictures with Matt when there was no more love or future. She still loved him. He might still love her, but there was no future for them anymore. The engagement was off.

Lynda, John, and the kids joined them, and Gloria pulled Lynda aside. "Don't force me and Matt together. We've broken up. We're not getting married."

"What?" Lynda asked.

But then Matt and his girls reached the group. Gloria couldn't take her eyes off him. He was so handsome in black slacks and navy-blue polo shirt, which showed off his strong arms. When Lynda took the group picture, she'd wanted to put her arm around him, but he didn't trust her and he might still be angry with her. Now she was going to stay away from him. She must learn to live without him, and his touch, in her life.

Dex told the hostess they were ready, and they filed into the restaurant. They took up one whole side of the room. Gloria was surprised when Julia sat by Gordy, who took center stage at the head of the long table. Lynda told him to sit there to make picture taking easier. Gloria sat by Gordy, and Dex sat next to her. She was a bit unnerved when Matt sat by Julia.

The waitress went by to take drink orders, and Gloria ordered a margarita. After all, this was a special occasion. When the drinks arrived, she noticed Matt ordered a beer. They placed the orders for the food. The place was noisy. Conversation wasn't really possible, especially across the table, so Gloria talked to Dex. Julia talked to Gordy a lot. The fact that Lynda held Matt's attention unnerved her. What was her sister telling him?

He smiled now and then, so maybe it was just something about the kids.

"I've always wanted a brother," Amber told Dex. "Now I won't have one."

"We can be friends."

"I'm only thirteen," she pointed out. "Right, Daddy?"

"Right." He smiled, and then Lynda grabbed his attention.

"It doesn't matter," Dex said. "What if we just say we're brother and sister? That'll be okay with me."

"Have you always wanted a sister?" Amber asked.

"Not really." He turned to grin at Gordy. "Having a pesky little brother was bad enough."

"I'm in a good mood," Gordy said. "Or I would punch you out."

Gloria laughed and drank her margarita. What was her sister telling Matt? John sat between the girls. "Lynda, why don't you trade places with Amber or Lisa, and talk to your husband?"

"Jealous?" Lynda asked and grinned.

Gloria peeked at Matt. "Oh for heaven's sake."

"Hey," John said. "I'm fine where I am. She'll find something to nag me about if we sit too close."

"Well, you insisted on wearing that ugly coat," Lynda said.

Gloria turned to look at John in a gray sports coat. "Isn't that the coat I gave you for Christmas?"

"You gave it to him ages ago." Lynda took a sip of her drink. "You were still with that Dumb Eddie. That alone will tell you how long ago it was. Gordy was a baby."

Matt cleared his throat. "You call him Dumb Eddie." He looked at Gloria. "And she lets you?"

"It's a term of endearment," Lynda said.

"Yeah, right." Gloria frowned. Matt was probably wondering why she wouldn't get angry with Lynda. Their problems, however, were all tied up in trust issues.

"We can't argue about the coat again," John said. "We've already made up, and it's my turn to nag you."

Lynda preened. "You'll find that a huge undertaking. I'm perfect."

"Matt, you should be grateful you dodged the bullet. These two are alike. You'd spend your entire married life arguing," John said.

Gloria met Matt's eyes for a second.

Lynda frowned. "I think you just used your turn."

"Let's go get another beer," John told Matt. "Maybe she'll calm down by the time I get back. Do you want another one, Gloria?"

"Margarita on the rocks." She didn't look in Matt's direction. His presence among her family seemed so natural, as if he belonged.

"Me, too, but frozen," Lynda said.

"I'm angry with you." John came around and kissed the top of her head.

"Then Matt will get it for me," Lynda said. "Right, Matt?'

"Sure. But I think I'd better check with John."

Matt walked away, and Gloria picked up a napkin and dabbed at her eyes. He stopped near the bar to talk to a man, probably a customer. She glanced at Gordy. He was having a good time talking with Julia. She hoped he still thought of her as a sister. Falling in love was too complicated.

"Are you okay, Mom?" Dex asked.

"I'm fine, *mijo*," she said.

John returned to the table, but Matt stayed behind with the man, whoever he was, talking and forgetting he was at a party with her and her sons. She was being unreasonable, but she couldn't help it.

When the food arrived, Matt returned to his seat and Lynda demanded, "Whose idea was it to break up?"

Gloria sighed. "This is not the place, Lynda."

"Because it's plain to see neither one of you is happy about it," she said.

Gloria didn't say anything. How could she tell her

sister she'd broken off the engagement because she didn't trust Matt due to the life she'd had with Eddie? And Matt didn't trust her because he'd believed she'd returned to Eddie, and he'd had an unhealthy connection with his ex. Matt didn't speak either.

"Let's eat," John suggested.

Gloria saw Dex and Gordy look at each other. "Yes, let's eat," she said.

"I cannot believe this," Lynda said.

"It doesn't matter who broke it off," Matt said. "We'll deal with it. Today is Gordy's day—graduation and dinner and whatever else happens."

"Yes." Gloria frowned at her sister, not stopping to think she was in agreement with Matt. "Focus on your nephew."

Lynda wanted to pursue the subject, but she started eating and talking to Matt again.

Gloria asked the waitress to take a picture of the group. Once this was over, she'd cherish these pictures, not only because of Gordy's graduation but because Matt had been present. She'd thought about Eddie and wondered if he'd attend Gordy's graduation. She wasn't surprised he hadn't gone. Which brought up the stark difference between him and Matt, who'd actually called her to say he wouldn't go because he didn't want Gordy to be upset. Tears threatened to spill out again.

She'd be fine after this was over. She would go home, and then as the days went by, the months, the years, she'd forget about Matt and that for a short time she'd believed she'd found a man she could share her life with.

They finished their meal. The kids urged Gordy to make a speech as the waiter placed a cake in front of him.

He stood up and grinned. "Thanks, everyone, for coming to my graduation and dinner because, you know, I'm the graduate and I graduated today."

"Lame, Gordo, lame," Dex said.

Julia laughed. Some of the other kids threw napkin wads at him.

Then Eddie was there. "Hey, my son graduated. Congratulations, Gordy." He put his arm around him.

Gloria couldn't believe her eyes. Gordy's smile faded, and he stiffened. Her son would rather be anywhere but with his drunken dad in a public place, ruining his special evening. She turned to Dex, and her older son's eyes were dark with anger, his body tense. He was about to get up and confront his dad.

She reached out and put her hand on his shoulder. "Don't get up. We can't make a bigger scene than your dad has already. I'll take care of it."

"As usual," Matt muttered.

Her heart ached. Matt would see this as another time she'd defended Eddie, but she had to get him out of there, and she didn't care how she had to do it.

She walked up to her ex and touched his arm. "Eddie, I'm so glad you could join us, but I think it's better if you meet us at the house. We're finished with dinner, and we're about to leave."

Eddie squirmed away. "You lied to me."

"What did I lie to you about?"

He pointed at Matt. "That day at the bookstore you said you'd lost the best man you'd ever met, and he's here. You lied to me."

She wished he hadn't said what he'd just said, but all she could think about was getting him out of there.

"Okay, I lied to you. I can't be trusted. Whatever you say. Let's go."

He refused to move and tried to shake off her hold. "I want to stay. I have every right. Gordy is my son."

The waitstaff eyed Eddie. The diners around them stared. Dex rose, but she held her hand up to him. Gordy looked down at his cake.

"John?" Gloria asked. But her brother-in-law was already walking toward her. For some reason, Eddie had always respected John. She suspected Eddie wanted to be like John, but he believed he could absorb through osmosis rather than work hard at being a good husband and father.

"Hey, Eddie," John said. "Come on outside, man. You can wait in my car, and you can join the party at the house." He led Eddie out of the restaurant.

Gloria leaned down to hug Gordy. "It's okay, *mijo.* I'm so sorry about this."

She left without looking at anyone else at the table. She reached the entrance and spotted Eddie sitting on a bench in front of the restaurant.

"He called a friend," John said. "He's coming to pick him up."

She slapped Eddie.

"Ow," he yelled, touching his cheek.

"How dare you ruin the most important event of your son's life? Why the hell did you come over here anyway? He doesn't need you now. Actually, he never has because he has me and Dex. I want you to stay out of our lives. You do nothing but mess everything up."

"I'm sorry, baby," he said. "I didn't mean…"

"Shut up, Eddie." She raised her hand to hit him again.

"Gloria." John took her hand. "Just let it go for now. He's drunk."

"I am so furious. I want to kill him."

Eddie continued to mumble apologies.

"Go back inside to your son," John said. "I'll stay here and wait with Eddie."

She took a deep breath and hugged John. "Okay, you're the best. Have I told you lately?"

John grinned. "I know I am. Everybody knows it."

She squeezed his hand. On her way back inside, she stopped and wiped her eyes. She had to pull herself together and not make things any worse for Gordy.

"Do you need anything?" a male voice she instantly recognized asked.

She turned to see Matt in the dim light. She wanted to rush into his arms and have him comfort her, feel his love, but there was no love anymore. "No, thank you. I'm fine. I have to go back, reassure Gordy."

She entered the restaurant and made her way back to the table. She caught both Dex's and Gordy's glances. "Everything's okay now." And she sat down.

"Are you sure, Mom?" Dex asked.

"Yes." She watched as Matt returned and sat down, not looking at her. He picked up his beer and took a drink.

"What happened?" Lynda looked from Matt to Gloria.

"John is waiting until a friend comes to pick up Eddie," Gloria said.

"But what else?" Lynda insisted. "What are you talking about?"

"Not now, Lynda." She forced a smile. "Why don't you take more pictures?" When Lynda would have persisted, she said, "Please, Lynda. We'll talk later."

After John returned, Lynda took a picture of Gordy with the cake. Gloria cut it and handed down a piece to everybody. Slowly, the party atmosphere returned to the table, helped mostly by the kids' chatter and laughter.

Gloria's body ached as if she had the flu. She stood up and went to the other end of the table to chat with Lynda's kids. Dex, Gordy, and Matt's kids joined them after a while. Lynda went around taking pictures.

"Congratulations, Gloria." Julia hugged her.

"Thanks, sweetie." She blinked at the flash of the camera.

"Special moments. That's my gift," Lynda said.

"Thanks, sis."

"I want to take a picture with Gloria," Amber yelled.

"Be quiet, you baby," Julia said, but smiled.

All three of Matt's daughters surrounded Gloria, and Lynda took the picture.

Then it was time to leave. The kids agreed, excited about the next phase of the celebration, this time without parents. The younger kids decided not to go since mostly grads or people close to their age were going to the party.

Everyone gathered their belongings. Somehow Matt was behind Gloria, and she bumped against him.

"I'm sorry." She looked up at him.

"My fault," he said.

The noise receded, and they were the only two people in the room. Could they just say those words and forget all the arguments and distrust and start over? Her body leaned toward him. He reached for her hand. A camera flashed. Gloria looked away.

"Time to go," he said."

"Yes, it is," she mumbled.

She turned away and met Lynda's eyes. "That's enough, Lynda. It's over."

Outside, she found Dex and Gordy. She hugged both of them and told them to be careful. She hugged Matt's daughters, who walked away with Matt, who didn't say another word to her. She hugged her nieces and nephews, and then she ran to her truck. She had to go home.

This was the last time she'd go where Matt would be. It hurt too much not to talk to him or touch him. It was over, as she'd told Lynda. And that was the saddest part of the whole thing.

Chapter Seventeen

"Let's go for a drive, Mom," Dex suggested.

"Oh, Dex," Gloria said. "I don't want to go for a drive. I'm too tired from last night."

Gordy entered the room, wearing a shirt he'd received for graduation. "You don't have to do anything. Just sit in the truck. Dexie will drive."

Dex punched Gordy a couple of times. "I told you to stop calling me that."

"Okay," she agreed. "Before you kill each other." She didn't change from the faded jeans and old T-shirt she wore.

She sat in the back of Dex's truck and closed her eyes. She opened them when Dex stopped the truck. For a minute she didn't know where she was. Then she saw the flowers and the brick house—Matt's house.

"Boys, what are we doing here?" So much for her vow never to go where Matt was. She was outside his house. "Take me home at once."

Ignoring her, Dex and Gordy jumped out of the truck. Matt's daughters ran outside. They gathered in a huddle and whispered, a further assault on her nerves.

She climbed out of the truck. "You know, I think I liked it better when ya'll didn't like each other," she yelled.

"I won't argue with that," Matt said from the front door.

He wore a T-shirt and jeans. Well, at least he wasn't dressed up. She hadn't even combed her hair. She couldn't be near him. It reminded her of all she'd lost. She wished she could get it back, but she didn't see how.

"Boys, if you don't come back here, get in this truck, and take me home, I'm going to walk down to the bus stop."

"Please come in, Gloria." Julia walked to her. "We need to tell you and Dad something, okay? Please."

Gloria stood still. She really couldn't believe Matt's daughter Julia, who'd been so against the engagement, would be the one to call her in. She looked at her sons. Then at Matt, who still stood by the door. "Okay. You know this isn't fair, five against two."

Julia put her arm around Gloria. When Gloria entered the living room, she remembered the last time she was in there, near tears breaking off her engagement. Matt had been drunk, half-asleep, angry. She glanced at the end table, but the ring was gone.

"Sit down, Gloria," Patsy said, and Gloria sat on a sofa chair.

"Do you want something to drink?" Amber asked.

"No, thank you, sweetie," Gloria said. Matt hadn't moved from the front door but stared at her. "Well, how about a bottle of water?"

"Okay." Amber grinned and ran to the kitchen.

When she returned with the water, Gloria opened it and took a sip. The kids gathered in the center of the room—Dex, Gordy, and Julia in the front, the younger kids on each side of them.

"Dad, sit down," Julia said.

Matt sat on the sofa next to the chair.

"Okay." Julia turned to Dex, then Gordy. Both boys motioned for her to speak. "We want to apologize for how we behaved when you first told us you were getting married. Dad, you said that was partly the reason things had gone wrong with you and Gloria."

"We understood, Julia," Gloria said. "Well, I did. I imagine it was a big surprise."

Matt didn't comment.

"And we know somehow that Dex and Gordy's dad and Mom had something to do with it, too," Julia continued.

"How would you know?" Matt asked, and Gloria ventured a quick glance at him.

"Mommy complained a lot," Amber said, "especially about Gloria."

"I'm sure she would complain to you, too, Dad," Julia said. "Mom is like that. She's hard to live with sometimes."

Matt nodded. "Your mom and I tried to make things as easy as we could for you girls after her diagnosis."

"I know you did, Dad," Julia said. Patsy and Amber nodded. "But I don't think you should have moved in, though we were all glad you did because it was so scary when Mom was diagnosed. But I think it hurt your relationship with Gloria."

Gloria sneaked a glance at Matt. He looked at her, too.

"As for Dad, he was always trying to get back with you, Mom," Dex said. "You had to fight him off all the time."

Gloria groaned and wished the water were a beer. She didn't dare look at Matt.

"He showed up at our apartment about two Saturdays ago, bleeding," Gordy said. "In a taxi. We had to help him pay for it. He didn't have enough money. He'd bought some beer."

"That no-good…I gave him enough money to go to his house."

"He said Matt had beaten him up," Dex said. "We asked him why, but he didn't say or couldn't remember."

Matt shifted in the chair. "I'm sorry about that. A little."

"He was drunk out of his gourd," Gordy said. "He kept mumbling he wanted you back and no one was going to take you away. He finally passed out. We drove him home the next day."

Gloria wondered if Matt heard. She almost pointed it out. The night he supposedly thought she'd spent with Eddie, he'd been with her sons. However, she'd already tried to explain it to him, and he didn't want to listen.

"So what we want you to do now is talk things out," Julia said. "We're going to leave for about one hour. Is that enough time?"

Gloria stood. "You can't leave. I don't have anything to say. I said it all the other day." She looked at Matt's daughters. "And, girls, your dad didn't want to listen to me." She stared down at Matt. "Tell them."

"I don't think we have a choice." He seemed so calm.

"Are you in on this plan?"

"Maybe I've had more time to think about it than you."

"We'll give you an hour and a half," Dex said. "It looks like you have a lot to talk about."

"I don't understand you kids," Gloria said. "When we first told you we were engaged, you went ballistic. Dex and Gordy walked out. Julia screamed. I feel like I'm on the edge of reality."

"That's how we felt when you told us, Mom," Gordy said. "It's always been just us three. All of sudden, all these people come into our lives."

"But we've had a chance to think about it," Julia said.

"And both of you are too sad," Patsy said.

"So that's why we think you have to talk—and be sure before you call it quits," Julia said.

"It's too late to change anything," Gloria said, but she sat back down and looked at Matt. She couldn't argue. She was sad. She didn't want to talk about it, though. Her body hurt. Her heart ached. She'd cried all night, and she really wasn't up to listening to Matt's accusations again.

"We'll be back." Dex leaned down to kiss Gloria. Gordy did so as well. Matt's daughters waved good-bye to him.

They filed out of the house. When the door closed behind them, she looked around the room and remembered the first time she'd been at Matt's house, the same day he'd tended to her garden. The first time he'd kissed her, but he wouldn't do that ever again.

"I'm going down to the bus stop. I'm sure a bus will pass by before the kids return. I don't have anything to say to you."

Matt grabbed her hand before she could open the door. She wrenched it away. "Please open the door."

"You can't do this to the kids. They really think they're helping us. At least wait it out with me until they return, and then we can tell them we tried, but it's over."

She closed her eyes, wishing again for what couldn't be.

"We can't hurt the kids," he said.

"I agree. But don't talk to me. Turn on the damn TV or something." She walked to the dining table and sat on a chair. They'd celebrated Amber's birthday there. For the most part, they'd had a good time. Then she remembered when she'd found Matt drunk and angry when she'd broken off the engagement—so unlike himself.

"Do you want something stronger to drink?" he asked.

"What?" Gloria brought her attention back to the present. He stood by the fridge, and she wondered why she was even at his house.

"Something stronger to drink?" he said.

"Oh, wine, I guess."

He poured white wine in a goblet and handed it to her. He grabbed a beer. "Should we toast?"

"Ha. Ha." She sipped her wine.

Gulping his beer, he walked to the living room and turned on the TV to a sports channel. Then he flopped down on a chair.

She opened her purse, straightened out some receipts, then took out a small spiral notebook. She flipped it open and saw the list she'd started the day Matt proposed to her. Tears threatened to spill out. She tore the page out, wadded it up, and aimed it at the trash can—and barely missed hitting Matt.

"Sorry," she said.

"No, you're not. You probably wish it'd been a

rock." He opened the fridge and got another beer.

"Don't give me any ideas."

"I'm glad I found out about this violent streak of yours."

She wasn't sure if he was teasing her or if he was serious. "What violent streak?"

"To hit men. Last night you slapped the shit out of Eddie. Today, you're throwing things at me."

"You're such a dunce." She almost smiled, but then she twirled her wine glass when she saw him grin. She picked up a pen and doodled on the notebook.

"I know you don't want to talk, but…may I tell you one thing?"

She raised her head to look at him. "What?"

"You look as you did on the day I first met you."

"My sons didn't tell me we were going visiting." She fiddled with her hair, which she had up with a clip.

He ignored what she'd just said. "The day I fell in love with you. I still am. Let's start over."

"You told me no," she said, her heart in her throat.

"I'm a jerk. A drunken fool. Like Eddie."

"You're not like Eddie." She doodled some more.

"I wanted to help you last night, but I know you needed to diffuse the situation." He sipped his beer, then sat down at the table with her. The sports anchor's voice sounded in the background. "I would have made it worse."

"Just doing what I do best. Protecting my worthless ex."

"You were protecting your son—and his celebration." After a few seconds, he said, "I trust you."

Gloria went over the doodle again, made it darker. "You're saying it because Gordy clarified exactly where Eddie spent the night after the fiasco at the bookstore. I don't want your kind of trust. You said you were only going to say one thing. Stop talking to me."

"Did you hear what I said?"

"You were reminiscing about the time we met." She sipped her wine. "I remember it, too. We should have kept everything businesslike."

"When I saw you with Eddie last night, everything made sense to me. The chaotic lifestyle you and your sons must have lived with. And I finally knew for a fact you didn't want to go back to it."

"How can you be so sure? How can you be sure you won't want to move in with Angela again?"

"Why are you making this so hard?" He stood and tousled his hair with both hands.

"So you think if you just say you still love me and trust me, I'll jump into your arms and we'll live happily ever after? You tore my heart into shreds when you acted like a jerk. I hadn't come here to break off the engagement. I wanted a second chance, and you refused. But now you're ready?"

"I was drunk. I know I don't have an excuse." He paced to the living room, then back. "You weren't exactly easy on me at the bookstore when I beat Eddie up, you know? How do you think I felt then?"

"You thought I'd chosen Eddie over you. The only good thing that came out of that sorry episode was I finally realized what I'd been doing with Eddie ever since I met him. I'd been enabling him to continue to not live up to his roles as husband and father. I realized I had to stop, and I had to tell him to get out of my life and stay out. You didn't believe me about that either."

"I'll never move in with Angela again. I made the

worst mistake of my life when I did. I don't want her or any other woman," Matt said. "I want you."

Gloria put her arms around herself.

"Throughout this time we've been apart, this is how I remembered you," he said. "You walked through the patio door with your hair up and blushing like a teenager. You're not blushing now, though. You look as if you want to throw something at me again." He grinned.

"Don't tease me. This is serious."

"We're making progress. At least you didn't tell me to stop talking."

She refused to say anything.

"I don't want to let you go." He took her in his arms before she could stop him. "From my life."

She stiffened and wanted to push him away. But then she felt the strength of his body and his gentleness. She realized again that this was where she wanted to stay. Her heart hammered in her chest. Warmth enveloped her. "You broke my heart." Tears filled her eyes, but she continued to hug him.

"I was still drunk. And very angry."

"I know." She felt the heat from his body, the hair at the nape of his neck so soft under her fingers. "I'd never seen you like that. You didn't seem like the Matt I knew."

"I'm sorry about every hurtful thing I said to you."

"I'm sorry, too." She leaned even closer to him.

"Do you want me to kiss you?"

He wasn't playing this time. Before she could answer, his lips were on hers, and the emotion and love in her heart and his threatened to overwhelm her.

"Once we're married, let's not go anywhere if

we're angry with each other," he said. "It hurts too much. During Gordy's graduation when I couldn't touch you…that was the most excruciating time I've ever spent."

"Me, too. I love you." She returned his kiss, then realized what he'd said. "We're getting married?"

"Do you want me to propose to you again?" He grinned.

"Only if you want to," she murmured against his lips. "I'll be happy just to be with you and feel as if you…

"I do love you."

He kissed her again, and she couldn't get enough of his warm lips on hers. They held onto each other as if they'd never let each other go. Only the sound of the kids' voices brought them back to awareness.

"Hey, I think it worked," someone said.

"Of course, it did," Julia said. "It was my idea."

"Just like a girl wanting to take all the credit," Gordy said, but not in anger.

"We have something to tell you," Matt said.

"What?" they all seemed to say at once. They looked at each other, frowning but hopeful.

Matt led Gloria to the sofa. He threw down a pillow, opened a drawer in an end table—the same one on which she'd thrown the ring—and pulled out the engagement ring. He knelt on one knee. In the background, the kids giggled and cleared their throats.

"Don't hurt yourself, Dad," Julia said.

"You should probably just concentrate on each other," Dex said. "Doing otherwise doesn't work for you."

Gloria stood, and Matt held her hand. "Gloria

Amaya, will you marry me?" He slid the engagement ring back on her finger where it belonged.

Gloria smiled through her tears. She couldn't say a word, but she managed to say yes.

The "yes" echoed in their children's voices. *Yes!*

Matt stood, pulled her into his arms, and kissed her. The feel of his lips was sweet, warm, and full of promise. They held onto each other while the kids high-fived each other.

Epilogue

Today is my wedding day.

Gloria stood in front of the wall mirror in the dressing room of the church and inspected her appearance. She could not believe she wore a lacy ivory dress with a flower piece in her hair. And the man she was marrying was the man of her dreams.

This time she really believed it was true. The first time—well, she wouldn't think of that. Comparisons were over. Nobody compared to the man who was waiting for her under the flowery arch of red roses, lilies of the valley, and greenery.

He's the man I've been waiting for all my life.

He had three daughters. She had two sons. And they were getting along. Something she and Matt had never dreamed was possible. They had even been instrumental in getting them back together. All of them were part of the bridal party, as well as Lynda's kids.

"I don't want to let you go," Matt had said when the kids left them alone to talk about whether to call it quits. Gloria thought he didn't want to stop hugging her because the kids were due back any minute.

Then he'd said, "From my life."

She hadn't wanted to let go either—ever, ever. But she'd believed there was no way to resolve the issues they had: trust, exes, kids.

Her dad entered the dressing room. "*Hija*, it's

time," he said. "You look beautiful. You couldn't improve on your appearance if you tried."

"Thank you, Dad." She hugged him, squeezing him tightly.

"I've always wanted the best for you. I love my grandsons. I wouldn't trade them for all the money in the world. But I want you to be happy, too. I think this is the time."

"Me, too, Dad." Her eyes filled with tears.

"Just like your mom, crying all the time. You're going to look all puffy."

Gloria laughed. "How do you know?"

He shook his head and took her hand. "How can I not know, living with your mom and you girls for most of my adult life?"

She kissed his cheek.

He led her to the entrance to the chapel. "Ready?"

"I've been ready for this all my life. I'm so glad you're part of my wedding, Dad."

His eyes welled up with tears. But then she heard the wedding music, and the usher opened the doors. Matt stood at the end of the aisle, at the altar, Wayne by his side. Lynda, her matron of honor, stood on the other side. Her gaze riveted on Matt, so devastatingly handsome in a black tux with a red cummerbund and boutonniere to match the red roses. He grinned. Then he sobered up and held out his hand. She walked down the aisle with her dad. The music swirled around her. The guests stood.

When she reached Matt, her dad shook Matt's hand, then put her hand in his. "Take care of my daughter." He kissed her cheek and walked away.

She held Matt's warm, strong hand. Their gazes

locked, and he pulled her close. She knew he wanted to kiss her, but they had to go through the ceremony first. And it was important to them.

The minister read the wedding vows. Gloria wanted to shout her responses.

"I do," Matt said.

He slipped his ring on her finger, next to the engagement ring she'd returned. Tears filled her eyes at the thought that she could have made the biggest mistake of her life.

"I now pronounce you husband and wife," the minister intoned. "You may kiss the bride."

Matt pulled her into his arms and kissed her.

She faintly heard sounds of clapping, cheering, and a couple of grunts from her sons. Mostly, she was aware of the strong arms of the man she loved holding her, his warm lips on hers.

When he finally stopped kissing her, he didn't let her go. They turned to their family and friends—Tanya and Wayne, Beatrice with Chavo still in crutches he really didn't need anymore—all smiling and clapping. Dex and Gordy grinned. Matt's daughters looked beautiful in their red dresses. And his family—his dad and most of his siblings had come to the church.

She held Matt's warm, strong hand and looked up into his eyes. The image of him coming through the wooden gate of her backyard appeared in her mind.

"Can you do something about my roses?" she had asked. They'd needed tender loving care, as she had.

"Sure, I can help you," he had replied.

Now he pulled her close. "I never want to let you go."

"From my life," she said.

The wedding music and cheers of the congregation swirled around her and Matt. Gloria's heart filled with gratitude that love had found its way into her life. In the background, their children laughed and grunted.

Her life was full. Matt picked her up and twirled her in his arms. She laughed in delight.

A word about the author...

L. M. Gonzalez lives in South Texas. She obtained a degree in Business Administration because her dad advised her to "get a trade." However, in college, she wrote her first story and has continued writing since then.

In 2001 she joined Romance Writers of America and her local chapter. L. M. loves to write love stories featuring heroes and heroines as single parents, and she adds a multicultural flavor.

http://lmgonzalez.wordpress.com/